SHOWTIME

RICKY RUSZIN

Published by Inkshares, Inc., Oakland, California
www.inkshares.com

Cover design by Tim Barber, Dissect Designs
Interior illustrations by Courtney Payne
Interior design by Kevin G. Summers

ISBN: 9781950301393
eISBN: 9781950301409
LCCN: 2022944313

First edition

Printed in the United States of America

For Clarine "Louise" Ruszin,
who always had a story to tell

PART 1

JORDAN, 2020

It's easy to forget that behind the smoke and the flames, behind each mother and sibling and grandparent who perished, there is a child who was robbed of the chance to say goodbye.

—*Michael Roberts,* Talent and Tragedy: An Oral History of the *Talent Now!* Massacre

1

JORDAN JONES WAS no stranger to rage. From the moment he opened his eyes each morning, he felt it humming just below the surface. Today he woke with baggy eyes as he staggered from bed, his clenched jaw sore from another night of grinding his teeth. The familiar rage had taken permanent residence inside him, a squatter that refused to leave. And it remained with him now in his tight fists and narrowed brows as he stepped through the doorway of his grandfather's brick row home.

Warm afternoon sun flooded the living room, illuminating dust motes floating in the nearly empty space. Though his footsteps were cushioned by the blue shag carpeting, he could still hear the echoes of his movements in the bare house—the creaks and squeaks and groans—that normally went unnoticed.

He hadn't gone to the viewing or the funeral or the Reading of the Will, the phrase spoken by his mother as if it were a proper noun. He'd been through it all with Granny years ago, and that had been enough.

Jordan slumped through the minefield of boxes filled with newspaper-wrapped china, hardback novels, and piles of faded jeans and jumbled dresses. His grandparents' material possession—table trinkets and greeting cards, the spreads of mail and opened bills and coffee mugs above chipped coasters—had been unceremoniously packed away. The house lay naked, stripped of its personality. Even the kitchen was alien, the once-cluttered countertops wiped clean and free of tarnished tea kettles, skillets, and Granny's homemade potholders. Also gone was the small, cross-stitched HOME SWEET HOME sign above the door, as well as the sampler box of Entenmann's donuts that Granny used to keep on the small kitchen table for unexpected guests. The absence of the box of treats upset Jordan the most.

"Kind of weird in here without Pop, huh?" His mother's voice chimed too cheerfully for the occasion of clearing out the last of his grandfather's belongings. She scanned the room through her acrylic-framed glasses, a museum patron perusing the art with disinterest. She wore ill-fitting beige pants and a loose floral top, the puff of curls atop her head more gray than black.

"Yeah," Jordan grumbled, rolling his eyes behind her back.

He exhaled noisily, surveying the white-walled room. Gone were Granny's tidy stacks of *Reader's Digest* that had once sat on the coffee table until his father's initial round of Keep It or Chuck It, as if the act of cleaning out his grandparents' home was some kind of morbid game show. Most of the stuff, Jordan knew, had fallen into the latter category.

"A lot has changed since I was last here," his mother said, running her slender fingers along the dusty dining room table with a smile. She picked up a stack of mail that had never been opened, then touched Pop's jacket hanging from the back of a chair with the tap of a tender palm. "It was a good place while they were here. Lots of good memories."

Every cheery syllable his mother spoke grated Jordan's patience. He felt his forehead grow hot but forced himself to close his eyes, take another breath, and push the anger back down, knowing that here and now was neither the time nor place for what he was tempted to say.

He stepped to the corner, shaking his head silently. He thought of the old, framed pictures that had lined the end tables—Pop and Granny on their wedding day, photos of their grandchildren, candid shots from their milestone birthday parties. One of Jordan's favorites had been of Granny's seventy-fifth, featuring Pop squinting with a jowly-cheeked grin as he shoved a hunk of white-frosted cake into Granny's face. Her eyes had been wide with surprise before the fit of laughter that would eventually overtake her. *Who had gotten those pictures?* he wondered. Were they just sitting in a box in some relative's attic? Had they been carelessly left in the alley for the next trash pick-up?

"It's like they never even lived here," his mom chirped, marveling wide-eyed at the lack of clutter.

Jordan plucked a flake of peeling white paint from the wall and watched it sprinkle the plush carpet with fine white crumbs. He looked up at the many other patches of chipped paint on the ceiling. The network of cracks made it seem like some invisible giant was squeezing either side of the living room with large, angry hands.

"It's so sad," his mom said from behind him. Her small voice choked with the coming of tears as she ran her hand along the darkened, dusty square on the wall where a family photo had once hung. "You think people will be around forever, and then . . . "

He felt the rage bubbling closer to the surface now.

"I remember when—"

"Cut the tears, Mom," he spat.

"Excuse me?" his mother said, her small voice rising to a higher register as her whole face—thin, unpainted lips; large nose; and colorless, slack cheeks—contorted in shock.

Jordan's eyes widened. He hadn't meant to speak those words out loud. But he couldn't take them back, so he pushed forward.

"You were never here," he said.

"*Excuse me?*" his mother repeated.

"I *said* you were never anywhere near this house. After you dumped me here, it was all you could do to run the other way." He shifted his back to her, one hand in his pocket as he picked at a hole in the seam.

"What are you talking about?"

Jordan scoffed. "You're unbelievable."

His mother fell silent, her brows knitted in confusion, though Jordan saw the dim flicker of realization slowly broaching the surface.

"When you and Dad needed to have your *time away*," he clarified.

She fixed her gaze on him, her now unblinking eyes boring into her son.

"What happened then was between your father and me," she said, her eyes darting away from Jordan.

Her voice had trembled slightly, pulling at the edges of Jordan's anger. He felt a rush of guilt as his mother struggled to meet his eyes, but he knew that if he didn't say this now, he never would.

"Maybe," he conceded, "but not when it involves your kid. Not when you'd tell me I was going for a visit, that you'd see me before I knew it, and I'd be back home soon."

"That was true."

"It wasn't, Mom, because parents don't drop off their kids with a fucking *backpack*—"

"Watch your mouth, young man—"

"—at their grandparents' house in the middle of the night if they're just visiting!"

"I always picked you up!" she said, her voice rising with Jordan's own.

"Yeah, Mom, you did. But how many days later? How many? There were stretches of days . . . *weeks* when you were just gone. I didn't know where you were or when—*if*—you were coming back. Even Granny didn't know." Jordan shook his head again in disbelief. "Do you know how many days I went to school in dirty clothes because you'd spent the night before drinking and had forgotten to wash them? How many times I got *myself* ready for the bus in the morning? How many times you forgot to pack me a lunch because you were passed out on the couch? I needed you, but you always chose the bottle over me."

"I dropped you off here to protect you when it got bad! To get you away so you wouldn't have to see or hear any of the shit that I had to!" She fell silent, but her drifting eyes betrayed that there was more left unsaid.

"Well, your genius plan didn't work out after all because I saw and heard plenty."

His mom ignored him. "And besides, you had Samantha here with you a lot of the time to keep you company."

"Oh, well, that just makes it all better then, doesn't it?" Jordan scoffed. "Sam wasn't my mother," he said. "It wasn't *her* job to raise me or make me feel safe or make sure there was food in the house. It was *yours*."

His mother shook her head, the corner of her mouth itching toward a wrinkled scowl. "And I didn't send you away. When you came here, you were just—"

"There were times you dropped me off in the middle of the night! I had no idea why or when you were coming back.

But you know what? Granny and Pop didn't make me feel like a burden, like I was interrupting their lives. They were the ones who told me that everything was going to be okay, that you and Dad would work things out, that none of it was my fault—"

"Don't you think I would've liked to do those things for you?" his mother bellowed. "Don't you think I wanted to be there for you? To be with you?"

"If you'd wanted to, you would've!"

"I did want to!" his mother shouted, her hands balled into fists at her side.

Jordan rolled his eyes, refusing to meet her gaze.

"But I couldn't. I knew I couldn't, and it *killed* me. I had a problem. A few of them. Between my drinking and your dad's anger and the divorce . . . " She trailed off, taking a shuddery breath. "I couldn't be the parent that I knew you needed me to be. That's why I left you with your grandparents. Not because I didn't want to be with you, not because I didn't want the responsibility of you, but because I knew . . . " She choked on the words caught in her throat. "Because I knew I didn't deserve you. I didn't leave because of you. I left *for* you."

"It wasn't just leaving." Jordan shook his head again, now slumped with defeat. "It was fucking abandonment."

His mother flinched as if visibly struck. "Watch your mouth," she said, but there was no fire in it.

"Once again it's all about you, isn't it?" Jordan's fingertips tingled with electricity. "But you know what I discovered those times when you finally decided to come pick me up? I didn't want to leave. Because Pop and Granny made this house a home. We had hot dinners around the table, where Pop asked me about my day and Granny helped me with my math home-work. I didn't have to listen to your screaming matches as I tried to fall asleep, I didn't have to walk in from school to see you sobbing at the kitchen table with a red handprint across your face and an icepack on your jaw, I didn't have to hear your lame excuses when I'd walk downstairs to see something broken—dishes or empty liquor bottles. '*Oh, I was just clumsy this morning.*' You said you wanted to get me out before things got bad? They already were bad. I knew what was going on then, and I remember it now."

His mother blinked rapidly, her tiny eyes narrowing behind her glasses. "After everything I've done for you?" she finally said. "All the things I've done to try to make up for it? Let you live at home while you commuted to college, fed you, not to mention paid for a good chunk of your tuition—"

"You and Dad paid for two semesters, Mom! A year!"

"And that's more than some people your age get, especially when they don't even know what they want to do with their lives!"

"I told you I wanted to go to art school!" he bellowed. "I need to get out of here!"

"Then what's stopping you?"

"Hmm . . . I don't know, Mom. Money?" he sneered. "Do you really think community college was my first pick?"

"Fine then. Leave. Just like your father!"

"Maybe I could've if you hadn't spent all your savings on wine and divorce lawyers. You and Dad always said that as long as I went to college, as long as I made you proud and kept my grades up, you'd help with the tuition. I did *my* part. So, what's the problem? Did I not make you proud? Did I fail to live up to the picture you painted in your head?"

"Jordan, that's ridiculous. You know—"

"So, when your friends ask you why your son dropped out of college after his first year, make sure you tell them that you dropped the ball. *You* did. *You* set me up to fail. *You* abandoned your son, *you* destroyed your marriage, *you* were the reason that home was toxic and—"

The *crack* sounded in Jordan's ears before he felt its effect, his cheek stinging as blood rose beneath his skin.

His mother eyed him squarely in the face, doing her best impression of Tough Mother—steeled eyes, straight spine, firm posture—but it didn't hold long before cracks began to appear in the armor. Her tiny chin began to tremble and when her eyes grew glassy and wet, her round cheeks began to soften. She stepped back as if not quite sure whether she was satisfied or horrified at what she had done.

The *crack* seemed to hang in the air like lightning, charged and electric.

She turned on her heels, grabbing her purse and car keys with trembling hands before storming across the kitchen linoleum in her scuffed Sketchers. The front door slammed behind her.

Jordan's jaw quivered with anger, that familiar rage now free from its bottle as he considered the repercussions of everything he had just said.

2

JORDAN SLOUCHED AGAINST the bare wall's peeling paint. The lack of personal effects gave the living room—and the house itself—a feeling of sterility. *Like a model home,* Jordan mused. *Or a hospital.* Without the salty, toasted smell of Granny frying catfish in the kitchen or the sound of Pop snoring in his recliner as *The Price Is Right* droned in the background, it was no longer *Pop and Granny's house.* It was just a house.

His pulse had begun to slow to its normal rhythm, though his cheeks were flushed from the argument with his mother as well as the temperature inside the house. He shouldn't even be here right now. Should've been deep in MICA's summer studio drawing courses—figures and nature and light and shadow. In a dorm or campus apartment, independent like the rest of his friends and cousins. Not here. Not stuck.

"Leaving?" one of his professors had asked during his last week. "Why's that?"

"I'm just taking a semester off," he'd said, embarrassed that money was the reason for the postponement of his dreams. Why he was frozen in place while his friends moved on.

He plucked his black Aerosmith T-shirt from his lean chest, fanning it back and forth. "Jesus, it's hot," he muttered, swiping at his sweat-matted bangs with the back of his hand. Even his ink- and charcoal-stained jeans were beginning to stick to his skin. He stumbled through the maze of filled cardboard boxes on his way to the wall thermostat, which he adjusted to a cool seventy. It was there, in the corner next to the staircase, that he saw the object he had come to see.

Pop's old secretary desk rose to his waist, the genuine oak stained a faded medium brown. The bottom had three drawers on each side, with a small space for an office chair between them. He allowed his fingers to glide over the upper portion's roll top, eyeing the top shelf's various knick-knacks and family photos covered in a thin layer of dust. Jordan had never known Pop to use it as a functioning desk, a place at which to work or write. Rather, it had been a place to drop miscellaneous pieces of mail and things he "might need for later" like old postcards and coupons for items he had never bought but might one day.

For as long as Jordan could remember, Pop had told him he'd get the desk when he died. He could remember leaving secret messages in its nooks and cubbies, locking and unlocking the bottom drawers with the tiny brass key, and sliding his Hot Wheels down the curved expanse of the roll top. Knowing that the desk would one day be his had made his six-year-old self giddy with excitement.

But despite his age—ten or fourteen or eighteen—Pop had given him the old reminder in the same matter-of-fact tone of a teacher reciting a fact his student may have forgotten: *You're gonna get that desk when I kick the bucket, you know that, dontcha?*

But as Jordan grew from a child to a young adult, his interest moving from toys to sketchbooks, there came a time when the desk was no longer enticing. The magic was gone, his Hot Wheels were long in the attic, and the desk was just a desk. Another outdated, bulky relic he had no desire to keep.

But he never could have brought himself to tell Pop.

In the three weeks since Jordan had received the faded manila envelope that had led him here, his feelings about it had boomeranged between dread and subtle curiosity. Jordan had suspected what was inside, and he hadn't wanted it. Hadn't been in the right state of mind to accept whatever his grandfather had left him. But now, as final preparations were being made to sell the house and the offers were rolling in, Jordan knew if he was ever going to confirm his suspicions about the envelope—and why Pop had been so insistent he have it—now was the time.

The crinkled envelope had frayed edges and a blotchy ink stain in one corner. Jordan's name was printed across the front in big block letters. The neat penmanship combined with the faded Sharpie lettering told Jordan that whatever was inside, whatever Pop had decided to bestow upon his grandson, it had been done long ago.

Now, staring at the desk and the envelope in his hand, Jordan was struck that, even in death, Pop was reminding him, *You're gonna get that desk when I kick the bucket, you know that, dontcha?*

Jordan tore open the envelope, tilted it downward, and watched as a small brass key fell into his waiting palm. Even though he knew what it opened, he couldn't help but wonder *why?* Keys meant safety and security. Why would Pop leave him a key to something so mundane?

Jordan guided the key into the desk's lock and turned. When he rolled up the top, he found exactly what he had been expecting.

Junk.

The entire surface was covered with it—papers, memo pads and pens from doctors' offices and senior centers, old coffee mugs, and a bright orange ceramic ashtray (Pop hadn't smoked since the eighties).

Jordan sighed as he leafed through a sheaf of old medical bills.

This? he fumed. *All this time—all those reminders—and this is what you leave me? Garbage?*

Thinking of the weeks it had taken to build up the courage to return here, to face the loss of a place that had once been his safe haven from instability and sleepless nights, his pulse quickened once again.

I came back here for this?

He'd made the foolish mistake of allowing his mind to wander, imagining that Pop had left him something meaningful. But there had been nothing. No inheritance to help him pay for art school or move out of his parents' house. No magic object to erase the horrible things he'd said to his mother. No box of photos or keepsakes of his grandparents to help ease his anger or fix the aimless present he was living in.

The fury he'd unleashed on his mother, which he had tried to damper, came bubbling back.

"Another few days," she had once muttered in this very room, her speech slurring. "A week. A week tops. After that—"

"A week tops?" His grandmother had been incredulous. "You gotta be kidding me! What am I supposed to do?" she'd said, unaware her grandson had been listening in the other room. "I've got Jordan and Sam here more days than I don't have them. I can't do this forever, Diane! You need to step up and be his parent!"

The memory sent Jordan's head throbbing. He raised his arm to the desk's surface and swept everything to the floor in one angry swoop. He balled his fist and sent it through the center of a framed family photo. The glass sliced his knuckles, but the sharp sting fueled his anger like gasoline. As he eyed the crinkled papers below, he saw one with a heading that made him pause: *Sandywood Elementary School—Report Card (Grade*

3). In Art, he saw, he had received an A. A wave of grief washed over him, remembering how Granny had proudly displayed each of his report cards on the fridge while his mother had been too drunk to care.

She kept them.

As if the surprise was too much to bear, Jordan cast the paper aside before opening the desk's many drawers and dumping the contents, eager to trash it all. But when he pulled on the last one, it didn't budge. His heart thumped, cheeks pink with exertion as he continued wriggling the handle.

It was when he stopped to take a breath that he saw the drawer's lock. Jordan fingered the rusted keyhole and noticed its similarity to the one above. He withdrew the small brass key from the metal lock in the roll-top, slid it into the one in the drawer, and turned. When he pulled the handle again, it opened freely. Jordan stared confusedly at the object inside.

The box was made of a hard, black plastic, nearly a foot wide on each side. With its top recessed handle and leather-padded corners, it resembled the kind of container that would have been used to hold old film reels or camera equipment.

What the hell?

Jordan tilted it back as his fingers found the dual latches on the front side and popped them open. He lifted the hinged lid backward and peered inside. The box was full of black VHS tapes, the kind that Granny had used to record TV shows and movies in the days before DVR and Netflix. Jordan assumed they were blank, unused, until he saw the first tape's faded white label in his grandmother's neat cursive:

Carol Burnett, '74

Then he remembered.

His grandmother had been a television junkie. Whether variety shows like *The Carol Burnett Show*, scripted ones like *Mary Tyler Moore*, or game shows like *The Newlywed Game*, she'd tried to attend as many tapings as possible, either with friends or with Pop. After they'd gotten married, she'd made it a point to schedule a taping of *The Price Is Right* into their honeymoon plans. "Why do you want to go to those things when we can eventually watch the exact same thing on TV?" Pop had often asked her. She'd smile, eyes glistening like a kid walking through the gates of Disney World for the first time, and say, "Because the magic's there."

Jordan remembered watching re-runs of those shows with her when he was younger, his grandmother using them to help him take his mind off what was happening at home.

Curious, Jordan slid over to the TV, inserted the tape into the slot of the ancient VCR, and watched it get swallowed up like some ravenous subterranean creature. The curved glass of the clunky, outdated TV fizzled a moment inside its hulking wooden frame before giving way to a black screen. Then the VCR timer blinked to life, and the video started to play. It was grainy at first, as some older recordings were apt to be, but good enough quality that he could see a glistening white stage complimented by an elegant black backdrop with pinpricks of bright white. The audience lights dimmed as the familiar musical cue began ("Carol's Theme," Jordan recalled his grandmother telling him one afternoon). Carol Burnett seemed to glide onto the stage. It was almost like magic, the way she commanded the large room. She smiled and waved, beaming at each person in the audience as if they were old friends.

After the show began with a joke and its signature Q&A portion, the camera returned to Carol as she scanned the audience for raised hands. Her eyes widened and she beamed with a nod as she pointed to a nearby woman with a poof of brown hair and a large-collared blouse.

Jordan froze.

But it wasn't the question, or even the woman who had asked it, that made Jordan stop. Rather, it was the woman sitting two rows behind her. She was close enough for Jordan to make out her emerald dress and faux pearl earrings, her high cheek bones and neatly combed brown hair. Although the teeth she flashed in the video were not the dentures she would have when Jordan knew her, the smile—the dimples and glowing, interested eyes—was the same. He would know his grandmother's smile anywhere.

Jordan remained still, jarred by the surprise of seeing someone long-deceased suddenly appear. He hadn't seen this tape before—hadn't even known it existed—but his grandmother had attended so many tapings that maybe she had forgotten to tell him about her little brush with fame.

Granny laughed, using her elbow to nudge the white-shirted woman beside her as their chests heaved in shared laughter at Carol's wittiness.

Jordan felt a strange mixture of joy and sadness, his heart caught between exaltation in seeing her for the first time in nearly ten years and pain in reliving her absence. The wounds had hurt but reopening them burned. Even in the muted studio lighting and fuzzy recording, a youthful energy radiated from her, radiant and carefree as he'd always known her to be, savoring each laugh, each smile, each second.

Nearly ten years, Jordan mused. He couldn't believe it had been that long since he'd heard her voice. And now, with Pop gone, too, the house's emptiness seemed to deepen, like gangrene settling into a wound.

Jordan blinked and his grandmother was gone from the frame, replaced once again by Carol as she scanned the audience for another participant.

A tease, he spat. That's what it was. Giving him just a taste before snatching her away, leaving him with a temporary memory that would no doubt fizzle and fade away like the others he had desperately tried to hold on to for years—how she smelled like roses, or the subtle lilt of her voice.

"Fuck you, Pop," he said, cursing his grandfather before rewinding the tape to watch it again.

There she was, preserved in the same twenty seconds. It was the only footage of her that Jordan knew existed. He touched a finger to the curved glass of the television and felt a subtle tingle of static as he patted his grandmother on the shoulder. *Clink, clink.*

The loneliness settled over him like a weighted blanket. Suddenly he was six years old again, listening to his parents arguing downstairs and wondering if his father would hit him, too.

He dropped the box of tapes and gripped the corners of the television's wooden frame, staring at the screen as if in a trance, transfixed by the soft studio lighting and the warm lull of Carol's voice. Everything felt so real—the cool, circulated air of the television studio, the bright lights, and the shining stage. He could almost smell a cloud of smog just outside the Los Angeles set's soundproof walls.

The last question of the show's opening Q&A was more of a request, as a young man with wavy hair and a denim shirt asked Carol if she would do her famous Tarzan yell. The audience clapped wildly, egging her on. Carol smiled and made a show of clearing her throat before raising a hand to the side of her mouth and honoring the man's request. She clung to the last raucous note, stretching it out before giving a theatrical bow and announcing the show's guests.

The camera pulled away and the exit music cued up, but something was off. The music had ended, but there was no cut to commercial. Instead of the picture fading out, the focus remained on the stage. With Carol gone, the studio lights brightened as stagehands wheeled out furniture and props for the first sketch of the show. Jordan felt as if he were trespassing, seeing the behind-the-scenes of it all. The *magic*, his grandmother would have said.

If the show had been recorded by an audience member, he could understand why it had continued to film without cutting to commercial, but the picture was too crisp and stable for that to be the case. He supposed it could've been an error on the studio's part, mistakenly broadcasting something that shouldn't have been. He squeezed his eyes shut against the beginnings of a migraine.

He looked down for the remote but couldn't find it. He knitted his brows in confusion as he ran a hand through his rumpled hair. Had he even used the remote to turn on the TV, or had he done it manually? And the box of tapes, he thought as he scanned the floor. Where was it? He was positive he hadn't moved it. And yet it was gone.

Jordan's palms grew slick as uncertainty struck him as suddenly as the slap that had been dealt from his mother. He stood on unsteady legs and turned to look for the box, but what he saw then was nearly enough to bring him back to his knees. His breath hitched in his chest, and he clutched at the ache blooming there. The world seemed to tip, a wave of heat spreading through his body as the realization hit him.

He didn't know how, but he was no longer in his grandparents' living room.

3

THE SPACE BEHIND him where his grandparents' couch and end tables should have been was replaced by a long row of black metal cabinets that ran the length of the room. They were scattered with knobs and blinking lights, branded with an outdated version of the CBS logo. Set between them was a low table filled with buttons and dials with wheeled chairs parked behind it. Grainy lunchbox-sized screens were set into the table and many of the tall cabinets. Looking at them and the images they featured, Jordan felt bile rise at the back of his throat.

With increasing anxiety, he glanced to the large rectangular window in front of the table and saw the same thing: the familiar, glistening white stage and black star-prickled curtains. Below, stagehands scurried to place furniture and props into their proper positions, while others adjusted the set lights and cameras.

Another hot prickle of fear spread through him as he looked down at the sea of heads floating below, the same faces he'd seen in his grandmother's tape. Her *recorded* tape. Of something that happened over forty years ago.

He must be dreaming. But he hadn't felt tired and knew he hadn't fallen asleep. Which left two possibilities: psychotic break or brain tumor. How else could he explain the impossibility before him?

He wasn't crazy. But then again, isn't that what all crazy people thought?

So, tumor it was. He didn't need WebMD to tell him that. Hallucinations combined with a steady, building pressure in his throbbing head gave him all the clues he needed. He'd always been a hypochondriac—each mole was melanoma, each headache an aneurysm—and he'd supposed it was just a matter of time before one of his nonsensical medical woes would actually become something to worry about.

Instinctively, he reached for his cell phone, but it was dead. He rubbed his temples and scanned the room for a phone, finally spotting one at the corner of the switchboard-looking table. He picked it up and relaxed a little when he heard the familiar dial tone. His first thought was to call his mother, until he remembered the way she had flinched when he'd snapped at her. He doubted she'd pick up the phone, and could he blame her? Instead, he dialed the three numbers that Granny had taught him at a young age. It rang only twice before his call was answered.

"911, what is your emergency?" the woman asked.

Where to start?

"My head hurts and . . . I'm feeling dizzy," Jordan began. "I'm-I'm seeing things that aren't there." The words sounded strange as they stumbled from his mouth, things he never thought he'd say.

"Okay, sir. What is your location?"

"My location?"

"Where are you right now?" she said. "From where are you making this call?"

"I-uh-I'm . . ."

Should he say where he was, or where he knew he *should* be? The operator's next question decided it for him.

"Where are you in the Los Angeles area?" she asked.

Jordan froze, gripping the phone as he pictured the woman at the other end of the line wearing a wide-collared shirt and flared pants.

Los Angeles?

"Sir? Are you still—"

Jordan's hand seemed to lose its strength and he dropped the phone back into its cradle, silencing the operator. It was then that he noticed it was a rotary.

His head banged harder than ever, the blood pounding in his veins.

A metallic rattling came from the corner, and Jordan looked to the wiggling knob of the door he hadn't noticed before. His eyes darted around the room as he searched for a place to hide. He settled on a small gap between the wall and one of the hulking pieces of machinery and wriggled inside. It was tight, and his feet became ensnared in a tangle of wires, but it was better than standing out in the open until someone showed up and asked the question to which he had no answer: *What are you doing here?*

Jordan heard the brass doorknob turn. A wave of nervous heat ran down his back as his arms prickled with anxious anticipation. He sat with his head pressed tightly against the wall and kept his hands on his knees to still their shaking against the metal surrounding him.

It wasn't long before the door opened, accompanied by the sound of male voices. At least two, Jordan thought. Maybe three. They entered quietly, and from the squeaks and metallic clicks ahead, he knew they had sat in the chairs at the switchboard-looking terminals below the wide window overlooking the stage.

"Roger that, Randy," one of them said into his headset. "Back from commercial in three . . . two . . . " When he reached *one*, the lights in the booth dimmed, leaving only the fuzzy screens and the constellation of glowing reds and greens on the various pieces of machinery.

Jordan snuck a peek at one of the screens to see Carol sharing the stage with Maggie Smith. He listened as they sang some song about London, looking like sisters from opposite sides of the pond. They had matching hair and wore loose-fitting jumpsuits and large silver-buckled belts. He recognized Maggie Smith from the *Harry Potter* movies, but it was weird to see Professor McGonagall forty years younger . . . and singing.

He didn't know how long he sat there, listening with his body scrunched up against the back wall, but based on his cramping legs, it must've been at least half an hour. He thought of all he had seen and heard—the 911 operator, the lights, the stage, the scent of the metallic machinery and cheap cigarette smoke that hung in the air. He ran his fingers across the gray shag carpeting. Hell, he could feel each fiber! He'd never heard of a hallucination like this.

The show took another commercial break, and when they resumed filming, Carol stood at the center of the stage after another outfit change and began singing her signature closing song, "I'm So Glad We Had This Time Together." Her voice was crystal clear, hitting each note perfectly. She held the last note and, as she let it go, tugged on her left earlobe in that familiar gesture to let her own grandmother know that she was thinking of her. "Good night. Thank you," she said, smiling into the camera. When the exit music cued up, Jordan peeked from his hiding place to see the credits rolling across the banks of small screens. Behind the names and titles, Carol was exchanging hugs and kisses with Vicki Lawrence, Tim Conway, and Maggie Smith, who signed Carol's guestbook.

The voice of the man closest to him startled Jordan and he retreated. "Okay," the man said. "We're gonna cut it in five . . . four . . . three . . . two . . . "

He reached *one* and an intense ache bloomed behind Jordan's eyes, wedged deep into his brain. He raised his palms to his eyes and kneaded them like balls of dough. When the ache finally subsided and he was able to open his eyes, he saw that Carol was gone, replaced by a static-filled screen and his hands gripping the wooden corners of his grandparents' television.

THE ROAR OF the audience's applause was replaced by the still silence of the near-empty row home. Jordan withdrew his hands from the television and scanned the room. The couch, Pop's recliner, and desk were back, replacing the hulking machinery of the room where he'd been just moments ago. He fished his cell phone from his pocket, expecting it to still be dead, but it was bright and awake, the battery indicator showing nearly a full charge. The screen flashed the time and Jordan froze. It was an hour later from when he'd pushed the VHS tape in, meaning that he'd watched the whole thing straight through.

An hour-long hallucination? He had never heard of such a thing.

Regardless of how it had happened, *something* had caused his slip from reality. Had there been a storm while he'd been watching the tape? Maybe lightning had struck the house, passed through the TV and into his body, frying the wiring in his brain. But he knew from the glaring daylight slipping through the windows that no such thing had occurred.

So, what then?

Jordan ejected the tape from the VCR and inspected it, but it was just a plain black tape with an ordinary white label on the side. A relic that time had made obsolete. He cautiously stuck a finger to the glass-fronted TV and felt a tingle of static before he jerked it backward, as if poking a sleeping monster. But nothing else happened. The dizziness was gone, his nausea and headache was abating, and he felt like he had when he'd arrived at the house—more or less normal. Maybe he just needed some sleep. Since dropping out of CCBC, anxiously drifting through the days and lamenting the life he wished he were living, he hadn't gotten much of it. Until recently he'd been working on his portfolio for his eventual application to MICA, filling his sketchbook with landscapes and figure drawings in charcoal and ink and watercolor, but he hadn't picked up a pencil in weeks. Didn't see the point of it anymore.

He looked down and saw that the black plastic box with the faux-leather corners was back at his side. Each tape looked the same, black and caseless. The only thing differentiating them from each other was the neat cursive on each of the skinny white labels. *Mary Tyler Moore '73*, read one. *Saturday Night Live '80*, read another. *Price Is Right '92. All in the Family '75*. Jordan pulled out these and half a dozen others, forming a small mountain on the blue carpet.

He caught himself glancing at the *Carol Burnett* tape again. Sure, his experience could've been brought on by stress, but . . .

What if it was something else?

Jordan plucked a random tape from the pile—*Super Password '86*—and stuck it into the VCR.

If it happens again, you'll know.

But know *what?* That he *was* crazy? That he was sane but *did* have a tumor? What good news, exactly, would a repeat experience bring?

He sat in front of the television just as he had before and pressed PLAY. Before long, he'd nearly finished the entire half-hour recording. Nothing happened. So, tumor it was. He drummed his fingers against the legs of his jeans and recalled that when he'd watched the last tape, he'd placed his hands on the TV itself.

What the hell? Jordan thought and shrugged. *If you're crazy, you're crazy.* He raised his palms and cupped them to the corners of the television set.

He watched. He waited.

Nothing.

This was stupid, and he knew it. The contestants on the stage continued their game, the rounds interspersed with witty remarks from the host.

Jordan sighed and checked his watch. Another minute or two passed, but it wasn't the time that made him pause. Looking down beyond his beat-up Timex, he no longer saw the deep blue carpeting of his grandparents' living room. It was instead replaced by an awful tan and black shag, the way he imagined cheetahs would look if God had created them with his eyes crossed.

He glanced up and a chill broke out across the back of his neck. There was a stage and a set and a studio audience, Bert Convy standing at the red and blue Password table between both teams. Each contestant was paired with a celebrity teammate, though Jordan didn't recognize either of them. Bert kept the game moving swiftly, while the announcer whispered the password to the at-home audience.

Again, Jordan was above, peering at the audience below through dimmed studio lighting. He'd been plopped into another technical booth, just as he had when he watched the *Carol Burnett* tape, but there was only one man at the switchboard-looking terminal this time. Thankfully, Jordan had appeared behind him.

Appeared.

Was that what someone would've seen if they were watching me? Did I just poof *into the booth, or slowly fade in, bit by bit, pixel-like?*

On stage, the final round concluded and Bert Convy bid the at-home audience farewell. "We're out of time today. We'll see ya tomorrow," he said, waving as the taxi yellow credits began to crawl up the screen. Before long, the set lights dimmed and the final credit—informing the audience that the show was *Videotaped at NBC Studios, Burbank, California*—appeared. Jordan had come in at the tail-end of the program, but he still had so many questions. Though he now had an answer to one of them. Because seconds later, when the screens in the tiny technical room faded to black and Jordan found himself once again clutching the corners of his grandparents' television, he knew he wasn't crazy.

HE SPENT THE next few hours in front of the TV, the pile of tapes at his side. He watched every one, careful to do so with his hands at his sides instead of on the TV itself. It could've been a coincidence that his hands had been on the set both times he'd been transported, but he didn't think so. He didn't know *how* it worked, just that it *did*. And that was all the knowledge he required to understand that he needed to be careful.

Each tape was a time capsule, a souvenir of the tapings his grandmother had gone to and the times she'd been featured on camera. Some appearances were obvious, like her being inside the frame during the Q&A portion of *Carol Burnett*, while others were like a version of those *Where's Waldo?* books he'd liked in elementary school.

When he popped in the *Price Is Right* tape, he didn't find her right away (she'd never made it down to Contestant's Row) and had to rewind each time the camera panned through the audience, looking for the person that Rod Roddy had called to come on down. It took him half a dozen tries to spot her—the camera only panned over her section of the excited audience for a second—but when it did, Jordan paused the tape. His grandmother wore a white T-shirt with some kind of phrase—something about Plinko or being one of Barker's Beauties, he would've guessed—and her signature wide-rimmed glasses. Her lips were painted a bright red, a sight that made Jordan laugh with surprise. In all his life, he'd never known his grandmother to wear such bright makeup. "Lipstick is for strippers and little girls playing dress-up," she'd say.

"Caught you," Jordan said with a slight smile. Not for the first time, he wondered what his life would be like if she were still alive. Would he have moved out of his mother's house, independent and removed from the toxicity he felt seeping into him with each passing day? Would he be at MICA, pursuing his art? Would he be happy?

He sighed and returned to the tapes at his feet, laying them out chronologically, a living timeline of his grandmother's life. It was a pleasant surprise seeing her again after so many years, but the happiness he'd felt began to ebb as he realized that this little taste, this *tease*, was all he would ever get. There would be no new visits or calls when he was overwhelmed or lonely. No new memories. Just the same brief glimpses the tapes offered. For a moment, it was as if she had been in the room with him, her reassuring presence filling the empty space. But then he felt her swiftly slip away like a wisp of smoke through his fingers.

Jordan's stomach soured. It wasn't fair. It wasn't fucking fair.

He knew why he'd gotten the desk, but why the tapes? What good did they do him? Which of his problems did they solve? And why the locked drawer? Locked drawers were for guns and knives, cash and secrets. Not old VHS tapes of game shows featuring his grandmother in the studio audience.

Jordan sighed. Who knew what got into the minds of the elderly? Sometimes they left their car keys in the refrigerator, while others left their grandsons a box of old videos.

The box's contents began to dwindle as Jordan came to the final tape. He picked it up and immediately saw that it was different from the rest. The corners were dinged and scratched, but it was the strip of film itself that Jordan noticed most. He raised the tape's back flap for a closer peek. The film was crinkled, and though all VHS film strips were thin, this one looked thinner than the others, like a hard candy that had been sucked down until all that remained was a small, opaque razor. He looked for the label to see which show it was, but there was none. His grandmother had been nothing if not organized, so the idea that she would purposefully not label one of her tapes struck him as odd.

Jordan examined the tape again, remembering his own VHS collection he'd had as a kid. Two of his favorites had been *The Fox and the Hound* and *The Lion King*, and he'd watched and rewatched them again and again until their film strips began to thin, the picture growing less crisp with each viewing. Why had this one been watched so many times? Was it another of his grandmother's audience appearances? A show that made her laugh more than the others? A favorite movie that had somehow gotten mixed in where it didn't belong?

His eyes narrowed as he moved the *Carol Burnett* and *Password* tapes out of the way and pushed the mystery tape into the VCR. There was only static at first before it was replaced by a black screen and garbled sound. In another moment, the picture appeared. The footage had a different look than the rest of the tapes. It was less crisp and a bit shaky, almost as if it had been filmed by an amateur rather than a professional studio cameraman.

What show is this? Jordan thought. *What year?*

As the camera zoomed in and the picture became crisper, Jordan began to recognize the setting he'd become obsessed with over the years. The black-floored stage spanned the length of the theater, dozens of bright spotlights causing its surface to gleam like volcanic glass. Behind it was the familiar red, white, and blue logo on the giant LCD screen that asked, "DO YOU HAVE WHAT IT TAKES, AMERICA?" Three bright exclamation points hovered above the stage, each ten feet high and one hundred pounds of Plexiglas and metal, rigged to the judges' table facing the stage. With the push of a button, those three Hollywood phonies—Larry, with his goofy dad jokes; Portia, with her painted-on face and fake enthusiasm; and Hans, with his thick German accent and aversion to smiling—could either make or break an act. Behind them and their powdered faces, the theater was packed with the excited, buzzy chatter of thousands of people nestled into the rows of red velvet seats.

Jordan's brow furrowed in disbelief above his glazed eyes. How could he be watching this? The show had never aired, and no clips had ever been made public to supplement the dozens of news reports, reflections, vigils, and anniversary remembrances that had played and replayed over the years. Jordan knew the show had been recorded to be broadcast later that summer, but he'd assumed that either the filming equipment had caught fire or the network had been completely barred—either by the FCC or lawyers of the victims' families—from showing even the smallest glimpse of what had occurred.

And with good reason. There was nothing about that day that should've been broadcast for the world to see. It would've been like taking someone's final, horrified moments trapped inside the World Trade Center and uploading them to YouTube.

Jordan didn't need a label on the tape to tell him what he was watching. The show was *Talent Now!*, a televised, country-wide search for America's next great talent. Though successful, it wouldn't be long before it was off the air. Because in what would later be known as the "*Talent Now!* Massacre of 2013," over four dozen people had died.

And Jordan Jones's grandmother had been one of the victims.

JORDAN SAT, CAPTIVATED by the recording. After a minute of steady filming, the picture went helter-skelter again, with the herky-jerky movements of someone operating a hand-held camera rather than a multi-thousand dollar steady cam used for television production. A muttered curse emanated from whoever was behind the camera. Whether due to the camera itself or the person filming, the recording's quality was horrible. If Jordan hadn't recognized the theater or the big *Talent Now!* stage backdrop in its patriotic red, white, and blue, he wouldn't have been able to tell what he was looking at.

The audience lights began to dim so that only the black stage was lit as the next contestant, a short lady wearing jeans, a red checkered shirt, and a white cowboy hat over her wild brown hair came onto the stage. The tape's audio was just clear enough that when Portia asked her name, Jordan could hear her proudly state that she was Cowgirl Judy, forty-two years old from Kentucky. The audience gave a collective chuckle. Jordan could not hear her answer Portia 's question about what she was going to do for them that day, one of the judges' many tactics for breaking the ice or provoking some kind of humorous or heartfelt response. But judging by her outfit and props, Jordan could guess.

Generic Old Western music began to play as she galloped around the stage on her very invisible horse, smiling madly as if she were having the time of her life. She stopped in the middle and cast her lasso around the neck of a wooden horse with yarn for a mane. The audience began to boo and hiss, urging the judges to buzz her off, but she ignored them and continued galloping about, lassoing more wooden horses and waving to the crowd.

Despite her precision, it wasn't long before all three judges (even Portia, who was usually the kindest of the three) slapped their buzzers. Each slap illuminated the judge's corresponding exclamation point above the stage in bright red accompanied by a bombastic *buzz!* to stop the music and act. Jordan didn't need to hear the judges' comments to know that Judy hadn't made it through to the next round, though she exited the stage with a huge smile on her face.

Jordan watched the fuzzy screen as a pair of production assistants removed her cowgirl paraphernalia, replacing it with several circular targets and a glass-topped table lined with black arrows. Jordan's pulse quickened when the contestant who would use them stepped onto the stage.

He was dressed in all black. And though that was nothing to hint at what was coming, it was something which the media would latch on to later (dark colors surely signaled depression or social deviance; some of the more extreme news programs went so far as to suggest Satanism). He wore heavy boots, had short, semi-spiked black hair, and several ear piercings that glinted silver. He stood on the contestants' mark—a large, white exclamation point—with stoic calm, his hands folded behind him as he looked out into the audience with the glazed eyes of a deer fresh from the taxidermist. It was easy to understand how that contemplative gaze could've been interpreted as excitement, maybe even shock or nervousness at the possibility that his life was about to change. But because it was expected to see such emotions on the contestants' faces, no one seemed to realize that inside his outward appearance of calm confidence was a core of cold calculation, his steeled brown eyes those of someone who knew exactly what he was doing. But one thing about that gaze was true: his life *was* about to change. And so were the lives of everyone in that theater.

After he introduced himself, the judges asked him one of the old standbys: "So, why are you here today?" The tape's sound faded in and out, and Jordan was thankful he couldn't hear his response. From reading and watching the old news coverage and articles when he was old enough to do so, he already knew what it was. A chill slithered down his neck.

The judges offered him the stage as dramatic background music began. He circled the stage several times without the showy, dramatic gestures magicians and other "danger" acts seemed to favor. Instead, he took short, measured steps before stopping at the small glass-topped table and raising one of the seven arrows placed there. He showed it to the audience and lifted the wooden bow from the adjacent table. Arrow against bow, he aimed at the target midway across the stage and, as the music hit a dramatic flourish, released the arrow, which landed in the outermost ring.

The audience was silent, unsure whether to boo or cheer, whether his off-center hit was unintentional or done purposefully to later shock them with his true skill.

The man raised another arrow and shot at the same target. Bullseye.

The audience cheered, but he didn't seem to feed off it, unfazed at being watched by millions of people.

He took another arrow and aimed it at a smaller target even farther away, drew a breath, and let it fly. It struck the center and the audience cheered even louder. The man was seemingly unmoved. It was the same when he brought two more arrows against his bow, fired both simultaneously, and hit a farther target dead center. He gave a thumbs-up to someone off-stage, and a smaller target descended from the ceiling as the dramatic music swelled. It stopped halfway between the floor and the ceiling, the stage lights dimming while two bright spotlights appeared: one on the man, one on the target. He withdrew a silver lighter from his pocket and held it to the tips of the remaining arrows. They caught fire instantaneously, and an awed gasp rose from the audience as he held one of them to his bow and aimed at the target.

Jordan's heartbeat quickened, knowing what was coming next.

The man adjusted his stance at the last second, swinging left and releasing the flaming arrow not at the target, but in an arc above the stage, above the judges' table, above the orchestra section, and up to the ceiling in a trail of orange light and smoke. *This must be part of the show*, some audience members were surely thinking. And some of them still must have been thinking it as the arrow found its home in something above the highest balcony level and exploded in a ball of fire.

The balcony erupted in a collection of screams and unintelligible pleas, the once silently seated audience now wailing as they rushed toward the exits. Large chunks of flaming plaster and concrete fell from the ceiling onto the people below.

The dark-clothed imposter remained on stage. Still. Silent. Watching. A pair of black-uniformed security guards charged up the short steps, but they didn't make it ten feet to where he stood before the man quickly fired an arrow into each of their chests. He shot another to the left of the orchestra section, and another into a balcony. Explosions followed each as somewhere off camera came the cataclysmic sounds of the sky tearing open—*BOOM, BOOM, BOOM*. But the recording's angle was crooked, and Jordan couldn't tell what had caused them. Only as the flaming arrows continued to fly did the rest of the audience seem to finally realize that it was not part of the act.

Another arrow flew dangerously close to the man recording the tape. He uttered a curse, and then a final explosion—this one the loudest and closest—emitted from the TV. The sound turned garbled, the screen went fuzzy, and the background was filled with the screams of all those who would soon be dead.

And then the picture went black.

JORDAN'S MOUTH RAN dry as he stared at the darkened screen. He had known about the event on the tape for over seven years, but seeing it was completely different, something for which he had been unprepared. The man's calm precision against the erupting chaos terrified him the most, Jordan's horror heightened by the fact that somewhere among the flames and screams and smoke, Granny had been there, fighting for her life with thousands of other people crammed into that theater. Despite its rich legacy of hosting vaudeville stars and Old Hollywood royalty, it would be known above all and forever more for the massacre that had taken place that summer afternoon.

Though Jordan had been a child, he hadn't been too young to understand what had happened. He'd known what a terrorist was, that a very bad man had done something terrible inside that theater. That the world had become a more dangerous place than it had been the day before.

For months, the media had featured non-stop coverage of the aftermath. Jordan remembered sitting in front of the TV next to his parents as his wide eyes reflected the chain of awful images. It was terrible, and yet he couldn't look away. People stumbled down the street with disbelieving, ash-covered faces as billowing smoke rose high above police blockades and caution tape. In the foreground, shocked newscasters attempted to provide information about the developing horror.

Clutching tissues and each other, his family had sat halfway between the television and phone, wondering which would deliver the news they were dreading.

The call didn't come until days later when they had identified the bodies.

Even then, as a child not quite thirteen, Jordan had wondered: *What now?*

With Granny gone, where would he go when things got bad? Would he be trapped at home with his alcoholic mother and explosive father? Would this be the tipping point, when his mother ran off for good or the abuse doled out by her husband was transferred to her son?

If only I'd gone, I would've been there with her.

It was something that had been spinning around his head for nearly ten years, the thought stuck in an endless loop like a record on a turntable, as if his mere presence in the theater could have saved her from the tragedy that was out of his control. On some level, he knew it was ridiculous, but that didn't help him forget—or forgive himself—that Granny had died alone.

He remembered how he'd caught her in her bedroom one day, rapidly filling a small suitcase with clothes. "Where are you going?" he'd asked.

"Granny just needs a little time away," she'd said in a huff without meeting his gaze.

"Away? I don't understand. Why—"

"I just need some time!" she'd snapped, one of the few times he'd ever heard her do so. He'd fled from her room in tears, suddenly certain that, like his mother, Granny was leaving him, too. Of course, there was no way he could have understood his grandmother's complex feelings about the sudden burden his mother had placed upon her. That Granny had felt the same nervousness and panic and anger as he did.

But more than grief, in that hell week between the funeral, televised memorials and vigils, and media that refused to let his family process their loss on their own time, Jordan felt hate. Hate for the man, the imposter, who had caused it all. The man, he hadn't realized then, who would cast a dark shadow over the rest of his life.

Once they'd identified his body, his picture was everywhere. He had a slim build and broad shoulders. Aside from a few acne scars on his tanned cheeks, the hint of a black goatee was the only adornment to his otherwise nondescript features. But more than the gelled tips of his spiked hair or the thumping of his black Doc Martens, his cold Mona Lisa eyes haunted Jordan the most when he closed his own at night. Even in sleep, they seemed to find him. He was only twelve, but his anger began to metastasize at realizing the man's death had likely been quick, that he hadn't lived long enough to suffer. That Jordan hadn't been able to kill him himself.

Print and online articles attempted to examine him—to make some sense of the tragedy he'd caused—and Jordan saved them, taping them to the inside of his closet door like a dirty secret. Before long, the door was covered in paper, the dark wood completely obscured.

It was that door he thought of now, taped with articles, pictures, and statistics from reputable newspapers and the more sensational ones. *AL QAEDA BEHIND* TALENT NOW! *MASSACRE?* Read one. TALENT NOW! *MASSACRE AN INSIDE JOB! GOVERNMENT EMPLOYEE TELLS ALL!* Read another. Another one mentioned his grandmother by name, and another a Baltimore woman who had survived with third-degree burns covering her face and body.

But most involved *him*: the few fragments the police and investigators were able to piece together about his history, why he had done what he'd done, and who, if anyone, had helped him.

Theories.

Speculation.

Nothing that would assuage Jordan's anger or bring his grandmother back.

In the numbing days and weeks after the massacre, though the hate had refused to recede, at least it made him *feel*. Because he—that eerily calm imposter—was the reason Jordan had been forced to grow up so fast. Why he'd grown angry and withdrawn, lashing out at his parents. Why he'd gotten into so many fights at school. Why he'd gone from playing outside with his friends to spending more time in his room, alone, knowing that anything good that happened to him could be taken away in an instant.

Granny would no longer be there to defuse his bubbling anxiety on the nights he was certain his parents were arguing because of him—because his grades weren't good enough or because he'd disappointed them in some way. "You didn't do anything wrong," she'd say. "Not a damn thing." On those nights, when his brain refused to rest and the anxious thoughts swam deeper and faster, her voice had been calm and leveled, her grandmotherly soothe mixed with a reassuring ferocity: "None of this is your fault, Jordan. You deserve better. You deserve so much better."

She'd never be there for him to confide in when he saw the red marks on his mother's face or his father's car missing from the driveway at bedtime.

Or pick him up from school with a smile (not the hard-edged, preoccupied gaze of his father) as she asked him about his sketches instead of pretending he didn't exist. "The figures look good," she'd say, not knowing how to be anything but completely honest, "but the faces could use some work."

He would miss how she contentedly hummed show tunes around the house and imbued each dinner with lively jokes and conversation instead of the heavy silences of home. He'd miss the joy he'd felt after opening her birthday cards bearing her neat cursive (*xoxo*) when his parents had forgotten.

If he'd only gone with her that day, everything might've been different. But now, because he hadn't, he would never have these things again. The things that he'd thought were untouchable and would last forever. Things he had taken for granted.

And while he had certainly grown to despise the man responsible for all the lives lost that day—he still couldn't bring himself to say his name, to taste it on his lips—there was only one that mattered. And *he* was the reason she had been taken from him.

Fuck you, he thought.

He sent the spread of VHS tapes across the carpet with a furious backhand, the hard edges scraping his skin.

"Fuck you!" he shouted. "Fuck you!" He raised a tape and sent it flying across the room with such speed that it cracked the glass door of the china cabinet. He raised another and threw it against the wall. The back flap broke off, sending the ribbon of tape fluttering behind it like a defective parachute. He repeated the action, throwing them as hard and as fast as he could, until his arm throbbed and the blood from his split knuckles coated the back of his hand.

Among the scattered and broken tapes, Jordan's eyes settled on the black box that had held them. He swung his leg and kicked it, the box tumbling across the carpet until it slammed into the corner of the desk. He'd removed all the tapes and assumed it was empty. But peeking out from the corner of the hinged lid was a small sheet of paper. Jordan reached for it and took it between his fingers. Old and discolored, it was like the many others in Pop's desk. It had been folded so many times that its horizontal crease had begun to tear, small holes appearing in the depths of the fold.

He unfolded the paper, expecting it to be another scrap of junk, and was surprised to find that it was an eBay receipt. The top of the page read, "Thanks for another purchase! Your order is now confirmed." Jordan's eyes narrowed in confusion as he scanned the sheet, reading the description of the purchased item. "This is ACTUAL FOOTAGE of the *Talent Now!* show tragedy that took place in New York City in the summer of 2013. A sad and terrible day!! I was in the audience during the show and personally recorded it from my seat before the terrible destruction started. I was one of the lucky ones! Unaired and authentic item!! Happy bidding!!"

Below, Jordan saw the winning bid of $256.

Jordan tried to wrap his mind around what he had read. *eBay? That's where Pop got the tape?* He didn't even know Pop had known how to use a computer, much less navigate online auction sites.

He flipped the crinkled receipt over to the backside, which was filled with Pop's familiar scrawl. In the upper right-hand corner was a date: September 12, 2013, a few months after the *Talent Now!* massacre. His brow furrowed in confusion. Each line of the half-sheet of computer paper was filled with only a few words and a date. Jordan read through some of them: *Mary Tyler Moore '73, All in the Family '75, Carol Burnett '77, Saturday Night Live '80, Super Password '86, Price Is Right '92.* The list went on until it stopped a few lines from the bottom.

It didn't take a genius to figure out it was a list of all the tapes in the box, all the tapings his grandmother had attended. But the list of tapes was not what confused him. Each show title had tally marks next to it. Some with one or two, some as many as a dozen. Jordan supposed it could be how many times Granny and Pop had watched the videos, but why would they feel the need to document each viewing? Besides, the note was dated *after* Granny's death in 2013, so it only could have been Pop watching the tapes. But why?

When he came to the list's end, his heart fluttered when he saw the last written line: *Talent Now! '13*. But what caused his arms to break out in goosebumps wasn't the title itself, but the amount of tally marks next to it. Running his finger over the pencil indentations, Jordan counted over two dozen. *Two dozen views. Why would he watch it so many times when he already knew what had happened? Guilt? Denial about losing his wife?*

The TV screen was still black. It seemed so long ago that he'd watched the *Carol Burnett* tape and felt the trill of pleasant surprise at seeing Granny in the audience. How he'd pressed his hands against the TV and—

It hit him all at once, everything crashing together—his traveling, why the tapes had been locked away (not forgotten, but secured), Pop's sheet, why the *Talent Now!* video had the most views of all. And then, looking from the paper to the TV and the tapes scattered around the floor, Jordan got an idea.

HE WALKED AROUND the room, gathering the tapes he had so carelessly thrown only moments ago. When he had returned them to a semi-neat pile, he went over each with a fine-toothed comb, searching for any nicks, cracks, or other damages he may have caused. There were a few with dented or scratched corners, but thankfully, only two seemed to be broken: one, the *All in the Family* tape (no great loss there, since his grandmother wasn't actually on screen); and the other, the *Price is Right* tape from '92. One of the tape's broken edges had caught on the film strip, ripping it in half. He set it aside. The only one that seemed to matter was the *Talent Now!* tape, which had the most tally marks.

He felt an electric jolt at the realization of the possibilities that lay ahead. And that he wasn't crazy. At some point, Pop must have experienced the same thing that Jordan had as he found out what the TV could do. Had Pop uncovered whether it was because of the tapes themselves? Faulty wiring in the walls? Or maybe some sort of weird electromagnetic energy upon which his grandparents' house sat? He didn't know and he didn't care.

The *Talent Now!* tape was still in the VCR, and Jordan hit the EJECT button to examine it, though it wasn't the plastic exterior he was concerned with. When he raised the back flap that protected the film strip, it was just as he'd suspected. The tape was faded in places, thinning to the point of tearing in others. If it was like this on the small piece Jordan had examined, he could imagine how the rest of it looked. Which explained why the tape's visuals were so uneven, the sound so garbled.

Jordan sighed deeply as he eased the tape back into the VCR and rewound it. He had no desire to sit through the carnage a second time, but if he was to follow through with his new plan, he had a lot of research to do.

9

IT WASN'T LONG after he pressed PLAY that he heard a rattling from the kitchen that he registered as the sound of the screen door opening. Footsteps followed.

"Hello?" someone called.

Jordan quickly pushed EJECT, gathered the tapes, and swept them back into their box.

"Jordan? You here?"

He shut off the TV and snatched a handful of papers from Pop's desk, pretending to read.

"There you are," the young woman said with a patronizing lilt as she walked into the room. "I was calling you."

Jordan barely made eye contact with his cousin as he stared at the wad of papers in his hands. "Sorry. Must've been in the zone."

"Sure looked like it."

Jordan suppressed a disgusted snort and clenched his fists upon seeing the result of her vanity. Waves of brown-blonde hair bounced atop her slender shoulders, her cheeks plump and perfectly powdered as the corners of her mouth upturned into a polite smile. Even if Jordan had not seen her enter, he would have known she was there by her perfume that smelled of crisp apples and salty ocean air.

Every ounce of her appearance screamed effortful perfection, from her artificially whitened smile to her Jimmy Choo flats, a stark contrast to Jordan's paint-stained band tees and scuffed Vans. Jordan eyed the sparkling diamond on her ring finger, fairly certain it was worth enough to feed a small country. *How much did that baby cost?* he came dangerously close to saying.

"Looks different without Pop here," Sam said as she looked around the room. Her voice was high and airy, resembling the tone of false modesty she used at every family function, regaling aunts and uncles and cousins with stories of which faraway island she'd been to recently, her promotion at work, or how she and Dave were close to picking a wedding date.

Jordan concurred with a half-hearted mumble, still looking busy with his pile of papers.

"It's so . . . *empty*," she marveled, hands on curved hips. "Like something's missing." She looked off wistfully. "Remember how much time we spent here when we were little? We'd sit together in Pop's recliner reading *Curious George*. I guess in a lot of ways, this place became home for both of us, didn't it?"

Jordan grumbled his assent, not in the least bit eager to reminisce with her.

"You know, I remember one time when you were little and Pop saw you in his chair and said—"

"Why are you here, Sam?" Jordan burst as he looked up from the papers, dropping his hands to the carpet. He raised his eyebrows in irritation.

His unexpected coldness seemed to jar Sam. "Pop left me the TV," she said. "I just came to measure it to see if it'll fit in the condo."

So much about that sentence infuriated Jordan. He clenched his fists and exhaled sharply.

She didn't even *need* the TV. Jordan was sure that the money Dave made from his fancy law firm job could buy them the biggest damn flatscreen that Best Buy could sell them. Not that Jordan wanted it anyway. But why should she get the TV when Jordan could think of at least four other people Pop could've willed it to who needed it more than her? Out of all the things Pop could have given him, he'd gotten the fucking secretary desk.

"That was nice of him," Jordan managed through gritted teeth.

Sam flashed her perfect smile and cocked her neck to the side as she said, "It was, wasn't it?" She wiggled her fingers into the pocket of her tight jeans and withdrew a small measuring tape. "So, what did he leave you?" she asked as she started measuring the length of the TV set.

He pointed to the desk.

"Oh, right! I remember he always used to say you were gonna get it when he died. Anything interesting?"

"What?"

She gestured to the open drawers and piles of papers on the desk and floor. "Did you find anything interesting in the desk?"

"No," he lied, looking down into his lap as he picked at a cuticle. "Nothing. Old papers and junk. You know Pop."

She finished measuring the TV and set the tape atop it as she glanced at her glittering watch, the metal face thick with chunks of gold and silver. Jordan sneered at the Coach band and reflexively rubbed the plastic face of the Timex on his wrist, the black fabric band creased and worn from years of wear. "Shoot, I'd better get going," Sam said. "Dave's out running some errands, and I need to sort through the rest of the engagement photos before sending them to the framer." She reached for the black Kate Spade purse she'd set on the table and slung it over her shoulder. "Well, take it easy."

"Will do."

"See you soon."

Hope not.

Seconds later, he heard his cousin's footsteps tapping on the kitchen linoleum, followed by the clatter of the screen door closing behind her. Then there was nothing. Jordan exhaled, closing his eyes as his shoulders slumped with relief and tension slowly left his muscles. He grabbed the *Talent Now!* tape from the black box and shoved it back into the VCR. If he was really going to attempt what was blossoming in his mind, he had questions that needed answering. Things he needed to know. And there was only one way to find out. After taking a few deep, calming breaths, he placed his hands on the sides of the TV, pressed PLAY on the VCR below, and watched.

10

SAM GOT HALFWAY into her car before she realized her mistake. She stepped out of the white BMW and started back up the sidewalk to Pop's house. She opened the door with a manicured hand, her shoes once again tapping on the cheap kitchen linoleum.

"It's me again!" she said. "Just forgot my measuring tape." She walked through the kitchen and into the living room to find Jordan where he'd been just minutes ago. The only thing that had changed was the television was now on. He stared into the screen like that little girl from *Poltergeist,* the bright glow shading his face.

"Jordan?" she said cautiously. "You okay?"

He gripped the corners of the TV with claw-like hands, though Sam couldn't see what he was watching from her angle.

"Jordan?" She wanted to tap his shoulder but was scared of what that might trigger, already thinking something was wrong with him. A thin line of spittle dripped from one corner of his mouth as if he was in some kind of trance. She watched the glow of the TV dance on his face, his gaze fixed on the screen, as his head minutely swayed left and right.

Dear God, she thought, the skin on her arms prickling with nervous heat, *he's having a seizure.*

A dark shadow fell over him as a quick burst of electricity—a craggy line that flashed pure white—sparked from the corner of the TV and into his fingertips. His rapt eyes reflected the screen's static flurry.

Sam flinched as Jordan began to take on a rapidly growing aura of that same white light. The color and shape of his features began to soften and bleed into each other, his body beginning to flicker in black and white like millions of microscopic pixels sparkling all at once. In a matter of seconds, Sam watched with rapidly blinking eyes as he grew lighter and lighter as if he were a photograph to which someone had applied an antique filter. His form grew more transparent as he faded in and out, and a high-pitched whine emanated from the television's speakers. The sound made Sam's eyes throb with migraine-like pressure, and she quickly closed them against the bright glow that had consumed her cousin. When at last she opened them, when the glow and buzzing whine had vanished, Sam's mouth ran dry. Jordan was gone, with nothing but a quick burst of hot air radiating from the empty space he had occupied only seconds ago.

11

THE NEW IMAGES that replaced the fuzzy ones Jordan had seen from the safety of his grandparents' living room were incredibly vivid, the sound no longer garbled. Everything had taken on a tactile presence. He felt the heat from the lights interspersed throughout the massive theater, smelled the cool, climate-controlled air, and heard the cacophony of thousands of cheering audience members. The noise was deafening, his brain pulsing inside his skull to the pattern of his heartbeat—throb, *throb*, throb, *throb*—until a flurry of white dots infiltrated his vision.

He expected to wind up in another technical booth as he had when he'd watched the *Carol Burnett* and *Password* tapes, but it was immediately clear that this time was different. He stood inside a small, red-curtained alcove near a center aisle where the roar of the crowd was ear-splitting. He only had to peek at the crystal-clear stage far below to realize he had been transported to one of the theater's upper balcony tiers. Fighting vertigo, he counted the tiers. *One, two, three.* He was on the third.

There was commotion a few rows below him as several audience members strained their necks to see past a man blocking their view, holding a video camera.

"Come on!" someone whisper-hissed. "*Move!*"

The disgruntled remarks continued until someone tried to grab the camera. "Okay! Okay!" the man conceded, lowering the silver Sony. "Back off. Jesus Christ."

It wasn't until Jordan heard the irritated utterance of *Jesus Christ* that he realized it was the same voice from the tape. Which meant that the cursing, camera-holding man was the one who had recorded it.

Jordan digested the revelation as he connected the dots. Both the *Carol Burnett* and *Password* tapes had been initially recorded from the sound booths he'd been taken to, which he thought explained the location of his materialization. But the *Talent Now!* tape had been recorded by an audience member's video camera. Is that why it had sent him, to this space, the spot closest to where this man had recorded it? Jordan wondered if each of Granny's tapes acted as a kind of homing beacon, sending the viewer to the vicinity of the recording. Which would be a good thing. At least he had a relatively firm idea of where he would end up each time. But there were more important things he needed to figure out. Like, where was Granny in this massive theater? And even if he could locate her among the thousands of other audience members, how could he save her? Could he simply warn her what was about to happen? Was that enough? Even if he found an option that proved to be even remotely feasible, he was sure Pop had already tried it. He thought of all the tally marks next to the line indicating the *Talent Now!* tape.

But what about *him*? Jordan hadn't even begun to consider the possible repercussions of his travels. What if he was caught or hurt or trapped? Could he ask anyone for help? Would they believe him?

Each question was valid and worth exploring, but only one stuck in his mind more than all the others: *Could I die?*

He couldn't begin to fathom the ramifications, and hoped like hell that he didn't have to find out.

The dull throbbing in his head returned, overwriting his dizzying thoughts of his own mortality. But it lasted only a minute before the ache and his terrible thoughts were eclipsed by a flaming arrow shooting up into the balcony.

12

THE SOUNDS OF people scrambling and screaming were the same as when he'd watched the taped version of these events, only louder. Now that he was *in* the theater, he could make out the panicked exclamations of individual voices—the moan of an old woman, the terrified cries of a nearby child—among the high-pitched screams of those who knew they were going to die. It was even more horrifying to watch because he knew help wasn't coming.

He retreated to the back of the alcove, suddenly realizing that the relative safety of the *Carol Burnett* and *Password* tapes had made him cocky—and careless. He watched audience members fleeing the flaming balcony below as the heat spread in invisible tendrils, probing through the cavernous space like the tentacles of a squid, curious and hungry. The man on the stage continued shooting arrows into the audience as if it were nothing more than target practice at summer camp. Watching the arrows arc and the danger they carried, it occurred to Jordan that he hadn't even considered how he would get out.

Another arrow shot to his left, reverting his attention to the man holding the video camera. The man jerked and jumped, trying to wriggle from his seat while filming the action below, so it was no wonder why the quality of the tape was so bad. He pushed through the crowd, cursing under his breath as he made it to the aisle. He closed the camera's small LCD screen, and—

A deep *swoosh*ing sound filled Jordan ears along with the sense of being pulled backward, like a roller coaster in reverse. But when he opened his eyes, he was no longer watching the terror from inside the theater. He released his hands from the television with a series of wheezing inhalations and took a moment to catch his breath. He said a silent prayer of thanks, grateful and relieved to see that he was back someplace familiar. The black-and-white static on the silent TV screen replaced the sardine-packed rows of flailing arms and legs and faces etched with panic and fear, the plain window shades in his grandparents' living room swapped for the flaming theater curtains. Although the cloying smell of smoke still clung to his clothes, his own horror began to dissipate as he clutched the blue carpet like an anchor. He swallowed hard and blew out a series of small, quavering breaths. Despite the noiselessness of the house, the audience's screams were clearly imprinted in his ears like a dark, echoing souvenir.

Though there had been no one in the room with him before, he felt a presence. Like he was being watched. There was no one beside him, and the living room door that led to the front porch was closed and locked. But when he turned around, away from the outdated television set, there she was: Sam. She sat rigidly on the edge of the couch as she stared at Jordan with wide, unblinking eyes.

13

JORDAN HAD TWO thoughts. The first was that he didn't know what to say to explain what she had just seen; and the second, much more instinctual, was *Oh shit*.

They were locked in one another's gaze. Then, in a small, numb voice Jordan had never heard her use, Sam said, "Either I'm crazy, or you have some explaining to do."

Jordan didn't waste his breath by spinning an elaborate lie, excuse, or suggestion that, yes, she *was* going crazy. Instead, he simply said, "I can't explain all of it."

Still in that childlike voice, Sam said, "Try."

Jordan rose from the floor, his legs numb from the hours he'd been sitting, and sat on the cushion beside her. He looked down at his lap and picked at a cuticle while he tried to settle on the right starting point. After a fumbling start, filling her in on Granny's box of tapes and what they could do, he told her about finding the *Talent Now!* tape and the sheet of paper with Pop's handwriting tucked into the bottom of the box.

"Look at the tally marks next to each tape's title," he said.

Sam looked at the crinkled paper, not yet beginning to see what Jordan was getting at.

"I think Pop knew what the TV—or the tapes, or the VCR, *whatever*—could do. Each mark is a time he watched the corresponding tape. But not just watch—"

"You think he . . . *went* there."

"Yes."

A contemplative silence fell upon the room, and from Sam's unblinking eyes and incredulous tone, Jordan already knew what she was thinking. "You think it's crazy."

Sam snorted. "Whether I think it's crazy or not is irrelevant. Whatever happened to you, wherever you went, I *saw* it. So, either we're having a shared delusion, or—"

"It's real," he insisted.

"So," Sam said, taking a deep breath, "what causes it?"

Jordan shrugged. "I don't know. Maybe it's faulty wiring in the house, or some kind of energy in the ground underneath." He realized the absurdity of both suggestions, as if his grandparents' 1950s row home sat atop an ancient Indian burial ground instead of poor, rocky soil. "All I know is it only happens when I touch the TV." He mimed clutching the top corners of the television with his palms. "Like that."

"Can you control it? Where you go and when you come back, I mean."

Jordan took a moment to consider and, as he did, realized this was the longest conversation he could remember having with his cousin since they were little, when the bitterness and disgust were still years away. "I don't think it works like that. It takes you to the location of the tape. The closest place possible to the source of its recording."

"And coming back?"

"It seems like it's whenever the tape ends. Whenever I . . . come back, the tape's over and I'm staring at a static-filled screen." He shook his head. "But I don't know for sure. I haven't done it enough."

Jordan imagined the cogs in Sam's head turning as she tried to make sense of what he was telling her.

"So, you just pop back in front of the TV?"

Her diction made it sound so simple, but it was true enough. He told her about the headaches and the fluttering in his stomach that accompanied the sensation of being yanked backward whenever he came and went. But he knew he didn't need to convince her. After all, she'd seen it firsthand.

"What did you see when you walked in?"

"You mean you?"

He nodded.

"You were in front of the TV, obviously," she said.

Jordan nodded to affirm that, yes, this *was* obvious.

"But it was like you were in a trance. After a few seconds, you started to look . . . "

"What?" Suddenly he was horrified of what she might have seen.

"Fuzzy. But not quite that. Just less . . . sharp. Fading in and out, like glitter in a snow globe. I thought I was getting a migraine, that my mind was playing tricks on me. But then you were drenched in bright, glowing light and were just . . . gone."

Jordan absorbed this new information, picturing his body fizzling and fading as he was sucked from one time and place and deposited in another. "And that was it?"

Sam nodded. The conversation seemed to take a toll as her bright, wired eyes began to lose their sheen. She pulled her hair back taut against her scalp in the stress-relieving gesture she'd adopted in her first test-taking days of elementary school. "Now what?"

"What do you mean?"

"I mean, what's your plan? What are you gonna do with this . . . information?"

Jordan's lips were pulled back in a shallow smile etched with cautious hope. "Go back and save Granny," he said.

"You can't be serious."

His steeled eyes, carrying not a trace of humor, conveyed how serious he was. "You don't have to approve."

"I'm not *dis*approving. I'm just saying it's not a smart idea."

"Oh," Jordan said, his smile growing crooked. "Because you know all about smart ideas, right? I'm sorry, for a second I forgot that I was speaking to Samantha Jones, doer of all things right and perfect."

Sam seemed to absorb Jordan's jabs and disses, pushing them aside with a deep exhale. "Look, even after what you know—what *we* know—think of the risks we're taking when—"

"First of all, what do you care about the risks? Second, there *is* no *we*. You walked in on me," he said, gesturing to the TV, "and I told you what was going on. That's it."

"Jordan, if you think I'm just going to go back home and forget what you told me, what I *saw*, then you *are* crazy."

"You know what," Jordan said, the pitch of his voice rising slightly in mock agreement. "Maybe that's a good idea. Actually, that's a *great* idea. Why don't you go get into your new BMW and drive back to your perfect condo? That way, when Dave comes home, you can go try out one of the hottest new restaurants in the city and congratulate each other on how wonderful and perfect you both are."

Sam adjusted her grip on her purse, her unblinking eyes blooming with uncertainty.

"You know," Jordan tried, his voice rising, "you're only five years older than me, but you're always the one looking down. Like I'm somehow less than you."

"What are you talking about? That's not true. I don't look—"

"Yes, it is," he countered, a hard edge to his words. "You mean to tell me you didn't judge me when I went to community college while you were blowing six figures to earn the same piece of paper from some liberal arts chalet in the middle of the fucking woods?"

"Jordan, I *worked* for that degree. I—"

"Or when you heard that I had to drop out while you got to live the college life in some hipster town three states away?"

"Drop out? I thought you were applying to MICA?"

"Yes, Sam. Drop out. I'm sure the phrase is foreign to you. It turns out that when you run out of money, your school runs out of reasons to keep you enrolled."

"I didn't know you dropped out," she said, her voice small. "But wait. What does that have to do with me?"

Jordan gave a disgusted snort. "Don't act like you don't know. You may be more successful than me, but you sure are shitty at playing dumb. How many times have you been to Thanksgiving dinner or family parties where you've bragged about the new places you've traveled to? You know the rest of us can't afford it, but that doesn't stop you from filling us in on everything we're missing."

"Jordan, I don't know where this is coming from, but my life isn't what you seem to think it is."

"Oh, Sam," he said, his voice mocking, "you've traveled the *world*." He spread his hands, gesturing wide. "But me? I don't go anywhere, Sam. Not to the beach, not to a fancy timeshare in Bar Harbor, not to the fucking Hamptons. But I guess it's not your fault. You just happened to fall into bed with money rather than earning it yourself."

Sam recoiled as if struck before turning to face Jordan. "The only time I went to the Hamptons was when Dave was invited for a work weekend with his colleagues."

"You would say that, wouldn't you?" Jordan's lips curled into a smirk as he shook his head. "Classic Sam Jones. But you know what? Forget I said anything. You didn't come here to hear any of this from me. You just came for the TV, right?" He gestured at the clunky square in the corner of the living room. "Go on. Take it. You already have everything else you could possibly want—the job, the condo, the vacations. What's one more thing?"

Sam seemed immobile under his glare, struck silent by his bitter words. Obviously, she didn't realize that he *had* meant what he'd said, and that he'd been harboring these feelings for some time.

Jordan's nostrils flared as the familiar rage bubbled closer to the surface. "Go back to your dream house and leave me the hell alone," he spat.

Sam still sat rigidly on her grandparents' couch as a plump tear rolled down her cheek. "You don't have to be such an asshole," she said, but her voice was small and lacking conviction. She grabbed her purse from the coffee table and headed for the door, only looking back when she said, "Pop and Granny took care of me when my own parents couldn't. They were my grandparents, too."

14

SAM DID GET into her new BMW and drive home, but Jordan had gotten one thing wrong. Dave wasn't there when she arrived. All that remained in the cream-carpeted living room was the black leather couch, end tables, and some family pictures on the walls, all the items she had bought herself. The rest (the sixty-inch flatscreen, leather recliners, and matching wine and magazine racks) Dave had taken when he moved out two months ago. Thankfully, the condo was in her name; otherwise, she was sure he would've taken that, too.

In the kitchen's bright light, her attention locked on the ring on her finger. The three adjacent diamonds sparkled with the brilliance of something twice their size. Despite the separation, she hadn't taken it off—or told anyone about the split. It wasn't that she was embarrassed (Sam had caught *Dave* cheating, after all), but she saw enough of the catty women at Dave's office parties to know that they would take one look at her and scoff through their plastered-on smiles. Like she was somehow tainted, erroneous for leaving a man who had the financial means to cater to her every whim. The same gossips who believed women could not possibly achieve happiness and fulfillment unless they were married, homeowners, and had a gaggle of children.

So, she wore her ring and a flashy smile at parties and family functions, making up excuses for Dave's absences. Somehow, embellishing her life seemed easier than revealing the truth.

It also became the norm.

There were times when her lies nearly fooled *her*, which only magnified the hurt when she returned home to an empty house. Though she had never been one to let a man define her, she couldn't deny the pain of being cast aside, like being repeatedly kicked in the stomach.

Instead of dealing with the pain, she dived deeper into her job as a junior marketing executive for Baltimore's office of tourism. She conducted and published interviews with up-and-coming restauranteurs, compiled her lists of the *Top 10 Things to Do in Baltimore*, and wrote more than her share of articles about the city's increasingly ridiculous goal to make the polluted waters of the Inner Harbor swimmable. It paid well, and she liked the work and her team, but as the calendar flipped months and years, she found herself being given the same cyclical assignments. She wrote the same "What's Hot in Baltimore?" columns every summer and compiled the same photo galleries of the Harbor's Christmas village—scarf-wrapped families ice skating as Santa waved from the throne inside his German-inspired chalet—every December. There were the same mundane interviews with aquarium employees about the new exhibits they were featuring, and the same rehearsed questions for the Orioles each baseball season. Despite her ability to write about the city she loved, it no longer gave her the satisfaction or sense of purpose that it once had.

She kicked herself for not applying for that feature writer job with the *Baltimore Sun* she'd seen the month before, though it hadn't stopped her from clicking on the job posting every couple of days, her mouse hovering over the apply button.

She knew she was qualified, knew it was a job she could do well—to write bigger stories, *important* stories. Ones that mattered. Not ones about fucking Christmas villages and base-ball games. So, why was she afraid? Why hadn't she applied?

Because you're an idiot, she thought. After all the years she'd spent being realistic—finding a job and building her emergency fund, playing it safe instead of shooting for bigger opportunities to avoid disappointment—where had it gotten her? Sam had looked around at her windowless, gray-walled cubicle and blinking cursor on the Mac in front of her.

In this box. That's where it's gotten me.

She glanced at the photos tacked on the thin, industrial walls—sunny shots of smiling, bikini-clad women clutching piña coladas on Caribbean beaches, extravagantly colored mar-ketplaces buzzy with activity, and a couple raising their arms in victory atop the ruins of Machu Picchu—all the pictures and postcards friends had sent her from their travels.

Why couldn't that be her? Wasn't it time to stop worry-ing and start taking chances? From writing about traveling to actually *doing* it? She had the time and the savings. And after that, when she was back from wherever she wanted to go, clear-headed and tanned, she would apply for that job with the *Sun*.

But after weeks battling with her remaining doubts about whether to take the plunge or remain with the relative ease, routine, and security of her current job, the decision was made for her. Her supervisor had informed her that profits for the last two quarters had been down, and they were letting go the least essential employees to compensate. As if being fired didn't hurt enough, she was now *least essential*. But what hurt most was that she had been cheated out of making the decision for herself.

She'd been given a decent severance package and, along with her unemployment, it was enough to live on. But in another few months, she knew she would have to start dipping into her savings. What would she do when it ran out?

Sam felt her stomach sink as the realization came with a sudden jolt of electricity: she would not be able to travel after all. If she didn't find a new job after her severance ran out, if she used all her savings on frivolous things like the trips she was planning (the brochures were still scattered on her coffee table), not only would she be unhappy, she would be homeless.

Her mind spun, blinking against the dizzying thoughts that had cycled on repeat for the past few months:

That she had wasted so much time on things and people that made her unhappy.

That she was useless—*least essential.*

That her job loss, like her separation, she had kept secret out of shame.

And this, she imagined telling her cousin as she stood in her near-empty home, *this is my perfect life.*

Sam opened a bottle of wine, picked up a book, and tried to read. It wasn't long before she tore her eyes away with an exasperated huff when she caught herself rereading the same paragraph over and over. She kept her narrowed eyes on the page with the intent of a student studying for an exam, but her mind was elsewhere, preoccupied.

Did Jordan really hate her?

Did she really brag and boast like he had accused her of doing?

She released a shuddery breath and set the book facedown, pages splayed on the adjacent couch cushion. Her eyes tingled with the impending threat of tears, but she forced them back, steeling herself. No. She would not let Jordan get into her head. Instead, she rose on wobbly legs and walked to the kitchen, to the marble countertop where she always set her phone. She doubted there'd be any messages from friends (especially those enjoying vacations in the Bahamas or skiing in Vail). She suddenly realized with the golden-hued enlightenment of perfect clarity that their lives had not stopped for her. She had separated from her fiancé and lost her job, and who among her friends—the friends she'd once shared late nights of wine and Netflix binges and promises to always be there for each other—had called to check on her? Had any of them offered to come over and order take-out and just talk?

She gripped the edges of the counter hard enough to feel her fingers tense atop the granite. She took a deep breath as she waited for the adrenaline to flush from her system. When it had, and she felt herself under control once more, she scanned the countertop for her iPhone—which she'd begun to check more frequently with each passing day—for good news, for a positive message, for a *win*. Maybe, she thought, as her heart trilled with a small jolt of adrenaline, she'd gotten a call from one of the jobs she had applied for. Or maybe there'd be a message from her old boss saying that the company's budget cuts had been reversed. Maybe they wanted her back!

But deep down she knew it was not true. When she swiped at the lock screen, there would be no missed call notification, no blinking envelope at the bottom of the screen to indicate an email from a potential employer or friend. Her eyes caught the five-by-seven plaque on the wall she'd had since college—YOU ARE ENOUGH, it said in raised black cursive. Once upon a time, she'd believed it. Years ago, backed by the voices of a dozen outspoken girlfriends and the promise that her whole career was ahead of her, that the best was yet to come, it'd been easy.

It wasn't until she reached for the space on the counter her phone usually occupied that she realized it wasn't there. It wasn't on the little table by the front door either, the only two places she'd ever left it. She began to retrace her steps as her mother had taught her whenever she'd lost anything—a stuffed animal or a special memento—when she was little. But now that she thought about it, she couldn't remember bringing it in the house at all.

She returned to the front seat of her car but did not find it there, either. Which didn't make any sense. She'd only gone one place today and was sure that—

She slowly closed her eyes as realization dawned on her.

You idiot.

With a deep exhale, Sam slid the key in the ignition and drove back to the one place she did not want to go.

15

JORDAN'S HEART RACED in the moments after Sam left, the clatter of the screen door sounding behind her. He'd never anticipated saying any of the things he'd said, but he wasn't sorry, either. Before he'd even known it was happening, his contempt for her had spilled out in a volcanic gush of vitriol so rotten and ugly that he himself was surprised that the words had come from his own mouth.

It was people like Sam who made Jordan wonder if life truly was unfair. She'd gotten the job she wanted fresh out of college, she was financially sound, and she effortlessly got along with everyone she ever encountered. By comparison, he'd dropped out of college, his summer job applications went unanswered, and each day he went through the same monotonous motions—mindlessly watching the morning news, scrolling through online job postings, and burying his nose in stacks of books borrowed from the library. He supposed because he was the youngest in the family, there was unfair pressure on his shoulders. Everyone else had stable, well-paying jobs, spouses, and homes. They'd started new chapters in their lives and had done Big Things. If these were the markers of success, what did that make him?

The sorrowful ache of underachieving, of being left behind, had swelled to the point where he'd even quit sketching and building his art portfolio—the one thing he had been banking on to be his ticket out of his mother's house and into a place where people shared his thoughts about life and art. He'd hoped it would bring him one step closer to animation illustration or designing art installations in big cities like New York and Chicago. The emptiness he felt, he knew, was something Granny would've known how to soothe.

He looked at the box of tapes. They were much more than keepsakes, more than memories of his grandmother to revisit whenever he felt the pull of the past. They were an opportunity. One that Sam or any of his other cousins did not have. A chance for him to do something great and extinguish his anxiety of not being good enough. To undo the damage done after Granny had died and the angry, bitter person he'd become when the stability of her presence had been stripped away from him. If he changed things, wouldn't that give him another shot at happiness, at saving for art school, a redo to plan the future he'd been neglecting? He didn't like to think of himself as running away from his problems, but what else would he call it? Wasn't going into the past to escape the future still running away?

Regardless, the strange and lonely thought had begun to solidify that there was nothing for him here, and Jordan became lightheaded with the dizzying prospect of becoming untethered from his own life. Even he had the wherewithal to recognize that the things that had once made him happy—going to the movies on a Saturday, bowling with friends, sketching in his bedroom or at the park while Rush or Jimi Hendrix blared in the background—no longer did.

He supposed that Sam was right about one thing: Granny had provided her with the very escape that she had provided him. But he couldn't help but feel bitter that Sam had gotten five more years with her than he ever would. She'd had time to ask Pop questions that her own father would never be able to answer, about car repair and career advice. Time for Granny to help her with her scholarship forms and study for her finals.

Jordan knew they had gotten along when they were younger, playing Frisbee in the backyard or walking to the snowball stand at the end of the street with the dollars Granny had slipped them. Or the nights when Jordan had padded wordlessly into her bedroom, Sam flinging back the covers and patting the empty space beside her. But then Sam had gone off to college, away from their middle-class Baltimore neighborhood and into the unknown. And although Jordan knew that she would be back on holidays and breaks, what stuck in his mind was that she had left him. Just like his parents, after the long stretches of days and nights when the yelling grew so loud it seemed to shake the walls.

Jordan's chest contracted with a sigh. He tried to clear his mind, but one thought wouldn't leave. The same question he had posed to himself in the minutes after Sam had left the house: If he'd said what he meant, why did he feel so guilty?

Jordan fiddled with the box of tapes for no other reason than to keep his hands busy and his mind off the guilt that plagued him. Somehow he wasn't surprised when he heard the kitchen door open as Sam crossed the threshold and stepped into the living room. She looked smaller somehow, her posture slightly hunched. Her eyes were red and puffy, and she was careful to avoid Jordan's gaze.

"Forgot my phone," she said. "Then I'll be out of your hair."

She grabbed her iPhone off the coffee table and turned, eager to be on her way.

"I'm sorry I said those things," Jordan said, noticing Sam stop in her tracks.

"You're not. You meant them. I could tell."

"I know," he said, not making an attempt to deny it. "But that doesn't mean I had to say them the way I did."

"Let's just forget about it."

But Jordan knew that neither of them would.

Jordan watched Sam eye the bare newel post, the wooden sphere conjuring the wispy memory of Granny's olive-green housecoat that used to hang there, the one with the big satin buttons. Seeing it gone, packed away somewhere, seemed to set Sam's bottom lip trembling. "She was something, wasn't she? I mean, I can't imagine the extra responsibility she took on by taking care of us." She wiped her eyes with the back of her hand. "For a lot of years, she was my grandmother as well as my parent after my dad overdosed."

"Wait," Jordan said as the dregs of his anger fizzled away. "Uncle Mike overdosed?"

The corners of her mouth dipped into a solemn frown as she gave a subtle nod.

"My parents told me he died. That he 'got sick.'"

"They were probably just trying to protect you. You were still pretty young when it happened."

"Yeah," he said, recalling all the horrible things he'd said to his mother this morning. "Probably."

"Granny told me years later that she knew he wasn't safe to be around. That she felt guilty she and Pop hadn't stepped in sooner before something worse happened. But she never badmouthed him in front of me." She shook her head. "The amount of restraint it must've taken for her not to call him every name in the book . . . " Sam trailed off. "The shitty thing is that he wasn't always mean." She absentmindedly touched a hand to her shoulder, the reminder of a bruise from a time and place long ago. "It was the Oxycontin that made him that way. I understand that now. Addiction's a bitch." Sam sighed. "After I dialed 911, Granny was the first person I called when I found him."

"You were the one to find him?"

"Yeah," she said. "Facedown on his bed. I thought he was sleeping—or drunk—until I started shaking him and saw the needle sticking out of his arm. When Granny came, she strolled right up to one of the policemen in her curlers and housecoat and announced that I was coming home with her. Like it wasn't even a question. Just wrapped me in an Afghan and cranked the AC as she drove us home." Sam looked off, eyes sparkling. "Sitting there in Pop's car . . . it was almost like a dream. I mean, I knew it was real, but I guess I hadn't ever really thought I'd leave that house."

"What do you mean?"

"My dad wasn't the most . . . peaceful. In my mind, I always knew that no matter how old he got, he'd need someone to look after him and keep him out of trouble. Even as a kid, I just assumed it would be me. He didn't have anyone else."

"But he was terrible to you," Jordan reasoned.

"It wasn't until I got here, to their house, that I realized what I'd been missing. There was no one screaming at the TV or at me, no crushed beer cans thrown at me for making too much noise playing with my plastic horses, no cigarette butts or glass bowls of God-knows-what littered on the countertops. No strange men delivering crumpled paper bags on the porch every other night. I remember that first night when Granny sat me down at the kitchen table and asked if I wanted something to eat. Her voice was soothing, even though cooking was probably the last thing she wanted to be doing at that hour. I just sat there and cried." Sam did so now as well, as if back in the moment, tears streaking her mascara as she reached into her purse for a tissue. "So," she said, "when you told me to leave earlier, that's why I got upset. That's what I was thinking of. Because if there's *anything* we can do to bring her back . . . that's something I need to be part of."

Jordan watched as Sam turned away as if embarrassed.

"Do you still feel like helping?" he blurted, the words tumbling from his mouth. "As crazy as it is?" He sucked in a shallow breath before expelling it. "I'm not sure I can do it by myself. For a lot of reasons."

Sam stared at the neat row of shoes lined against the bottom of the staircase—Granny's scuffed white sneakers and black church flats beside Pop's brown penny loafers and ratty house slippers. They were coated in a thin layer of dust, waiting for the time when they, too, would be unceremoniously stuffed into one of the big cardboard boxes marked for Goodwill.

She turned to the box of VHS tapes on the floor. In her wistful gaze, Jordan saw the same longing in her that he felt. It could be weeks, maybe months, before the house was sold, though soon the place that had overwritten so many of their bad memories would no longer be open to them. But if there was something they could do to change things . . . if there was even a *chance* to erase the past . . .

Jordan looked at her expectantly, his eyes pleading for her help.

He didn't know if she could forget the things he'd said, but he hoped that she could forgive them. If not for him, then for Granny. He watched as Sam's eyes fell upon the lone picture of their grandmother—mid-laugh, cheeks rosy above her Christmas sweater—atop Pop's desk. Then she turned back to her cousin and said, "What do we do now?"

16

AS THE CONTEMPLATIVE silence between them waned, Sam's question seemed to have only one answer.

"We go back there," Jordan said.

Sam turned from the VHS tape jutting from the VCR to her cousin. "But there's still so much we don't know."

"Exactly. Which is why we'll take it step by step. One trip at a time. We can make a list of what we need to do and what precautions to take."

Though she was all for being cautious, Sam wasn't certain that a safe way existed. Her brain still buzzed with the dregs of shock at seeing Jordan fizzle and fade like millions of pixels in front of her eyes. "Okay, so just for the hell of it, what questions would be on this hypothetical list of ours? What do we need to know?" She swept a lock of hair behind her ear as she glanced at the darkened television.

"The theater," he said. "That's the main obstacle. If we were transported somewhere public, somewhere outside, it might be a different story. But inside . . . " Jordan trailed off, shaking his head. "There's so many variables that it almost seems impossible."

Sam chewed her lip, considering. "Hit me," she said.

"Okay, for example, how do we move around the theater unseen? Where are the exits and entrances? How many employees are patrolling the place? What if we're caught?" He sucked in a breath. "And those are just off the top of my head."

"And even after all that, how do we save her?" Sam offered.

"Even before that," Jordan corrected, "how do we *find* her?"

"Well," Sam grinned, "we'll just look for the lady with a purse full of hidden cigarettes."

"Oh, God!" Jordan's lips stretched into a smile. "I forgot about that. Remember when we caught her behind the house?"

"You mean when she tossed the cigarette into the rosebush and it caught fire? Then she tried to tell us it must've been a miracle like that burning bush in the Bible."

"'I only smoke once in a while! When I get stressed!' Even then she made us promise not to tell Pop."

"I never did," Sam chuckled.

"Me, neither."

"So," Sam said, "just in case *that* plan doesn't work . . . "

"Well," Jordan said, "we can't exactly check row-by-row. That would take . . . I don't even know how long."

"More time than we have," she added. "And we probably shouldn't take the risk of asking anyone who works there. With our luck, they'd know right away that we weren't supposed to be there, though they'd probably just think we'd snuck in off the street, not from another *time*."

"And it wouldn't be smart to call out her name, either. There are thousands of people in that audience. Hell, she could be anywhere for all we know."

"Plus, if we wanted to avoid calling attention to ourselves—"

"Which we do."

"—then that's probably not the best idea."

And so, they decided that the aim of their next trip would not be of rescue or prevention, but of location.

They sat in front of the TV, the *Talent Now!* tape still protruding from the VCR. They'd decided that since Jordan had traveled three times already, he'd be the first to go. Sam would stay behind and make sure that nothing went wrong—though she wasn't entirely sure what that might be, especially when so many things could go wrong, or how she would fix them if they did.

Sam bit the corner of a cracked lip as she watched her cousin once again place his hands at the corners of the television.

Jordan took a deep breath and exhaled. "I'll be careful," he promised.

With her fingers poised on the front of the *Talent Now!* tape, she said, "You've got seventeen minutes. Make it count."

And then she pushed it in.

17

THIS TIME, IT didn't take Jordan long to recognize his location. He was back in the same red-walled alcove. The lighted sconces around the theater's perimeter barely cut through the darkness, more decorative than illuminating. Jordan quickly pressed himself against the wall. Although no one had seen him last time, it wasn't an impossibility that it could happen. He looked down at his watch and set the timer for seventeen minutes.

Everything was as it had been the last time: the darkened balcony, the red velvet audience seats, the high, curved ceiling, and the giant white exclamation points hanging above the shining stage. Though the amazement of being here once again was not lost on him, time was literally of the essence.

He peeked into the aisle and knew he wouldn't likely be able to spot his grandmother regardless of his angle or vantage point. It was too big, too dark, and too crowded.

He had to focus.

On stage, Cowgirl Judy's act was winding down. Though her audition was not successful, Jordan knew that it would end up being a blessing. After the massacre, she would appear on a local news broadcast saying that being eliminated from the competition probably saved her life since she didn't have to stay backstage to fill out paperwork for her progression to the next round. And everyone knew how things had turned out for the people backstage.

For a second, Jordan considered blowing the protocol he and Sam had discussed of avoiding calling their grandmother's name. He knew it was a long shot, but the rapid *thump thump thump* of his heart that accompanied the bubbling urge to shout, "Thelma Jones!" grew harder to ignore. It wrapped around his mind like a tempting serpent. *Do it. Just do it and see what happens.*

He closed his eyes and shook his head as if to dislodge the thought. But knowing that his grandmother was out there somewhere, in the same room as he, only heightened the jittery prickle racing down his spine. The nervous energy he felt in his clenched stomach grew stronger and more electric as Jordan saw *him* walk onto the stage.

The man's posture was straight, his steps measured and soldier precise. *Almost as if he'd practiced this,* Jordan thought. The man held his chin high as he took long, purposeful strides across the shining black stage. His microphone amplified his heavy-booted footfalls, which were not unlike the elephantine *thump, thump, thump* of his parents' on the hardwood stairs as they galumphed around the house during a fight, each of them eager to get the last word in before retiring to their separate bedrooms.

"Mom and Dad are screaming again," he'd quietly breathed into the phone on many sleepless nights. "I don't like it, Granny."

"It's not your fault," she'd soothe with the calm precision of a 911 operator, and Jordan would swear he could feel her warm breath emanating from the receiver. "How about I stay on the phone with you awhile?"

Jordan hadn't thought about that phone call in years, and he forced his lips to steel against their quivering. He had cried back then, huddled under his Pokémon bedsheets with the phone pressed against his rosy cheeks, but he would not give this man the satisfaction.

Jordan pulled his eyes off the stage as the temptation to call his grandmother's name fluttered up again. He quickly scanned the crowd for women who resembled her short, plump frame. She would have glasses, for she could barely see anything without them, and most likely a long-sleeved top of some sort. She was always cold, especially in large buildings like theaters and casinos where they pumped in cool air to keep people awake and alert.

He focused on one woman in particular, not because she looked anything like his grandmother in clothes or size but because of her smile—that same wide, joyful grin. It was almost enough to make him think it could be her. But as his heart fluttered, the comingled applause and music in the theater seemed to soften into an expectant silence that fell upon the audience like a freshly laundered blanket. Jordan watched as the smile vanished from the woman's face when a piece of flaming debris fell from the ceiling and onto her head with a meaty *crunch*. Her mouth opened dumbly, as if she had been presented a particularly challenging math equation she could not solve. Her eyelids fluttered, and her limbs kicked and jerked. Her seatmates flocked to her, placing their hands on her shoulders as blood poured from the open wound at the flattened top of her gray-haired head. It cascaded over her slender nose and thin lips before streaming into her open mouth, the people around her not yet realizing that she was a lost cause, that she would lose consciousness within thirty seconds and be dead within sixty.

Jordan froze. He didn't think he would be able to move ever again. But after a moment, the audience's screams snapped him out of it.

His watch continued to count down. In another few minutes, he'd be back in his grandparents' living room. And what had he accomplished? All he'd done was eliminate a few dozen women from consideration. He'd have to tell Sam that they were still completely in the dark.

He peered from his hiding place as flaming hunks of plaster fell from the ceiling, smoke mingling with the cool theater air as the enormity of his efforts hit him. It would be impossible to find Granny unless they did something drastic.

Jordan looked past the many balconies and the judges' table way below, then to the man standing on the polished stage with his chin held high in defiant victory. But the contestant's Zen-like composure was broken as his lips betrayed the sliver of a wry smile, his eyes closing as if in response to some sort of euphoric electricity humming through his body. When he finally opened them, he exhaled as if satisfied by the work he had done, God looking at his creation and finding that it was good, before he calmly turned and exited the stage.

And then, as Jordan watched screaming people struggle beneath hunks of fallen metal and plaster, the man disappeared behind a screen of heavy smoke, and Jordan knew what he had to do.

18

HE LOOKED AT his watch as it counted down the final seconds until he would be plucked from the theater and deposited back into his grandparents' living room. He would tell Sam his idea, how wrong their focus had been, how there might be another way. A better way.

He heard the stampede of people beyond his alcove and squeezed his eyes shut, steeling himself for the nausea and whopping headache and *whoosh*ing that would soon fill his ears. But moments after he should have been returned to the safety and quiet of his grandparents' living room, all he heard were the incessant screams of the scared and dying. He opened his eyes to see that he was still in the theater, the shouts of those beyond the curtain growing louder and more pained. Jordan coughed as the smoke roiling through the gaps in the curtain found him. It obscured his vision but not enough so that he couldn't see the small digital readout at the center of his watch.

No, he thought, looking at the four blinking zeros, two on each side of a stationary colon.

The countdown was over.

His eyes widened, his scalp prickling from the wave of confusion that swept over him. He sucked in jagged, wheezing breaths as his empty stomach churned with the rise of hot bile at the back of his throat.

He'd accurately set the watch, had known exactly how long the *Talent Now!* tape lasted. What was going on?

I should be back by now, he thought, his chest tightening as he tried to ignore the panic clawing like a bear at his chest. It wasn't working.

Mostly everyone had fled from their seats and now crowded the theater's various exits. They pressed tightly against each other's sweat slickened bodies, shoving away those who tried to squeeze in front as if they could somehow navigate the mob quicker than anyone else. The cacophony of wails formed a deep-toned wave of panic that swept over each row in the theater.

Jordan could no longer see the stage through the enveloping smoke. One of the unoccupied balconies that had caught fire began to crumble, chunks of charred plaster and velvet seat fragments breaking away and cascading into the aisle and seats below. From the screams and injured moans beneath him, he assumed that the pieces of jagged-edged debris had smashed onto the heads of those who had been unfortunate enough to sit below. What he knew for sure, though, was that this was the most he had seen of the terror here. The tape always ended when the view-obstructing man had shut his video camera, sending Jordan back to his present. But that had been minutes ago.

His panic continued to spread, but he couldn't help thinking that he had only himself to blame. He had been naïve, meddling in something he didn't understand. If he died here, what would happen? Would it be like he was never born at all, like George Bailey in *It's a Wonderful Life*? Or would Sam be putting up missing flyers for her cousin who had disappeared into the TV? Jordan dug his nails into the carpet as he closed his eyes and waited to find out.

19

THE LIVING ROOM was quieter than Sam would have liked it. She'd always found comfort in noise at home—the tinkling of jazz from a nearby speaker, the muffled sound of an afternoon talk show on the television in the background. It calmed her, made her feel she wasn't alone. Which was why the noiselessness of Pop's living room jangled her nerves. She'd put in the tape and pushed PLAY, watching in disbelief as her cousin faded and fuzzed and disappeared before her eyes again. After he'd vanished, she grabbed the VCR remote and muted the recording. Knowing what was coming—the screams, the chaos, the bloodshed, and the fear—churned her insides intensely enough that she clutched her stomach

Sometime after Cowgirl Judy had left the stage, Sam checked the watch she had synched with Jordan's. In another few minutes the tape would be over, and Jordan would appear in front of her. Then they could discuss what he'd seen and how best to proceed.

On the TV, the screen was stuck. Had she not already seen the video once before, she might have believed it was over. But there was still commotion to be shown, the videographer capturing the chaos from crazy angles as he fled. Plus, the tape would cut to black when it was over.

And Jordan would've come back.

Sam hovered a finger over the PLAY button of the VCR, waiting a moment, then pressed it.

Nothing happened.

She pressed it again.

Click.

Again.

Click click click click.

Nothing.

The screen showed the same still frame, the edges quaking slightly like the building fizz inside a shaken soda bottle.

She thought back to the days before Blu-Ray players and iPads, when the highest level of technology she'd had was a VCR. The tape wasn't over, Sam knew; rather, it was a problem she'd faced many times as a kid, calling her parents from her bedroom on a Saturday night to come fix it. Now, staring at the television as she contemplated the ancientness of both it and VCR, she shouldn't have been surprised that the screen was frozen.

"Shit!" she exclaimed, continuing to press the PLAY button like she had as a kid, as if it would magically unfreeze the screen.

Click click click click.

She held her hands in front of her as if she no longer knew what to do with them and slapped the wooden sides of the TV with an open palm. "Come on!" she said, her tone first pleading, then commanding. "*Come on!*"

The only result was the hot throbbing in her palms as her panic slowly churned into fear.

How am I going to explain this?

If she couldn't unfreeze the TV, if Jordan never came back, what would she do? She sure as hell couldn't tell anyone about this. And even if she did, what would she tell them? That

Jordan had been sucked into Pop's TV while they were trying to change the past? They'd think she was having a nervous breakdown and had lost her grip on reality. *Jesus, they'll try to get me committed.*

"Fuck!" she shouted, striking the center of the glass screen with the side of her fist.

As if instigated by her profanity, the TV blinked back to life, unfreezing as the final few minutes of footage played. Sam stared at the screen as the tape switched over to the shaky filming and weird angles that signaled its coming to an end. *Come on. Just another few seconds. Don't freeze up on me again. Just another few—*

The tape abruptly cut to black, and Sam gaped at the TV as her cousin began to materialize in front of her.

20

JORDAN SCREAMED AS he tore his hands from the sides of the TV. He lay on his side with his eyes squeezed shut, clutching the sides of his head.

"Jordan," Sam soothed. "You're okay. You're back. What's going on? What's wrong?"

"My head," he said, palms pressed against his temples.

Sam sped into the kitchen and returned with a glass of water. "Drink this," she said, extending the glass. As he reached for it, a crumpled Hershey bar wrapper fell from his hand. He stared confusedly at the chocolate-slick paper before realizing he must've grabbed it when clutching the theater floor. *Ten-year-old chocolate,* he mused. *Wonder if it's expired?* He reached for the water and chugged it with his eyes closed as some dribbled down his dry lips. At last, the throbbing in his head began to dissipate and he was able to sit up.

"What was that?" Sam asked.

Jordan's hand shook as he brought it to his nose and wiped away the blood that had begun to trickle down.

"It's getting worse," he said, rubbing at the dark bags that had appeared beneath his eyes.

"What do you mean? What's getting worse?"

"The headaches. The pressure." He kneaded his fingers into his eyes as if simply speaking had caused him pain. "It builds and builds and then it just . . . bursts."

"Wait," Sam said, "are you saying this has happened *before*?"

Jordan nodded, knowing she wouldn't like that he hadn't told her about the side effects.

Sam's expression was stern, her jaw set. "How often?"

"Every time." Then, as if it was somehow supposed to make her feel better: "But this is the worst it's ever been."

"Jesus," Sam muttered, shaking her head. "That's it. We're done. No more field trips."

"Sam—"

"No, Jordan. This is going to *kill* you. If this is happening to you after, what, three or four times, who knows what the next one will do to you?"

Jordan scrambled to the toppled black box that held the VHS tapes. "The tally marks," he said, grabbing the eBay receipt and holding it out to her. "Look at them. All the times Pop did it. He must've found a way."

"Yeah," she said, "or maybe there are different effects for different people. Did you ever stop to think that *this* is what killed him?" She motioned to the scrap of paper. "This is hardly a case study."

"But we're so close."

"We're *not* close. We're nowhere in the vicinity of close."

"I thought you wanted to help."

"I did," she said slowly, as if afraid that an angered tone would set him off. "But there were some things you left out the first time, like the increasingly debilitating headaches and nosebleeds. Not to mention the possibility you might not come back."

Jordan froze.

"Yeah, I know about that, too. Was it as scary for you being there, waiting to come back, as it was for me here?"

"What caused it?" he asked as the last of his headache faded away.

She pointed to the TV. "The damn screen froze. Something else I guess you didn't consider."

"How'd you unfreeze it?"

"I hit it a couple times, but who knows if that even did anything?" She shrugged. "There are just too many variables in play, and we don't know enough to make them any less dangerous. Not even close. And the more I think about it, the more I think that nothing good can or will come out of this. I can't speak for whatever Pop did, but what I know with absolute certainty is that if something happened to you, I wouldn't be able to forgive myself."

Jordan smirked. "You didn't even ask me," he said.

"Ask you what?" Sam said, grabbing her purse, ready to leave.

"What I saw when I went there."

"Whatever it is, it doesn't matter. I'm done."

Jordan began to sit up, afraid she might actually leave. "You might want to wait to decide that until after you hear what I have to say."

Sam sighed. "Fine." She crossed her arms, looking down at her cousin. "What'd you find out? A new way to get us killed?"

"No," Jordan said, not appreciating her sarcasm. "Pop tried to save Granny. Obviously, he wasn't successful. But I don't think it's anything he did wrong. He failed because it's not possible. Here," he said, again showing her the paper in Pop's handwriting as if she had not seen it already. "Just look at the tally marks. If there was a way, there wouldn't be so many. He would've figured it out."

"He was already in his eighties when Granny died. Who knows what he was thinking?"

"Everything I can think of, from calling her name, to searching the audience, to clearing the theater or pulling the fire alarm, all of that stuff he would've thought of because they're the easiest solutions. And you're right. Who knows what was going through his mind? He could've tried each possibility ten different ways and still failed."

Sam stared at him blankly.

"Think of the audience. There were thousands of people in that theater. The number of women alone makes it impossible to locate Granny. Like finding a needle in a haystack. But what if instead of saving someone, there was someone we could stop?"

"Stop who? And from what?"

Jordan smiled. "This whole time we've been focusing on saving Granny when we really needed to focus on someone else." He paused to make sure he had Sam's attention, that she wasn't merely waiting to shoot him down. "To save Granny, we have to stop that lunatic from blowing up the theater."

21

"NO, NO, *NO*."

"Sam," Jordan started, "this is different. Now that we know *who* to focus on, it won't be like the other times."

"Oh, it won't? And how can you guarantee that? Hmm?" She kneeled on the floor with hands on curved hips, lips pressed tightly together below eyes narrowed with a schoolteacher's severity. "Who's to say that us meddling in the past won't cause things to turn out even worse? Is that a chance you're willing to take?"

Jordan was silent, knowing he'd been backed into a corner.

"Jordan, you didn't see the TV from your side of things, but I did. The picture and sound faded and fizzed like someone scanning stations on an old radio. Not to mention that it *froze*, nearly trapping you a decade in the past. And you know what that means? The tape is bad. I doubt the quality was good to begin with, but after seven years of views and exposure to heat and sunlight . . . " She shook her head. "I'm surprised you even came back at all."

All of what she said was valid, but he couldn't *not* do something just because there was danger involved. He trained his steady, desperate eyes directly on Sam's. "I can't just give up."

Sam stepped to the VCR and pushed the button marked EJECT.

"Woah!" Jordan cried. "What are you doing?"

Sam silently extricated the tape from the VCR, flipped the back cover open, and smiled knowingly. "Just like I thought." She turned it around so Jordan could see. "It's falling apart."

Jordan practically jumped the distance between them, eagerly grabbing the tape from her hands. "No," he said. "It can't be."

But it was. He looked at the faded strip of tape beneath the plastic flap and saw that it was even worse than he'd remembered. There were sections that were crinkled, and what looked to be a small hole near the bottom edge. If he unwound the entire film strip, what other damage or defects would he find?

Sam fixed him with a pitying look. "If the tape were new, it might be a different story. But who knows how many views this one's got left in it? You could try it again and maybe get there fine, but coming back . . . " She trailed off. "That would be another story. A story you might not have the opportunity to tell."

"What if we can fix it? There's got to be a way."

"I majored in digital media," Sam said, "but we examined plenty of VHS tapes to see how technology has progressed over time. And all I know tells me our tape is just about shot. I think we'd be lucky if we got another view out of it before it froze again or went completely haywire."

Jordan's heart sank. He'd known this is what the outcome would be, but he'd tried to push it from his mind, choosing instead to believe the more optimistic alternative. He inched from the couch and set the tape on the chipped coffee table, looking at the black rectangle with disappointment as if it was a magical object that had become disenchanted.

"Pop must've watched it more than we thought," she said quietly, as if the possibility of failure scared her more than she was willing to admit.

Jordan continued staring at the tape, as though his gaze would cause it to magically repair itself. "Do you know that sometimes I have to look at pictures to remember what she looked like? And then when I do, I find that my mental picture—my *memory*—was wrong." Jordan looked helplessly at his cousin. "She's fading, Sam. I was twelve when she died. It's been a long time."

"I know. It must have been hard."

"She was one of the only people to ever encourage my art. Who told me to take chances. After she died, I thought that if there was ever a way to bring her back, I'd do it." He looked around the living room that now smelled of dust and stale air and closed his eyes, choosing to remember how it had been instead of how it now was. "Remember how we used to play games back then? The four of us around the dining room table?"

Sam smiled at the memory, as if forgotten until this moment. "Of course I do. You tried to cheat at Yahtzee."

The hard edges of Jordan's face softened into a grin. "I can still hear her humming as she let me help her make stuffed peppers. I think she knew that it calmed me, being in the kitchen with her."

"What about when she'd take us to 7-Eleven to get Slurpees and held up the line because she insisted on paying in dimes and nickels?"

"That," Jordan said, nodding, "was embarrassing."

"No more than watching her hurry to hide when she saw the Jehovah's Witnesses walking up the sidewalk."

Jordan smiled, caught up in their joint reflections. "When I couldn't sleep, I'd think about how she'd stay on the phone with me on the nights my parents' arguing got really bad. Either reading me a story or just telling me about her day."

She was the first person I'd ever lost, he thought. *How can you grieve if you're never shown how?*

"We had a way to bring her back," he said, examining the fading strip of film before tossing the tape onto the coffee table with a clatter. "But now it's gone."

Sam wiped her eyes. "I know how you feel. I thought she'd be around forever," she said, raising her shoulders in a childlike shrug. "She was always there. It just never occurred to me that one day she wouldn't be. I was too concerned with dumb stuff like boys and concerts to appreciate her."

To Jordan, it seemed as if the feelings Sam had either repressed or ignored because the truth was too difficult to accept came flooding back to the surface.

"I was at the mall when it happened, Jordan. The fucking *mall*." She sighed, taking a deep breath. "I didn't believe it. Not at first. It didn't sound possible. Then I rushed home and saw that every TV news channel was the same—the smoking theater and exploded windows, bodies on stretchers, streets blocked by ambulances and caution tape, people with hands pressed to their mouths in horror. It was like watching 9/11 coverage all over again." She nodded. "Then it hit me. But even then it was too much to process. Too much *noise*. So, I pushed it away."

She nibbled on a fingernail. "What if you're right?" she said, looking to Jordan, her eyes glistening with cautious hope. "What if we did try again, one last time?"

He eyed her quizzically. "What about the tape? You said it could freeze or tear."

"It might," she said. "But maybe we'll get lucky."

"You're willing to do that?"

"It scares the hell out of me, but yes. We owe it to Granny."

"But even if we planned ahead, thought everything through, what would make this time any different from the others?"

"Well," Sam considered, "you already said the main one. We'd be saving Granny indirectly by stopping that man from blowing up the theater in the first place. Plus," she said, "you'll have something that you or Pop didn't have before."

"And what's that?" he asked.

"Me," she said, her eyes shimmering in the low light of the living room. "We'll go together." Sam stuffed her tissue back into her pocket and placed a reassuring hand atop her cousin's. "We're going to save her, Jordan."

His smile dropped. "And what if we can't?"

"Then we'll have done the best we could."

For now, that seemed to satisfy both of them.

"I don't know about you," Sam said after a while, "but I've had enough excitement for one day. Let's meet back here tomorrow and we can start talking things through to get some semblance of a plan together."

"Sounds good to me," Jordan said. "Wait, don't you have to work?"

Sam shifted uncomfortably on the couch, her cheeks growing red. "I'll just take a sick day," she said without meeting Jordan's eyes" She shrugged. "It's been a slow week anyway."

They gathered the tapes and returned them to the box and the locked drawer in Pop's desk. Jordan slipped the small brass key into his pocket, feeling its shape through his jeans to double-check it was there. As he and Sam walked through the kitchen and out the door, for the first time since Jordan could remember, they said their goodbyes with an embrace that felt neither forced nor obligatory.

One last time, Jordan thought to himself on Pop's porch, the high summer sun warming his face. *One shot to get it right.*

They would plan and account for as many variables as possible, using whatever they could: maps of the theater's exits and entrances, eyewitness accounts, newspaper clippings, and YouTube videos of that grim day. Because this was the time that mattered. And if they could change things . . . if they could go back to the way it used to be, away from all the bitterness and anger and uncertainty . . .

Jordan smiled hopefully, considering it. And as he watched Sam walk away with the parting promise to return tomorrow, for the first time in a long time, he had a good feeling about things to come.

22

AS SAM WALKED to her car, she struggled to push away the thoughts that had been swimming through her mind for the past couple of months—how everything she'd once held dear had suddenly been swept away: the partnership she'd built, the career she'd worked for, the financial stability she'd achieved. It was all gone. Even five years ago, if someone had given her a list of the possible ways she'd be spending her mid-twenties, this one—this loneliness, this isolation, this fear of taking chances—would have been her last guess.

There's always light at the end of the tunnel was the expression she'd always heard (and offered) when others were in times of crisis. But now that she was on the other end of it, she couldn't foresee a future, near or distant, in which the crumbling of her carefully constructed life would start to rebuild itself, where the light would become brighter until it was strong enough to make her forget the darkness had ever existed in the first place.

But maybe that was about to change.

What Jordan had told and showed her was nothing short of miraculous. She didn't know how it worked or why it was possible, or why this chance had been afforded them, but she didn't care. They had a chance and intended to make it count.

There were extensive plans to discuss, preparations to make, but Sam relaxed, knowing they could take the time they needed to get it right.

Still, she couldn't help but wonder that if they could change the past, how would it affect the present? If they were successful and Granny lived—if the *Talent Now!* show had gone on as planned—who was to say that something worse, some other tragedy she could not predict nor control, would occur as a result of their meddling? Would there be more lives lost, more destruction, somewhere else in the world? The possible implications sent a tremor of fear through her, goosebumps rising on her arms.

There were risks, yes, but the chance of success was enough to push them aside. Just the possibility that she would once again see her grandmother's wide smile and feel her tight embrace was enough to keep her going. A chance to make up for the years of lost time she had never appreciated as a teenager. A chance to prove to herself that she wasn't a coward, that she wasn't afraid to take chances.

She shoved the day's happenings from her mind as she unlocked her car door. She had just sat down when the shrill *brrrriiiiiiing* of her cell phone made her jump. She plucked it from her pocket and, as she glanced at the screen to see who was calling, was ashamed to find her heart leap at the possibility that it might be Dave. Calling to say that he'd made mistakes, that he was sorry, that he was coming home, and that everything would go back to the way it was. But it wasn't Dave, and she swiped the screen and said hello to her Uncle John.

"Hey, Sammy," he said in his usual cheery manner. She could picture his dimpled grin at the other end of the line. "Sorry to call so late. I just wanted to know if you've had a chance to get the TV out of your Pop's house yet."

"No," Sam said. "I haven't. I'll probably get to it soon, though."

"Well, if it's too heavy for you, I'm sure Dave can—"

"Dave's busy," she snapped. "I can do it." She lowered her voice and tried again. "Why do you ask?"

When he told her, Sam felt her heart freefall into her stomach. It wasn't the news itself that shocked or scared her, but what it implied. So, after they said their goodbyes and the connection was broken, Sam exited the car and bounded back up Pop's sidewalk, her heart still galloping in her chest. Her legs, it seemed, could not move fast enough.

23

"COME ON, COME on, come on," she mumbled as she tapped her foot on the landing, each unanswered knock ratcheting up her nerves.

"Didn't you get enough of me today?" Jordan joked, answering the door.

But Sam was not in a joking mood. "Tonight," she said, talking fast, voice grave. "It's got to be tonight."

"What are you talking about?"

"I just got a call from Uncle John. He's in charge of Pop's will and asset distribution," she explained.

She paused for a moment, and Jordan leaned in expectantly. "They sold the house," she finally blurted. "They're clearing it out in the morning. We have to do it tonight."

Jordan fell silent, his eyes growing wide as he seemed to process her words. "But we're not ready!"

"I know," she said. "Believe me. But if we're ever going to do this, it's got to be now."

24

THE HOUSE WAS dim when they walked back inside. Dusk was approaching. Sam clicked the black knob on the neck of a floor lamp, casting a dim, ethereal glow throughout the room. The blocky television with its wooden exterior sat in the corner, a dormant monster waiting to be awoken.

"This isn't the way it was supposed to be," Jordan said.

"I know. But we've got to do the best we can."

If they knew how it worked, it would have been different. They could've moved the TV to Sam's house and tried to replicate their attempts, but because they didn't know, whether it was the TV itself, the videotapes, faulty wiring, some weird energy beneath the house, or a combination of things, they couldn't justify taking the risk.

"There's still so much we don't know," Jordan said, defeat coating his words. "So much. How do we get backstage? How do we get to *Him*?"

"Hey," she said with a cautious smile. "We can do this. You've done it before. That already gives us a head start." Her words seemed sincere but uncertain, as if trying—and struggling—to give him a pep talk. "Failure is one thing, but not trying? What would Granny think about that?"

"She'd tell us to keep going," he said. The memory of his grandmother's words brought a smile to his face. His eyes began to mist, and he rubbed them with his palms as he considered the possibility of hearing them once again.

In the darkness, Sam gave him a reassuring smile, though her eyes betrayed a degree of skepticism. "All right," she said. "Let's get started."

They spent several hours online researching and reading all that was available about the *Talent Now!* Massacre, most of which was old news Jordan had committed to memory nearly a decade ago. By the time they'd grown weary of the subject, they could relay all the key facts: the number of dead and injured, how many first responders had arrived at the scene, the number of weeks it had been a headline news story, and so on. They knew the accused's name, age, and the simple rouse that had allowed him to successfully commit such an act of terror. They knew about the theater itself, its architecture and exits, and how the ancient fabric of the curtains and audience seats had proved a natural accelerant for the flames that would engulf them. They also knew about the survivors and their stories (always horrifying, always brutal), including one familiar to Jordan about a young woman who had suffered third-degree burns, knocked unconscious outside the theater's mezzanine exit. They knew these facts like the backs of their hands, but what they didn't know far outnumbered what they did. As such, they were resigned to find there was not much information that would help them with what they were planning. How would they blend in and travel undiscovered? What would happen to them if they couldn't? As they continued skimming articles and news stories, one thought persisted in Sam's mind.

"How does one person manage to do all this by themselves?" she asked. "I mean, maybe he could've done *most* of it, killed a few people, but did you read how long it took for security and first responders to scramble into the theater and down the aisles? How no one seemed to be able to get out? I mean, for God's sake," she said, scrolling through an article on her phone. "This one says all the mezzanine level doors inside the theater were *locked*. What the hell, Jordan? How can one person do all that by himself and not get caught?"

It was a good question, and one which Jordan had considered many times over the years.

"What if he didn't?" he said. "What if he had help?"

"An accomplice?"

Jordan shrugged. "Nothing was ever reported in the press, but that doesn't mean it didn't happen. The idea of an accomplice was something the police had hung on to for a while but gave up on the theory after they couldn't find any evidence to support it."

"Great," Sam considered. "As if one psycho wasn't enough."

"But who?" he said. "And why? Who's crazy enough to go through with something like that?" Jordan pictured the flaming theater, the screaming children, the crime scene photos of singed teddy bears and toddler shoes.

"Who knows? There's a lot of unstable and messed up people in the world. And what about M—?"

"Don't say his name," Jordan interrupted, holding out a palm to stop her. "He doesn't deserve it. And what about him? He's dead."

"Yeah, but who killed him? And why?"

"I don't know *who*, but I'm guessing the *why* had something to do with him blowing up a theater full of innocent families."

"I know, but his body—what was *left* of it, anyway—makes it seem like there was more to it than that. It's not like he died of smoke inhalation, Jordan. He was *stabbed*. Multiple times."

"I don't know," Jordan said numbly. "I'm just glad he's dead."

Sam sighed. "I think we've just about exhausted our research resources. What information we have, we already knew. What information we need, we'll never have. It's now or never."

Jordan solemnly nodded his agreement.

Sam rose to lock the kitchen door as Jordan turned on the television. The picture was dark, left on the blank station that allowed them to connect to the VCR. He withdrew the black box from Pop's desk, anxiously rummaging until he found the *Talent Now!* tape, acutely aware these could be his last moments in 2020. When he'd left the house that morning, he hadn't realized it might've been for the last time. "It wasn't just visiting," he'd spat at his mother. "It was fucking abandonment." Even now he recoiled at the thought that he had actually said those words aloud, that they might be the last ones he'd ever say to her.

He glanced at his cousin. They were sitting inside the dim circle of illumination cast by the lamp on the floor, stage actors in the spotlight. "You ready?" He pressed the necessary buttons on the VCR and readied himself to push in the tape. "All right," he said with a grim smile, "let's try not to die."

Sam cast her gaze downward, readying herself for what she was going to say as much as Jordan's reaction to it.

Jordan lined up the tape with the VCR slot. With the slightest of pushes—and good fortune, he supposed—the familiar visuals would emerge on the screen from the flood of static and muffled sound. He would put his hands on the television like he'd done each time before and he and Sam would—

"Wait," Sam said, seizing Jordan's hand. "How exactly are we planning on stopping this guy?"

"We need to get backstage somehow. Use one of the employee entrances. If we're quick enough, we might be able to get to him before he even makes it onto the stage." Jordan fiddled with the tape, leaving its edge jutting from the slot in the VCR. "We need to tell someone what's going to happen. Maybe they'll stop the show. Maybe—"

"Maybe they'll think we're crazy."

Jordan didn't disagree. "The priority is to get backstage before it's his turn. If we get that far, and if no one believes us after we tell them what he's going to do, well . . . we'll have to take things into our own hands."

Sam grimaced at the prospect but didn't argue. "Keep in mind, we've got less than twenty minutes. Once the tape is over—if it even makes it to the end—that's it."

"I know. We'll do the best we can." He looked back at the TV. "You're gonna want to put your hands here and here," he said, placing his palms at the corners. "I guess it'll take us both back together. I don't see why it wouldn't."

But Sam made no move to touch the television as Jordan reached out with his fingers on the tape, ready to push.

"Jordan," she blurted.

He craned his neck toward her, eyeing her expectantly. "Huh?"

"I-I don't think I can do this," she said, her eyes trained on the floor. "I can't go with you."

"What are you talking about?" His small smile revealed he thought she was joking. But when her stony expression held and he realized she wasn't, Jordan withdrew his hands from the television. "We were going to do this together."

"We were," she said, her hands shaking as she picked at her cuticles. "But I'm scared. So fucking scared."

"Scared?" Jordan said. "And you think I'm not?"

"I know you are," she said. "But I keep thinking of what could happen to me. To *us*. Then I picture Granny in that theater, and I think, 'Wasn't she scared? How selfish are you?' But I can't help it, Jordan. I can't help it." She began to tremble, her cheeks reddening as warm tears brimmed in her eyes. "So much of my life has gone wrong," she said, throwing up her arms in weak surrender. And if I go with you . . . if something happens and I can't come back . . . I think I'll lose it. I think I'll lose my damn mind."

Jordan's rigid posture loosened, surprised at seeing her so vulnerable. This wasn't the Sam Jones he knew, the Sam who spoke of exotic vacations and flashy cars, bragging about adventures with friends and how great her life was. Then again, Jordan considered, maybe she had never been *that* Sam at all. Maybe it was a version of her he'd cooked up and vilified over the years, and out of what? Jealousy? Insecurity? Now, sitting in the darkened living room of their grandparents' home, which would belong to a stranger in less than twenty-four hours, the image of her he'd conjured began to melt away, and what he saw before him was not an entitled braggart, but a woman consumed by fear.

But he still couldn't stop the bubbling rise of hate and betrayal, the kind of rage he had felt many times before, knowing it was only a matter of time before he said something he would later come to regret. After all that he had shared with her, all the feelings he had tried to put aside, *now* she was deciding not to go?

"Are you fucking kidding me?" he spat.

Sam's tears flowed as she began to mutter a low apology, but Jordan's ringing ears prevented him from hearing it.

"Now," he said. "*Now* you decide to chicken out."

"I'm sorry," she said. "I'll stay here in case something goes wrong with the tape, but I can't go with you. I can't. I'm just so—"

"Yeah," Jordan said. "Scared." He shook his head in disbelief. "But you want to know the good part? I actually thought I had been wrong about you. But it turns out that you're still the same selfish, self-absorbed bitch I remember."

Sam flinched as if struck, her eyes wide with shock.

"What?" he mocked. "Is it time for you to go on one of your 'vacations'?"

Sam's face whitened.

"You think I never noticed? You're not as mysterious as you think you are. You always run away when things get hard. You did the same thing at Granny's funeral. Where were you that time?" Jordan scoffed. "Fiji? The Caribbean? Did you even go to Pop's funeral?"

Sam looked up at Jordan with ferocity in her eyes. "How dare you."

"How dare *me*?"

"I know for a fact that you didn't go to Pop's funeral, either, so yeah. How dare you belittle my grief."

"Grief," he mocked, shaking his head. "You don't know a goddamn thing." He didn't know whether he wanted to cry or scream as he turned back to the TV and the waiting tape jutting from the VCR. "Forget it. I'll do it myself. And when I come back with Granny, make sure you let her know that you were too scared to give a shit."

"Wait." Sam wiped her eyes as she grabbed her purse from the dining room table and dug around before finding what she was looking for.

In the darkness, Jordan couldn't see what she held. But once she got closer and he saw it in the glow of the television screen, he instinctively drew backward.

"You just happened to have this with you?" he said.

"I always have it with me. I had a stalker in college," she said and sniffled. "I was going to bring it anyway, just in case." She extended the hand that held the gun. "Take it."

"I don't want anything from you."

"Please," she pleaded, as if his refusal would be his final rejection of her.

Tentatively, Jordan moved closer, as if the weapon was a snake he'd been promised would not bite. "I've never shot before."

Sam's hands shook as she showed him the bullets from the small silver revolver, and how to load and unload them. "See? Easy. It's for short range, though, so if you think you're going to use it, make sure you get close enough."

"Have you?" Jordan asked, his tone softening.

"Shot it?" She wiped her nose on her sleeve. "Only at the range." She placed the gun in his hand and fixed her eyes on his. "Do whatever it takes to save our grandmother."

Jordan carefully placed the gun in one pocket and the bullets in the other.

"And promise me you'll be careful."

"I can't do that," he said as he turned back to the TV. "It's not too late to change your mind, you know." The soft way he said it was almost hopeful, the terror of doing this alone replacing his anger. Despite what he'd said, he wanted—*needed*—her help.

Sam shook her head, averting his gaze.

"Care to do the honors, then?"

25

SAM PUSHED THE tape into the VCR. As it was sucked in, she got the feeling that something irreversible had been done. She moved away from her cousin, kneeling as she observed his face in the glow of the TV. Before long, the snowy static faded and coalesced into the familiar picture on the screen. Sam just hoped it would last long enough for Jordan to get there and back.

And alive.

They synchronized their watches with dual *beeps,* and Sam watched as Jordan placed his hands at the corners of the television and stared silently into the screen.

"Get him," Sam whispered as the remnants of shame faded from her pink cheeks. "Get that sonofabitch."

And tell Granny I'm sorry.

She sat in the lamp's yellow glow as Jordan's body began to grow simultaneously transparent and luminous, his image pulsing and fading in and out. Soon he would be gone, and she would be alone in the darkened house. If all went as planned, it would be less than twenty minutes before he returned. But then again, she thought once more, if everything went as they hoped, would she even have memories of this, or would there be some kind of cosmic reset?

Seventeen minutes. So much can happen in seventeen minutes.

As she hoped they were doing the right thing, Sam was spellbound by the pulsing figure of her cousin flickering like a flashlight in need of new batteries. And then he was gone in a crackling burst of white light as if he'd never existed at all, leaving her alone in the glow of the television.

26

SEE YOU SOON, Jordan had been tempted to say, but he no longer felt a return trip was guaranteed. As he steadied his breathing, he pictured the fading memory of his grandmother's face and felt himself falling down the rabbit hole of memory to a time when worries of art school and jobs and debt were light-years away. He thought of the countless summer afternoons they'd spent on the sunken-in couch with books and lemonade or watching the very TV show he was about to travel to. He could almost smell the freshly cut grass that had once wafted in through the cracked windows as Granny tapped his nose and called him *Peanut*. When the doorbell rang, announcing the arrival of his mother or father, Jordan would feel his stomach prickle with anxiety, looking up at Granny with wide, pleading eyes: *Do I have to go?* But he already knew the answer. *Please don't make me.* If he had known then that she'd been gone in two short years, he would've spent a few extra seconds looking back at her, savoring the sight of her standing on the porch with the sun glinting off her glasses as she smiled and waved.

But now, instead of looking back as he had been compelled to do for so long, he was *going* back. And if what he and Sam had theorized to be true, for the last time.

He swallowed his fear, focusing.

Now or never.

Sam's revolver was a weight in his pocket, pressing down on his wallet. Inside was the folded, yellowed newspaper article he'd kept tucked there for years, the one he'd nearly memorized. *57 Dead, Hundreds Injured in Talent Show Massacre*, the headline said. When—*if*—he came back, if it was different from its Internet version, he'd know that he'd been successful. That things had changed.

He'd told his cousin the truth about mostly everything. He *did* want to save Granny by stopping this madman. And though he'd said that he was content to find him backstage and alert security about his plan, Jordan had lied. It wasn't enough. Not even close. Because after seven years of built-up rage and yearning for this moment, Jordan wanted to do more than just stop him. He wanted to be the one to kill him.

Sam had given him the gun as a precaution, for self-protection, but he had no interest in passivity. He'd known it would have to be this way since his last trip, understanding that there was no other possible way to save Granny or stop this psycho with the limited time they had. Killing him would be the easiest way—and the most satisfying.

With his hands gripping the corners of the television, he stared at the screen, breathing deeply. *I'm coming for you*, he thought, as he waited for whatever was going to happen.

PART II

CHARITY, 2013

You will be heard. You will be seen.
And your life will never be the same.

—Talent Now! *promotional flyer*

27

CHARITY SPARKS HAD gotten to the convention center early, wanting to be there even before the line officially opened at 7:00 a.m. Even with her precautions of setting her alarm early, choosing her outfit the night before (a loose white top and her best pair of blue jeans), and taking the bus route she'd known was the fastest, she hadn't been sure she would get a spot.

Her palms began to sweat from nerves as much as the temperature, and she wondered if it was even worth standing outside in the heat for just a chance. It was a little after 6:00 a.m., but many early risers had arrived ahead of time. *Look at them all,* she marveled, staring at the winding stretch of people caged like cattle between the steel dividers that wrapped around the block. Having survived nineteen Maryland summers, she knew it would be a few more hours before the heat began to take its toll.

She took an anxious, sideways glance at the people ahead. She could tell this was not the first time for many. Some sat in collapsible sport chairs with cloth bags filled with Doritos and Gatorade and well-thumbed paperbacks, looking ready for a day at the beach rather than auditioning for a talent competition. Charity, on the other hand, hadn't brought much with her. She had a bottle of water in her small purse (which she had bought specifically for today), along with a few packs of Keebler peanut butter crackers. And her iPod, of course. Always her iPod.

Today wasn't just a new experience, something fun to do. It was an opportunity. Her opportunity. And she would not blow it.

She hadn't fully anticipated the amount of people that would be here, and now the hundreds of bodies crowding her began to intensify her anxiety. Her heart thumped and her fingers trembled as she scrolled through her iPod, hit a song at random, and began her breathing exercises while Petula Clark cooed at her through her earbuds. *You are fine*, Charity thought, eyes closed as she blocked out the sensory overload. *You are safe.* She repeated the mantra as Petula listed all the reasons she should go downtown. *You are fine, you are safe. You are fine, you are safe.*

When she felt calmer, Charity fished the square of paper from the back pocket of her jeans and unfolded it.

THINK YOU HAVE WHAT IT TAKES TO BE THE **NEXT BIG THING?**

it asked at the top.

TALENT NOW! AUDITIONS COMING SOON TO BALTIMORE!

Below was the date and time, which she had committed to memory weeks ago.

Just looking at the page and running her fingers over its glossy surface made her heart flutter with the possibility that someone like her, a nobody from Baltimore, could have her dream come true in an instant. That she could move out of the city to somewhere she felt safe, where the afternoon summer sounds she'd hear would be the tinkling bells of the ice cream truck rather than the *pop pop* of gunshots. That people—strangers—would come to see her perform. That she would be heard and loved.

Which is not to say that she wasn't loved already. Her mother loved her, and her father had loved her, but she had no friends, only acquaintances, and she'd always felt uncomfortable around extended family. She saw how they stared at her, the furtive glances and higher-pitched tone they used when speaking to her, as if she were a child. Sure, she mumbled with her neck bent low to avoid eye contact, rocking back and forth to self-soothe when things got too loud or bright or fragrant. She was unable to control her nervous tics even when everyone else around her was still, but when the mere prospect of person-to-person interaction made your brain race and your heart flutter, what did you do? What was the solution? There was no easy fix for the anxiety that had plagued her all her life. It didn't matter if there were three people or three hundred. Her mind would begin to race—*Are they looking at me? Will I have to talk? What will I say? What if I say the wrong thing?*

For as long as she could remember, she had been asking for a sign. Something to tell her that she would be all right. That she could one day go to the mall without staring at her feet to combat the fear that every eye was on her. That she could go grocery shopping and not rush out of the store, leaving her cart behind when it came time to check out. That she would be able to count money on the spot or make small talk with the cashier without feeling pulse-pounding dread.

She needed a sign that she wouldn't be this shy, anxious girl forever.

Then, one day last month, she got it.

It had been hot and muggy and, with only a window unit in the small city rowhome she shared with her mother, Charity had spent the night as she always had during summer months: parked in front of the television with a grape popsicle in one hand and the remote in the other. It was Tuesday, the highlight of her TV week, because amid the horrible summer programming of reality TV, cop procedural reruns, and game shows, there was one bright spot in the lineup: *Talent Now!* She watched it every year, eager to see the various talents, the razzle-dazzle production values, and the reminder that anyone, anywhere, could do anything. It was the only show both she and her mother could enjoy together, laughing at comedians and shielding their eyes at the danger acts.

Once the show had finished, Charity got up, threw away her gnawed popsicle stick, and prepared to climb the creaky stairs to her room when she paused at the booming voice coming from the TV.

"Do you have what it takes to be the next big thing?" the announcer bellowed. "*Talent Now!* auditions are coming soon to the Baltimore area. Now is your time to shine!"

She turned, nearly slipping on the throw rug at the bottom of the steps on her way back to the TV.

"What's gotten into you?" her mother asked.

"What was that commercial?" Charity said in a rapid monotone.

"Looks like the show's coming to Baltimore," she said, looking into her daughter's eyes. "Why?"

Charity's eyes grew wide and bright beneath the straggles of her blonde hair. They brightened her pale, freckled complexion and softened the hard edges of her petite features as the corners of her mouth rose in a cautious grin.

"Oh, honey," her mother said, using the tone Charity equated to someone talking to a puppy who had just pissed on the carpet, a cross between disappointment and pity. "I just don't know about that."

"Mom, it might be fun," she said.

"And what would your talent be?"

"Singing," she said, doubt suddenly coating her words. "I would sing. There's lots of singers on the show."

"Those people are professionals, honey. People who have been doing this their whole lives. People who—"

"Don't you think I could do it?"

Her mother frowned.

"Baby, thousands of people will try out. You have to be realistic. The odds of winning are—"

"I'm just talking about auditioning. Trying. Isn't that what my social skills classes are for? To get me out of my comfort zone? To help me be more comfortable around people? To be part of the world?" Then, as if an enticing prospect had crossed her mind, she said, "Somebody's got to win it . . . right?"

Karen Sparks gave a nasally exhale, her mouth scrunched in a pouty frown as she looked down at her daughter. "Somebody's got to win it," she confirmed, holding Charity's hand. "I just don't think it would be you."

Auditioning for the show was outside Charity's box in every way, but she'd fantasized about being a singer and being on a stage ever since she was eight years old, sitting on her bed surrounded by posters of Carrie Underwood and Taylor Swift as she sang along to their songs with a pink microphone clutched in her hand. And then she'd seen Kelly Clarkson win *American Idol*, and that had cinched it. It was all she wanted and more. To be loved for being herself, not for who someone else thought she should be.

Regardless of what her mother said to keep her cooped up here—even if it was, as Charity suspected, because her mother was afraid of being alone—Charity would no longer allow herself to be collateral damage. She vowed to spend the next month practicing—her voice projection, her stage presence, her appearance. With enough time, she could be ready. No, she would make herself ready.

Now, standing between the steel dividers outside the convention center, only miles from home, Charity closed her eyes as the first rays of Baltimore sun kissed her cheeks. A smile formed on her lips and, as she opened her eyes, her heartbeat slowed as the line began to move.

By nine o'clock, the excitement in the crowd began to wane as the heat became relentless. Charity was tempted to pull her hair into a ponytail but didn't want to risk messing up the blonde locks that, against all odds, had fallen the way she'd wanted. After all, first impressions were important.

As she turned the last corner of the building, she could see the distant forms of registration tables and clusters of red, white, and blue balloons. Again, she felt that combination of nervousness and anticipation. "Uncertainty makes me anxious," she'd often admitted in her social skills group, where she was encouraged to share her fears and anxieties.

"And what makes you feel better?" the lead therapist had asked. "What makes those feelings go away?"

For once it was a question that she knew the answer to right away. "Singing," she'd said with a meek smile. "Singing makes me feel better."

She tried to push her worries aside, and it wasn't long before she found herself at the front of the line. She looked behind her, considering how far she'd come since she'd arrived and the many hours spent wrapped around this massive concrete building. It would have been so easy to give up, to turn around and go home, but she had not. She was quiet, but she was not a quitter. She would prove everyone wrong—all those people who'd ever said she was too anxious and timid to be a singer, all the kids who had laughed at her in her elementary school talent shows as she'd butchered the words (and pitch) of Kelly Clarkson's "A Moment Like This."

She was so caught up in her thoughts that she didn't register someone saying, "Miss? Miss?"

The man behind her tapped her shoulder, startling her. "I think she means you," he said, pointing to the check-in table and the blonde-bobbed woman in the white *Talent Now!* T-shirt sitting behind it. There was something about standing in front of her that made Charity feel as if she was already being judged, either in appearance or personality.

Charity fiddled with her hands while the sausage-fingered woman finished filling out a white form. "Okay, darlin'," she said with a Southern twang once she'd set down her pen. "Let's start with your name."

Charity smiled.

That's an easy one. Maybe this won't be so bad after all.

"Charity Sparks," she said, forcing herself to project her voice.

The woman wrote it on the form. "And what's your talent?"

She felt the urge to plug in her earbuds but forced herself to look in the woman's eyes when she said, "I sing. I'm a singer."

The woman seemed pleased with that answer. "We like singers on this show. They tend to do well."

Stupid! Charity thought, berating herself. Why didn't she say what she was really thinking and feeling, what her mind was shouting? *I've wanted to do this since I was eight years old!*

"I . . . uh . . . " she stammered nervously. "I sing."

"Got it." The woman smiled, as if she could sense the anxiety behind her repetition, that she was new to this.

Charity spent the next few minutes feeding the woman—Cheryl, Charity discovered—information about herself (birthday, address, contact information) as she wrote it on the application. When she'd finished and it seemed there'd be no more questions to answer or boxes to check, Cheryl took a Sharpie and wrote #6170075 in a box at the top. She also withdrew a long red, white, and blue label with the same number and handed it to Charity along with a red *Talent Now!* wristband. "This is your contestant number," she said. "Just peel it back and stick it somewhere on yourself. Shirt, leg, it doesn't matter. Anywhere we can see it. Just don't lose it."

Charity stuck the label below her heart as her lips curled cautiously into a smile, already feeling as if she belonged here. Cheryl told her to follow the other contestants into the building and wait for her number to be called.

Charity thanked her as she walked past the table to enter the convention center.

"And, honey?"

She glanced back to find Cheryl grinning at her.

"There's nothing to be nervous about," she soothed with a warm smile. "Just go in there and sing your heart out. Besides, what have you got to lose?"

She weaved through throngs of costumed jugglers, dance troupes, magicians, and animal acts, until she found a seat in one of the hundreds of folding chairs placed throughout the main floor. The once-neat rows she'd imagined had been disassembled as contestants had moved them around to sit with family or, in the case of those more socially outward than Charity, the new friends they'd made over the course of the morning.

When she'd walked through the doors of the convention center, the atmosphere had nearly taken her breath away. The gray carpeted floor stretched hundreds of feet in all directions, and natural light spilled through the large glass panels that made up the building's walls. To her right, a large gleaming flat screen hung from one wall, with dozens of blinking, colored arrows directing visitors to the locations they were looking for. BALLROOM 1, it said next to a flashing green arrow that pointed left. EXHIBIT HALL A, it said next to a blinking blue one that pointed right. She craned her neck up to the cavernous space above the massive TV and felt a tingle of nausea at the many intersecting escalators and walkways above her. It was like the mall on Black Friday, she mused, though the convention center had more natural light and more people bustling around.

Bunches of balloons flagged the entrance to each of the glass doors, while the judges' faces stared down at her from the large *Talent Now!* banners that swayed from above. Glossy, marquee-sized posters in red, white, and blue were plastered everywhere. DO YOU HAVE WHAT IT TAKES TO BE AMERICA'S NEXT NEW TALENT? read one. NOW IS YOUR TIME TO SHINE, read another.

The large size of everything in the massive space made her feel like she had been miniaturized, her mind swirling at the overwhelming cacophony of excited voices filling the room. She'd been tempted to plug in her earbuds and listen to some of the sixties music she'd downloaded, something else she'd discovered as a way of coping with her anxiety. Some people closed their eyes or counted backward or used a stress ball. She had her iPod.

But now, as she sat in a folding chair by the aisle, hands holding her purse in her lap and humming the opening bars to The Chiffons' "One Fine Day," a strange contentment came upon her. There was no one here she knew—no parents, no family, no acquaintances. She was free from judgmental stares and downward cast glances, from shame and fear. Free to be who she wanted. To start over as the new Charity Sparks who looked people in the eye and spoke more confidently and even carried a purse.

She relaxed and crossed her right leg over her left, feeling her posture straighten. Now, she wondered, as she watched the many performers around her, who would look at her and see a timid girl of nineteen? Because with her inner calm and purse and numbered contestant label, she looked (and felt) like she blended in just fine. She'd wait here until her number was called, watching the practicing performers all around her. After all, it was free entertainment and, as her mother always said, you can't beat a free show. And who knew, Charity thought, high on her newfound confidence, she might even make a friend.

It turned out she didn't have time. After forty-five minutes, the now-familiar voice boomed over the loudspeaker: "If your number ends anywhere between zero-zero-six-seven and zero-zero-seven-seven, please begin making your way to audition room number two. Again, if your number ends anywhere between . . . "

Charity once again consulted the label on her chest: #6170075.

That's me! That's me!

She grabbed her purse and shot up from her seat, frantically looking around the room as she realized that she had no idea where to go.

"That's me!" she said to the large woman next to her. "Where do I go?"

"See over there in that corner?" The woman gestured. "Just follow the crowd. That's the audition room."

"Wait," Charity said, confused, "I thought *this* was the audition room."

The woman laughed, seemingly delighted at her response. "You must be new to this," she said. "This is the *holding* room. We're just a bunch of cattle out here. Back there," she said, pointing to a far-off corner, "is where you wanna be. They got different audition rooms for different talents."

Charity mumbled her thanks before running off, barely hearing the woman yell, "Good luck, honey!"

She nearly sprinted across the main floor to the door with a bolded "#2" on it. She showed her wristband to the man standing outside, who motioned for her to enter. It was much smaller than the main exhibition space. By Charity's estimation, there were only a few dozen people. Gone were the flashy outfits, costumed animals, juggled objects, ventriloquist dummies, and large groups of dancers she'd seen before. Instead, Charity watched as they cradled real guitars and pretend microphones, tuned their various instruments, and sang lowly to themselves or with small groups clustered in loose circles. She'd barely sat down when a man with a black T-shirt and headset called her number.

"Six-one-seven-oh-oh-seven-five?" he asked.

Charity nodded.

"Perfect. You can follow me."

She obliged and they walked through another door, down a sloped carpeted hallway. "How are you feeling?" he asked, alternating glances between her and the hallway ahead. "Nervous?"

"No," she lied.

"Good," he said. "There's nothing to be nervous about."

Charity found that very hard to believe. Obviously, he'd never been through this process before.

"So, let me quickly tell you what to expect when you go in. Normally, you'd be auditioning in front of a few of the show's producers before being selected to audition in front of the judges. That's what will happen with most of today's contestants. However, we're doing things a little differently today." He gave a boyishly mischievous smile. "In addition to the acts already screened and put through by the producers, we've randomly selected some acts from today's pool to also audition in front of the judges. You know, to add some flavor to things."

Charity slowed her speed as she processed what he was saying. "So, you're saying I'm going to be performing in front of the judges?"

The man flashed a smile of perfectly white teeth. "Pretty cool, right? Normally contestants have to pass the producers' audition first, but you're skipping right through."

She'd known from watching the show that if she made it past the producers' round, she'd be auditioning in front of the judges. She just hadn't expected it to be *now*. She felt herself propelled forward as if by some invisible force, no longer in control of her own feet as she followed her escort down three separate hallways before stopping outside a pair of blue double doors with a laminated sign that read, STAGE DOOR. AUDITIONS IN PROGRESS. NO NOISE BEYOND THIS POINT.

"Stage door?" she said quizzically.

"Yeah," the man said. "We were lucky enough to find a convention center with an adjacent theater. That way you'll get the authentic *Talent Now!* experience right away."

Charity's eyes widened, the look of an aquaphobic child about to be tossed into the deep end of a swimming pool. What had she gotten herself into?

"And you know the best part about a theater?" he said, his playfully mischievous smile returning once again.

"A live audience," he said, opening the door.

The backstage area of the theater was freezing, the bite of the cool air chilling the beads of nervous sweat on her arms and forehead. Everything was as unwelcoming as a hospital room, only instead of white walls and sterile appliances gleaming beneath artificial lights, everything was black—metal beams and apparatuses, curtains, and crates with TALENT NOW! in white stenciled letters. Charity turned as she heard the heavy *click* of the door closing behind her. There was no going back now, only forward. She felt like Dorothy landing in the middle of Oz.

Throngs of people sped across the glossy floor, most with clipboards and T-shirts with crew printed on the back. As Charity advanced through the bustle and the dim spotlights above, she heard someone singing the opening bars to Whitney Houston's "Greatest Love of All" and found that it eased her nerves enough to take her mind off running in search of an emergency exit. She became so entranced by the silky smooth vocals that, for the second time today, she didn't notice when she had been spoken to.

"Charity Sparks?" a man holding a clipboard asked.

She nodded.

"Looks like you're next."

She looked down to where he had led her, a section of the black-tiled floor marked with an "X" in white tape.

"Keep your eye on the stage," he said. When she exits,"—he continued, pointing at the current contestant with the smooth voice—"I'll give you a thumbs-up and you'll be clear to go on. Sound good?"

She stood firmly planted to her "X," unmoving.

"I'll take that as a yes," he said. "Now, any questions?"

Yes, Charity wanted to say. *Plenty.*

What did I get myself into?

Am I really ready for this?

Why did I have to be randomly chosen to perform in front of the judges?

And the biggest one of all—

What if all of this was a big mistake?

But instead, she said nothing. The man seemed to pick up on her anxiety when he said, "You'll do fine."

Charity tried to summon a smile and reminded herself to breathe.

You are fine, you are safe.

"You'll have ninety seconds to perform and afterward the judges will decide what comes next. Now," he said, flipping through the pages on his clipboard, "it looks like we *do* have the song you brought, so no problems there. Just stay on your mark and wait for the current contestant to exit the stage. Pop quiz time—what am I going to give you when you're good to go on?"

"A-a thumbs-up," she stammered.

"Perfect. Just wait for my signal and you'll be good."

Charity was glad this man seemed to have so much confidence in her because she wasn't so sure. From her mark behind the long black curtains, she could see what waited ahead. The stage wasn't as large as she'd anticipated, which was good, but she was unable to see the size of the crowd and couldn't decide whether that scared or soothed her.

Applause sounded from the audience as the big-haired young singer jumped up and down before turning to leave the stage. Charity assumed she must have gotten a *yes* from all three judges. She hugged Charity on her way out, shocking her with the physical contact.

In the silent seconds that followed, Charity searched for the man in the black T-shirt. *Now?* her nervous eyes asked.

He held up one finger, spoke something into his microphone and waited for a response. Then he looked at Charity and held up three fingers on his right hand.

Then two.

Then one.

Then, after the longest fifteen seconds of her life, came the gesture she'd been waiting for.

His thumb flicked upward with a smile as he mouthed, *You're on.*

Charity looked from him to the stage, straightened her top and heat-frizzed hair, then walked out into the spotlight.

You are fine, you are safe, she reminded herself as her heart thumped in her ears, focusing only on her steps. *Don't trip. You're almost there.* She walked to the microphone stand at the center of the stage as if it were a sailor's beacon. If she could just make it to that point, she might be all right.

After five seconds that seemed much longer, she made it, one hand clutching the microphone stand, the other on the strap of her purse. She looked out at the raised judges' table on its little island set back from the stage. There they were—Hans, Portia, and Larry. She'd watched them on TV so many times but couldn't believe she was actually standing in front of them. They looked resplendent in their designer clothes and makeup that, she was sure, was professionally reapplied after each contestant left the stage, much unlike her sorry attempts to apply her own off-brand blush and eyeshadow at home. The judges seemed to glimmer regally, Portia especially, their sight reminding her that she was alone in the middle of the stage under bright lights and the gaze of strangers. She heard the familiar *bzzz* in her ears that, along with her dry mouth and tunneling vision, signaled the beginnings of a panic attack.

But then Portia's lips were moving. "What's your name?" she inquired in a cheery voice.

Portia! Charity mentally screamed. *Portia is talking to me!*

"Charity," she mumbled with her head bowed low, bumping the microphone with her chin. "Charity Sparks."

"And what are you going to be doing for us today, Charity?" Portia soothed.

Easy questions so far. Keep 'em coming.

"I'm going to be singing."

"Why do you think you're the next winner of *Talent Now!*?"

For a moment, caught up in the Hollywood glamor of the three people seated before her in their expensive clothes and artificially whitened teeth, she didn't know. She couldn't think of a single good reason she deserved to win. But then it came to her. The truth. "Singing helps me," she said softly. "I want to sing for people. I've wanted this since I was eight years old." Then she remembered the words she'd spoken to her mother weeks ago. "Somebody's got to win it." She shrugged. "Why not me?"

This elicited a smile from Hans. "I like that honesty," he said in his thick German accent. Obviously, he was used to more generic, heartstring-pulling answers about contestants following their dreams or wanting to make their dead parents proud. "Well, if you're ready, show us what you've got."

Charity smiled politely and glanced backstage, anxiously nibbling her lip as she waited for her selected song to begin. A moment later, she relaxed as the soft, melodic opening bars of Mama Cass's "It's Getting Better" started up.

Charity had loved Mama Cass the moment she heard "Make Your Own Kind of Music" on one of those Time Life CD compilation infomercials a few years ago (which she'd quickly purchased), and it wasn't long before her posters of Taylor Swift and Kelly Clarkson had been joined by those of The Mamas & the Papas, Charity wrapping herself in one of her grandmother's tie-dyed shawls from the sixties as she twirled and sang along to "I Saw Her Again" and "Dream a Little Dream of Me." They were songs with messages that Charity related to, optimism she just didn't find in the music of today. Mama Cass understood that it was okay to be different, to do things your own way and live your own life, no matter what other people thought. To make the world adapt to you and your uniqueness rather than the other way around.

But now Charity had a bigger task than listening, and she was no longer in her bedroom. She took a deep breath to wash away the cobwebs of nerves that still clung to her and, with sweaty hands at her sides, opened her mouth to sing.

She began by imitating Cass's low sweetness, Charity's voice sounding a little rusty to start. But as she hit the chorus, she sung louder, and her anxiety abated as she found comfort and confidence in Mama Cass's lyrics from nearly forty years ago. *I'm doing it,* she marveled, unknowingly replacing her old mantra with a new one. *I'm really doing it.* She sang without any stylistic flourishes of the raspy-voiced or high-note-holding singers she'd seen on the show, thinking the judges would appreciate her simplistic approach. And, by God, she was having fun. She felt her lips creep into a smile as she eased into her favorite part of the song, stopping in horror as her voice cracked on the last note. She slapped a hand to her mouth, cleared her throat, and prepared for the next verse. Her eyes were closed so she didn't see Hans raise his hand in the air, as if to stop traffic, as she continued to sing.

When she realized that the music had stopped, she opened her eyes, confused. *What happened to the music? Is something wrong?*

"I'm sorry," Hans said, rubbing his temples as if he'd been subjected to the blaring sounds of highway roadwork. "I just couldn't listen to that anymore." He took a long, deep breath. "How do you think that went?"

Wait a minute, Charity thought, confused. There were more verses. She hadn't finished. "I thought I had ninety seconds," she said meekly.

Portia was usually the judge on the contestants' sides, but a grin blossomed on her face. She clapped a hand to her mouth as a giggle made its way into the microphone, sending high-pitched echoes throughout the theater.

"Honestly," Hans said, "it sounded as if your vocals were on a rollercoaster—up and down, up and down. Like you were singing to yourself in your bedroom. There was nothing unique about it. No spark."

Charity was glued to the floor. What did they mean it wasn't good? She hadn't even been able to finish! Didn't they like any of it? Hadn't they seen that she'd *tried*?

Hans's words and Portia's laughter combined to create a crushing blow. Charity's mouth hung open. She was too shocked to defend herself or say anything at all. She'd put herself out there, gone after what she'd wanted, and for what?

To be judged.

To be ridiculed.

And now, instead of the excitement and the thrill of fulfilling her dream, of changing how people saw her—not as a timid, socially awkward weirdo, but as someone with confidence and a backbone and something to offer—the only thing she felt was defilement. Mama Cass was wrong. There weren't good people in the world, ready to accept her one day. Even now, years after being ridiculed by the giggling audience in her school talent shows, nothing had changed.

Everyone was rotten.

Before, she'd been too starstruck by the judges' glamor to notice the crowd of hundreds. But now, stripped of her song, her chance, she listened as ripples of varied, Portia-instigated laughter spread through the audience. Charity could imagine the rows of sneering, amused faces, but all she was able to see were the innumerable, shadowed figures above and below. Her eyes were wide as she hyperventilated, and suddenly she felt very small, a caged animal struck immobile by the sensory overload of taunting zoo patrons. She grew hot beneath the stage's spotlights and pressed a jittery hand to her forehead that was slick with oil and sweat. There she was, the star of their mockery, squinting against the bright lights in front of laughing strangers. Her skin prickled and her head spun as she realized that there was nowhere to hide but behind the skinny microphone stand.

Her lower lip began to tremble, and she struggled to hold back the building tears as she considered how long she had prepared for this moment and how quickly it had been taken away.

The audience laughter weakened just enough for Portia to shrug and casually say, "I guess we'll vote?"

It was a no from Hans, an opinion which he punctuated with, "Obviously."

It was a no from Larry, his raised eyebrows and scrunched-up mouth betraying his embarrassment for her.

And, as much as it pained her to do it, Portia said it was a no from her as well. "But keep singing," she offered with a wave.

Charity only half-processed what they'd said, consumed instead by the animalistic scream trapped inside her. But she'd heard enough to know that she would not take Portia's advice. She would tear down her posters, throw away her CDs, and burn her grandmother's shawl. She would never sing again.

Charity clutched her purse with trembling hands and hugged herself, her arms crossed over her chest in an X. Her whole body shuddered as if breaking from the inside out. With a fragile hand to her mouth, she finally tore herself from her spot and ran across the stage, back the way she'd come. She withdrew her iPod and hurled it against the polished stage. The screen cracked, sprinkling the floor with clear splinters. As she collapsed backstage by the long black curtains, she let the tears come as she cried harder than she ever had before, her mind not yet clear enough to be aware of the piece of her that had been so quickly destroyed.

28

CHARITY'S EYES STUNG as the last two minutes of her life replayed in her head like a song stuck on repeat. Her head spun as she felt the quick rise of hot bile in the back of her throat, startled when someone reached out and tapped her on the shoulder.

"Miss?" a man said. "You okay?"

She shot out her arm and pushed him away.

Why won't they leave me alone? Why can't they just let me be?

Suddenly she was back in middle school with kids calling her Mumble McGee and "accidently" getting wads of Juicy Fruit stuck in her stringy hair, imitating her nervous tics, and spreading rumors about her cleanliness so that she would get picked last for group science projects. "Hey, Ass Burgers!" they'd taunt after she wore the same shirt twice in one week. "Dontcha got anything else to wear, or do they not sell new clothes to freaks?"

"Go away!" Charity snapped now. Her throat was lined with mucus so the words came out thicker than usual. "I don't want to talk to anyone."

The man did not reply, but Charity could still feel his looming presence.

"You know," he said in a low, calm voice, "that was rotten what they did to you. Really rotten."

Charity's hands remained pressed to her face, but the intense trembling of her shoulders lessened.

"I watched the whole thing," he continued. "Was it the greatest singing in the world? Probably not. But what they did to you . . . you didn't deserve that. No one does."

His kind words caught her off guard as she cautiously withdrew her hands from her reddened face. Her blurry vision cleared as she saw the man kneeling beside her. He had a black T-shirt that said CREW and muddy brown eyes that seemed focused both on her and somewhere else. His black hair was short and tipped with sweat, the freshness of his most recent haircut just beginning to fade. Charity could not tell his age, just that he was definitely older than her, maybe in his mid thirties.

"Here," he said, withdrawing a tissue from his back pocket.

Charity eyed him cautiously. "No tricks?" she asked.

The man nodded. "No tricks."

Charity slowly extended her hand, cautious of any kindness offered by anyone in this place.

The man waited until she had blown her nose before asking, "Charity, huh?"

"What?"

"Your name. It's Charity?"

She nodded shamefully at the thought that her embarrassment had been linked to something as inextricable from herself as her name.

"I like it," he said. "Kind of old-fashioned. You don't come across too many Charitys. Anybody call you Cherry?"

She shook her head to indicate that no, no one did.

The man looked out onto the stage. "I know what you're going through. I've been in plenty of situations like that."

Charity's eyes lit up. "You sing, too?"

"God no." He laughed, scratching his cheek. "The world doesn't want to hear that. I just mean generally. People don't accept what they're unable or unwilling to understand. People who are unique. With spirit. With drive. People like us. The world is a cruel place, Cherry. And what you got out there?" He grimaced, gesturing to the stage where a new contestant was belting out the chorus of a pop song that Charity found insufferable. "I know it feels like the end of the world, but that was just a taste of how people will try to put you down. They'll step on you and laugh while they do it. Try to stifle your ambition and talent and what makes you special until they mold you into what they want you to be."

Yes, Charity wanted to say. *That's exactly it. That's exactly what they do.*

She'd never heard anyone voice her own feelings so openly, so completely, every syllable of every word ringing true.

"And when others crush ambitious people," he said, his hands balled into fists, "how are they treated? Are they told that what they did or said wasn't appropriate or kind or polite? Hell, look at the people who just laughed at you. Did they get punished? No," he answered for her, "because in this messed-up world of ours, what just happened to you wasn't an assault. It was entertainment.

"Now," he said, eyes focused intently on hers, "explain to me how that's fair. In a country that prides itself on honor and justice, where's the justice for those who are mistreated for being different or not fitting into the mold of what society thinks they should be?"

Charity's tears had stopped. Now, listening to this man saying the things she'd always felt but hadn't known how to put into words, the hurt she'd felt before his arrival seemed to lessen, like a weight had been lifted from her chest.

"Do you want to live in a world where people like that get to win? Where they're allowed to?"

No. I don't. Not Anymore.

"What can I do?" She shrugged. "Nothing I could do would make a difference. Especially after . . . " She pointed to the stage. She could not yet look back at the place that had been the source of so much embarrassment and hurt.

"No," the man said, smiling and shaking his head, "that's what society tells you. But you are—and could be—so much more."

She looked at him with wonder in her eyes, as if someone had confided in her that there was alien life on Mars. "I could?"

"Absolutely."

"What could I be?"

"Anything you want. That's the beauty of it. It's up to you." He fixed his gaze on her. "You could change things, Charity. You could change the whole world if you wanted to. You could be the judge for once, be in on the joke instead of the butt of it. If you embraced the hurt and anger that the world has told you to push down and be ashamed of . . . " He looked out at the stage. "You could make them pay."

The world beyond their tangle of black curtains seemed to fade away. It was as if nothing else existed.

"And those people out there? Don't they deserve to feel what they made you feel? Isn't that fair? Isn't that justice?"

It was all so clear now. She'd been trapped inside herself and the prison that a society of cruel kids and unsympathetic adults had constructed for her. But what she felt now was more intense than sadness or regret. She felt the feeling she'd pushed down for so many years: hate.

"We can make them suffer," he whispered, his hot coffee breath tickling her ear. "For what they did to you. For what they'll do again and again until the end of time. Is that what you want?"

Charity was quiet for a moment as she contemplated the revelation that she'd felt this way all along. All it had taken was someone to verbalize it. To tell her that it was okay. And with a new kind of tears in her eyes, those of a burden being lifted from her, Charity gave him her answer, the one word that thundered in her mind.

"Yes."

29

THEY SAT ON the loading dock of the convention center amid the cooing of French fry-pecking pigeons and the familiar stench of the nearby Inner Harbor—an unappetizing mix of saltwater and sunbaked garbage. During the short time she'd been with this man—Matt, he'd introduced himself with a smile and a handshake—she had felt a palpable change within her. Listening to him say all the things she'd long felt but had never been able to voice was like drowning and being tossed a life jacket at the very last moment. She no longer felt as if the waves were crashing over her, the current dragging her along. With the new fire that burned inside her, she felt as if she could bend the waves at her will, finally equipped with the strength to have a say in her own life.

"So, what are we gonna do?" she asked. "What's the plan?"

Charity did not move as she listened to his proposal, hanging on to every word as if it were gospel.

"Are you up for this?" Matt asked once he'd finished. "It's fine if you're not, but now is the time to say something."

Just this morning she'd woken up early to stand in line for a talent competition and now she was sitting in a back alley loading dock with a man she'd just met. The old Charity would never have done that, she thought.

No, she wouldn't. Which is why the old Charity is dead.

She usually avoided socialization if she could help it, knowing that it would only trigger her anxiety about what to say and how to act, but in talking to Matt she hadn't noticed her mouth run dry or her thoughts swirling. Hadn't felt her heart hammering or the all-encompassing urge to run away. So, if she could do *this*, she thought, something that had always been a challenge, what else was she capable of?

"Because from this moment," Matt warned, waiting for her response, "there's no turning back."

Charity shook herself from her thoughts and swept aside any remaining doubt for what she was planning to do. "I am," she said. "I'm ready. After what they did to me . . . " She trailed off as the tears threatened to come again, but she pushed them back down. "I would do anything."

Matt nodded.

"Good. Because it may come to that."

30

THE MAN WHO introduced himself as Matthew Manson had been watching Charity as she walked out onto the stage with the small, timid strides of a baby deer. Her eyes had darted all around as she cast furtive glances at the microphone stand ahead, the spotlights above, and the judges to her left. As if she was forcing herself to do something she wasn't completely comfortable with. He cringed as she sang, hitting all the wrong notes in all the wrong places, and again as the laughter and insults followed. And when she ran off the stage into the tangle of curtains in the corner, he walked over to the brittle-looking girl with her head in her hands and offered her a tissue. After all, he wasn't a terrible person. Because although he did terrible things and had terrible urges, it didn't mean he was responsible for them.

He'd grown up on a tiny patch of land that had once been lush and green, complete with fresh air and the sounds of roaming cattle and cooped chickens. His father was a third-generation farmer and had inherited both the property and the land, though his combination of laziness and casual alcoholism usually caused the farm's regular duties and upkeep to fall on Matt's small, bony shoulders.

He could not work the machinery or herd the cows, but there were plenty of jobs that an eight-year-old could do. While his classmates in town spent their summers swimming and fishing and going to camp, Matt spent his mornings rising with the roosters, his afternoons picking row after endless row of corn and tomatoes, and his nights by returning to the shed to put away whatever tools his father had left scattered haphazardly around the farm. He did these tasks six days a week without complaint. Then again, routine had a way of making you blind.

It took years for him to realize that in making his own dinner and cleaning his room and getting himself ready for the bus each morning, he'd become both a mother and father to himself. But when the realization came, it did so not with the bitterness or anger of his childhood having been lost to the pressures of adulthood, but with the quiet contemplation of learning something new, the knowledge of a fact that just *was*.

And when his chores were finished and his father was passed out on the couch as the dregs of daylight faded from the sky, he relished the time that he had to himself to do as he pleased. But the farmhouse had no Internet, cable, or any of the electronic gadgets that would appear years later under every suburban roof, so Matt was forced to be creative to keep himself occupied.

He tried marbles. He tried cards. Whiffle ball. Soccer. Bean bags. Chalk. Anything he could find in the dusty shack they called a home. And while such games diverted his attention for a time, he bored with them easily. They were juvenile, Matt would have said had he known the word, far below his intelligence and interest. And though he could not express it with words in a way that others would understand, such games failed to scratch the itch he felt deep inside that had been there as long as he could remember.

But one night, as he was cleaning up his father's messes, a shaft of blood-red sunset shone through a crack in the shed's tin roof and illuminated an object in the corner covered by loose hay. Matt, always curious, picked it up. He admired the old, darkened wood that created its Y-shape and thick rubber band stretched across the wood with the small cloth pouch in the center. As he examined it in the light, he found that it fit perfectly in his hand. As if it was made just for him.

He locked the shed and, knowing that his father was passed out somewhere in the living room, took it to the back porch. For a while he just stared at it, appraising the feel of the grained wood, but his caress was soon interrupted by the wispy sound of scurrying in a patch of tall grass ahead. He squinted and saw the angled brown nose of a rat peeking out to sniff the air, as if trying to decide if it was okay to enter the dirt clearing nearest Matt or if it should remain in the relative safety of the yellowed grass.

As he watched it scurry and sniff, Matt became increasingly aware of the itch in his body, his skin prickly with the hum of electricity. But no, that wasn't completely right. Because it wasn't on the surface, somewhere that it could be relieved by scratching with his dirt-caked fingernails. No, it was buried deep, out of reach from any object or limb that could relieve it. And as his heart thrummed and his head grew dizzy, he realized that it wasn't even in his body.

It was in his *brain*.

Unable to take his eyes off the rat, he felt his fingers twitch as they scrambled in the dirt below the warped porch step, placed a tiny, jagged object in the slingshot's small pouch between the rubber bands, and let it fly.

The rat squealed as the rock hit it. Judging from the fine spray of red, Matt could tell he'd hit its eye. He stood on the porch as his breathing grew so heavy that it was nearly a pant. He placed his open palm against his chest, felt the rapid pounding of his heartbeat, and watched the blood dribble from the rat's eye socket. A shudder ran down his spine as if someone had slid an ice cube down his shirt. Matt scrunched his shoulders up to his neck as his arms tingled with pleasure.

But there was no smile. There was no joy. No fear or horror of *What have I done?*

Instead, his pupils dilated as his brain exploded with sensory input, each sensation suddenly heightened. He inhaled the scent of dry, crumbling soil and freshly mown grass, his ears picking up the whistle of the wind as it blew through the rusted weathervane on the barn roof. His vision began to blur at the edges until he had to sit back down on the dry-rotted porch steps. When, at last, it had returned to normal, he looked back to the sunbaked clearing where he had watched the rat flail and scurry off to die in whatever hole it had come from. It had been alive then, but now it was dead, Matt thought with a nonchalant shrug.

His father's booming voice beckoned him back inside, but Matt did not protest. He bent down to pick up his new toy and silently walked back into the house to get ready for bed with the quiet, contemplative nature that was his usual manner in all things. But something, he knew, had changed. His skin was still buzzing with electricity, emitting a subtle hum audible only to him. His fingers trembled as he brushed his teeth and lay on his lumpy mattress, but that unquenchable fire inside his brain that had begged to be extinguished began to retreat as if draped with a wet towel.

Matt closed his eyes, baggy with sleep and relief. For the first time that he could remember, he felt himself begin to grow weary the second his head touched the frayed edges of his pillow. Sleep would come soon. And as his brain fired off one last jolt of euphoria, his extremities tingled beneath the sheets as he drifted off to the thought that the deep itch he'd felt inside him for so long had finally been scratched.

31

MATT EXPLAINED THAT because he was part of the stage crew for *Talent Now!* they would have a ride to the next audition stop.

"And where's that?" Charity asked.

"New York."

"City?" she asked with a mix of wonder and fear in her eyes.

"Yeah," he said. "You'll be fine to come. Guys bring girls on the busses all the time. No one will think twice."

"But you can't audition, can you?" she said, a tinge of anxiety creeping back into her words. "Isn't there something in the rules about prohibiting anyone affiliated with the show from auditioning?"

"There is," he confirmed, smiling his charming smile. "Which is why when we get to New York, I'll be putting in my resignation."

Besides, he thought, but did not tell Charity, he had reason to believe that if everything went as he had planned, it would be the last job he ever had.

32

IN THE FINAL moments before the bus with the *Talent Now!* logo and judges' faces plastered to the side pulled away from the curb, Charity contemplated whether this was something she really wanted. Because like Matt had said, it wasn't just a commitment to a decision; it was a commitment to a new life.

The bus would leave at 5:00 p.m., only hours after the Baltimore auditions, so she would not have time to go home and pack whatever few belongings she'd felt were important. As she'd snuck out her window in the pre-dawn hours, it hadn't struck her that she had left the house for what may have been the last time. And the strange thing was that she didn't mind. The more space and time between her new self and her old life made her realize there was little to miss about it. What was there to miss about being unemployed? Or her social skills classes, learning to make eye contact and conversation, to utilize her coping strategies when the world got to be too loud and bright and overwhelming? Or being told to push down her anger as if it was something to hide?

She supposed she would miss her mother, but the one person in her life whom she loved was not enough of an anchor to keep her here. And during these moments when guilt of leaving her behind began to creep up on her, she just had to remember the bank statement she'd found on the dining room table shortly after she'd told Karen Sparks that she wanted to audition for *Talent Now!* The statement for the bank account into which her mother had said she'd deposit Charity's Supplemental Security Income checks, the money that was supposed to be for her food and clothing and housing. For her *future*.

She'd looked at the account's total of thirty-seven dollars with confusion. After all, she'd been getting the checks for over a year. There should've been *thousands* in there. Shock came first, then anger. She considered approaching her mother with the statement and asking where her money was, but as she thought of their new premium cable subscription, the jewelry Charity had seen her mother wearing, and the flashy Mazda in the driveway, she realized that she didn't need to. There would only be excuses and lies:

That she'd picked up extra work.

That she'd taken from her own savings.

That she'd won big on a scratch-off.

She'd always trusted her mother—after all, she'd had no reason not to—but now that she knew what her mother had been doing, Charity came to the horrifying realization that the dishonesty and defilement she'd been so scared of in the world had now invaded her own home.

And why? What purpose had it served? Was her mother trying to hold her back, fearful that if her only daughter finally moved out, she would have no one to monitor and manage? Charity was grateful for the roof over her head and food on her plate, but she didn't need anyone to make her dinner or draw her baths, to call her *sweetie* and *baby* or pour her morning cereal. No, it was time for Charity to live her own life. And when Karen Sparks came home to find that her daughter was neither in the house nor at her social skills class, she would undoubtedly call the police to report her missing.

Let her call, Charity thought. *I'll be long gone.*

And at nineteen, she was a legal adult. She had done nothing wrong and had committed no crime. There was nothing they could do to force her back into the padded cell she had been naïve enough to call a life.

Now, standing at the threshold of a new life, becoming the person she'd always known she could be, the temptation was too great. Matt was standing inside the bus's open doors, waiting for her with an extended hand. She only had to reach out and grab it.

After a moment, she did.

And stepped onto the bus.

They barely spoke for the full three-hour ride. Matt slept on the seat beside her, while Charity stared out the window at the passing scenery. Lush trees lined both sides of the interstate, the bright summer sun seeping through the branches and seeming to light them from within. In another few months, the colors would begin to change, and she would've given anything to see them. There were no trees in her own backyard in the city, the seemingly endless beauty of the natural world kept from her.

She did not have her iPod during the ride (and immediately regretted smashing it), but so far had managed to keep her anxiety in check. The trees helped. Pretty soon, one of the roadies said, she'd be able to see the New York skyline.

She'd never been to New York—or anywhere, really. The only other state to which she'd traveled was Pennsylvania, and that was only to visit her grandmother for Thanksgiving and Christmas. But if there was an expiration date for child-like wonder, Charity did not know it. The scenery and long, winding road stretching out before her was so fresh and new that she felt more like a child looking through the glass of a zoo exhibit rather than the windows of a bus midway through a drive from Baltimore to New York City.

The auditions would be tomorrow, which meant another morning of waiting in the heat. But unlike the Baltimore round, everyone who auditioned would do so in front of the judges and a full theater audience. She searched the venue on Matt's iPhone and read that the theater held over two thousand people. Her heart fluttered and her palms sweat thinking of how she'd felt at being in front of just a couple hundred.

You can do this. You can do this. She owed it to herself to retaliate against those who had taken away her dream, who had caused her so much embarrassment and hurt. *You are fine. You are safe.*

She heard chattering in the seats ahead of her and looked out the window to see what the fuss was about. She saw the many skyscrapers of the New York City skyline piercing through the early evening fog like a dream, each one seeming to rise higher than the last as if they were in direct competition. Although Charity had never visited the city, she knew where all the prominent buildings were. She spotted the Empire State Building, the Chrysler Building, and felt a jolt of sadness as she looked at the empty space in the sky where the dual towers of the World Trade Center had been.

When the bus passed through the Lincoln Tunnel (which was both longer and more terrifying than the Fort McHenry) and emerged into the city, New York was just as she pictured it after seeing it on TV. She marveled at the many crisscrossing streets and avenues clogged with yellow taxis, as well as the bright lights of theaters advertising musicals like *Cats* and *Wicked*. And as she saw hordes of business professionals lined up behind hot dog carts, and the bus passed dozens of store signs boasting AUTHENTIC NEW YORK SOUVENIRS!, Charity felt the electricity of the city pulsing through her. Like it was set to a different frequency than Baltimore. It hummed beneath her feet as the bus inched forward, a special kind of magic.

A horn blared, and she looked below to see a cigarette-smoking cab driver flash his middle finger at a jaywalking pedestrian.

Yes, Charity thought with a smile. *This is New York.*

33

THE SUMMERS OF Matt's youth were much quieter than the city in which he now found himself, beside a girl he'd just met.

He'd perform the chores his father had assigned him before retiring to the porch with his slingshot until his aim grew better, his hand steadier, waiting for new unsuspecting creatures to enter his clearing—rats and snakes and crows.

He never felt remorse.

What he did feel was the heightening of other things—intense smells and sounds and the ability to feel everything so fully, all at once. Along with the skin-tingling euphoria that caused his fingers to tremble and doused the fire in his brain, there was the realization of what had been missing from all the games he'd played by himself before the day he'd found the slingshot: cause and effect. The idea that something could be living one minute, then dead the next. And that he had the power to make it happen.

After he finished bedding the horses for the night, Matt went into the living room and stood in front of the flames his father was tending in the stone fireplace. The fireplace, Fred Manson was always eager to relay to anyone within earshot, that he had helped his grandfather build when he was younger. Matt stared raptly with the involuntary intensity of a mosquito attracted to a bright light, hands loose at his sides as he inhaled deeply. He'd seen fires before—when his father had burned pots of beans on the kitchen stove or built a campfire on the occasions his drinking buddies would come over—but this was different. This was inside the house, big and bold and crackling. His throat was dry as he swallowed, watching the logs pop as the flames danced.

"What the hell you think you're doing?" his father spat in his dry-throated grumble.

Matt fixed his unblinking stare on his father. "Can I watch?"

Fred assumed that his son meant the TV in the corner of the room, but Matt had no use for the cheesy black-and-white Westerns his father favored. Had no use for television at all, really.

Fred turned in his armchair to reveal his rumpled hair and dirtied overalls stained with black motor oil and a spray of red that may have been blood. A half-empty bottle of Jack Daniels sloshed in his hand. "After the shit you did?" he said plainly.

Matt stared at his father with confusion, registering that his father looked unhappy. He wondered why.

"My kid thinks it's funny to kill God's creatures, is that right?" A mixture of whiskey-tinged saliva and tobacco juice dribbled over his yellowed teeth and cleft chin.

Matt understood then, picturing the scattered mounds of dead things he had accumulated in the backyard: rats and birds and frogs. Small swarms of flies had formed around the piles of creatures and their leaking fluids, creating an incessant *bzzzz*.

His father shifted in his chair, and Matt waited for the beating that was surely coming. Instead, he only said, "No TV for you tonight, Matty."

"But I did all my chores," Matt said, stepping closer. The warmth of the flickering flames caused his skin to break out in a pleasant tickle. His pulse quickened, his little nose twitched, and his eyes grew wider at the sight of the dancing fire. "I did everything you wanted. I fed the cows, I bedded the horses, I picked the tomatoes, I—"

"Keep it up and I'll give you something to whine about," he warned with a crooked finger. "Our actions got consequences, Matty. And you know what yours'll be if you take another step." He took another swig of Jack and belched. "Get out of here and leave your father be. You know how I am about my fireside time."

But Matt didn't want to go. Didn't want to leave the warmth or the brilliant yellows and oranges of the flames' perfect ribbons. They danced higher as they ate through the logs, leaving them blistered and charred. Despite the smoke drifting his way, Matt's eyes shone as he looked on, his breathing shallow and jaw slack. He could watch for hours.

A floaty feeling buoyed him as he extended his hands to feel the heat generated from the blanket of crackling fire. He wanted to lay there beside the flames, run his stubby fingers through the logs and ash, feel the waves of heat that—

Matt felt a sharp pain across his cheek and looked up to see his father looming over him. "You deaf, boy? Get outta here!"

Matt tore himself away from the blaze and began to plod away, but evidently his retreat was not quick enough for his father.

Fred Manson stormed toward him across the wood floor of the living room. It was so quick that Matt did not have the opportunity to run before his father gripped a fistful of his shaggy hair and began to drag him backward across the floor.

Matt wriggled and yelped against the pain radiating from his scalp, but his father only pulled harder, grumbling and cursing as they crossed the threshold between the living room and kitchen.

"No!" Matt shouted, looking back longingly at the fireplace as he was dragged toward the kitchen. "Stop!"

"My kid thinks it's funny to kill God's creatures and expects a *reward*? Well, let's see how fun this is."

Matt couldn't remember ever having cried, or what it felt like, but he knew that if there was ever anything that would bring the elusive tears from his eyes, it was this. But the only thing he felt was shock and surprise as his father's alcohol-induced rage made the muscles in his face tremble and his cheeks turn beet red.

"What, no tears, huh? We'll work on that."

Matt twisted his shoulder as his father shoved him onto the kitchen's stained linoleum, grabbed him by the ankles, and dragged him to the corner of the room. He gripped Matt's leg with one hand and, with the other, began removing six of the loose wooden slats that made up their kitchen floor.

Clank.

Clank.

Clank.

Again and again and again.

"Get off!" Matt yelled as he tried to paw his father's hands off him, knowing what was coming next. "Get off me!"

But it was no use, and it was only a matter of seconds before his father dragged him over the dark opening and let him fall to the cold dirt two feet below.

"You stay there and think about what you done," he bellowed, spittle dripping onto Matt like holy water. "Little freak."

But Matt did not cry, and he did not scream. After all, it was not the first time he had been put beneath the floor. He lay quietly as his father nailed the wooden boards back into place, staring up through the cracks of weak light between the slats.

He didn't need his drunken father or his stupid stone fireplace, he realized. Because on the hard dirt below him, looking up through the boards inches from his bloodied nose, Matt had made up his mind. One day, he resolved, he would make his own fire.

34

THE SHOW ALWAYS paid for its crew members' hotel stay, and Charity stayed in Matt's room. It was on the eighteenth floor, giving them a perfect view of Midtown Manhattan and the organized chaos below. From her vantage point, it was easy to see the perfection of the city's ever-evolving landscape of hotels and theaters and apartments, the hectic streets and avenues that seemed so much more organized when viewed from above. Orange light began to brighten the façades of buildings on the opposite side of the street, the sun casting its setting glow on the specks of people bustling in compact hoards on the steamy sidewalks below.

Matt had spoken little as they checked into the room in which they now stood. And who could blame him? There was planning to do, questions to consider.

What if they didn't get an audition slot tomorrow?

What if he messed up and blew their cover?

What if there was something he had forgotten?

But they were only possible threats to the mechanisms of their plan. A million things could go wrong, but it didn't do any good fixating on them. Instead, Charity watched as Matt unpacked the sparse contents of his duffle bag and savored the pleasant *zzzzzp* of the zippers as he opened the bag's many compartments.

"You still haven't told me," Charity said, interrupting his calm.

"Told you what?"

"What we're using."

She was right. He hadn't told her.

"You never asked," he said, summoning a playful smile.

It wasn't like he was hiding anything. He was waiting for the right moment, when he was sure that she was in this for the long haul rather than merely looking for an escapist road trip to the Big Apple.

Now, he unzipped a compartment that ran the entire length of the duffel bag and reached inside for the one item from his childhood with which he had refused to part. He'd taken it everywhere, starting from the day he had left home for good. He pulled its edge from the bag and tugged it out the rest of the way, the orange-pink light from the setting sun giving the wood an eerie glow.

"Oh my God," Charity said with a whisper of awe or horror or both.

"Cherry," he said kindly. "I told you. If this is too much for you—"

"It's beautiful," she said, involuntarily reaching out to take the object from his hand. "Where'd you get it?"

"I made it."

"Wait," she said, tearing her eyes from the bow to look at him. "You *made* this?"

"Yeah. In high school."

"I love it." She caressed its curvature as Matt himself had first done all those years ago. "No one appreciates good craftsmanship anymore."

Matt pointed to the bow with a frown. "You know they made fun of me for that?"

Charity raised her brows. "Well, they're fools not to admire something so . . . perfect." She ran her hand over the lacquered finish. There were a few nicks in the wood here and there, but otherwise it was in perfect condition.

"So, this is it. This is what we're using?"

Matt smiled at her. It seemed friendly enough but when paired with his faraway gaze, there was something distantly sinister about it.

"They shot insults at you," he said to Charity. "Let's return the favor and shoot something back."

35

IT WASN'T LONG before Matt outgrew the slingshot, though not what it was capable of doing. What *he* was capable of doing. He just needed a new tool. But like all kids, his interests and hobbies took a backseat to the unfortunate annoyance of federally mandated education.

He didn't have any friends (not that he had use for them) and didn't particularly care for any of his classes, either. But the one that gave him the closest approximation of pleasure was Introduction to Carpentry and Technology (what they would've called "woodshop" back when his father was in school). He loved the sounds of the apparatuses—buzzing and scraping and sawing—and the way the orange sparks flew, threatening to grow into dozens of small fires. The room always featured the sharp sweetness of sawdust and paint fumes, and he savored it along with how connected he felt to the tools surrounding him, as if they were not separate things, but extensions of his hands. It was the only class in which he had taken any interest, so when Mr. Bixby saw Matt constructing a hunter's bow instead of the birdhouse they'd been assigned to build for their final exam, he did not protest.

Matt cut and carved the wood, sanding it down so smoothly and delicately that his movements resembled caresses. It took him all three hours over the course of both exam periods to finish his project, and once he had stained the wood with a light varnish, he beheld the beauty that he had created.

But the chattering voices of his classmates broke him from his reverie, Matt only catching lowly spoken fragments.

"What a freak."

" . . . can't believe he made that thing."

" . . . like a serial killer or something . . . "

"Probably offed his mother, too."

" . . . Michael Myers with that blank stare."

"Fuckin' weirdo."

" . . . I heard he killed his own dog."

" . . . part of that weird hippie cult from the sixties."

Matt sighed at his classmates' juvenility. They were just like the creatures piled in his backyard: expendable. He'd always hated his last name (especially during history classes) and the imagined association with the very family he was being accused of being part of. But then one day in his fundamentals of art class, he'd come across the works of another famous Manson, and one painting in particular. The mix of watercolors showed the frail torso of a naked woman with her hands wrapped tightly around her emaciated arms as if she were shivering. She had full red lips and almond-shaped eyes, dark with sleepiness or disinterest, below a white, bald head. Surrounding her were splotches of orange and yellow and red, the woman unflinching as she burned alive.

"What's it called?" Matt had asked his art teacher with an interested lilt to his voice that surprised even him.

"Exactly what it looks like," Mr. Fields had said with a gruff chuckle. "*Baby on Fire*. Marilyn isn't exactly known for giving his works creative titles."

Since that day, staring at the painting of the naked, burning woman, he'd long wondered why it spoke to him so much, and why the deep itch inside his brain—a part of him that also felt like it was on fire—seemed to dull the longer he stared. As he did, his relief was always accompanied by the mental image of his house's fireplace and the wish that his father was burning inside it.

But after listening to his classmates' continued comments and insults, Matt couldn't say that he was surprised. He was used to people talking about him. How he was quiet and often stared off into space. How he lacked emotion or empathy or friends, instead choosing to be alone as he drew or read or stared intently at the blue flame of the Bunsen burner in science class, turning the dial higher and higher. Even his teachers noticed, often worried or uncomfortable enough to alert his father about his son's *tendencies*. There were countless messages left on the answering machine stating that they just wanted to make sure that everything was okay at home and that the school would be happy to provide any additional support or counseling services that he deemed necessary. Of course, Matt could have told them it was useless. That even the promise of a free keg of Budweiser wouldn't be enough motivation for his father to get his intoxicated ass off the couch.

After many calls from the school's pupil personnel worker, when it became clear that his father didn't care about his son's wellbeing or mental health, when Matt's *condition* escalated and he retreated deeper into himself and spoke to no one, there was little else the school could do. Even his middle school counselor, Ms. Katie, who said she was "worried" and "concerned" and wanted him to "feel safe," could not reach him. As time wore on, her efforts intensified as Matt's dark, greasy, black bangs began to hide his deepening blank stare. Each of his teachers knew that when he eventually graduated or dropped out and went on to commit some awful crime when he'd put himself or others in danger—another Columbine, maybe—Matt Manson would be the kind of student they would realize as having slipped through the cracks, the public school system failing him.

He knew he was different, but a freak? Well, if everyone else thought so, maybe he was. Though the taunts did not affect him, the conclusion wasn't lost on him that kids were cruel. Why should he continue coming to a place where the vermin of the world were allowed to roam free, without fear of extermination? A place where he was not wanted nor understood, where the only important things seemed to be graduation followed by four grueling years of high school? And then what? College? A job? A family?

Why?

Why would he want to spend the rest of his finite existence in an office cubicle with people like the arrogant and pimply faced morons he already spent every day with now?

As the bell rang and the rest of his classmates left the warehouse-looking classroom, Matt stared down at his bow with the intensity of a decision made:

There is nothing for me here.

One day I will leave this place.

I will leave this place and never look back.

It would be another four years before he did just that. Another four years of kids' taunts and teases and stares. Four years of high school that might as well have been fourteen. But there was one highlight. Matt's county required all high school students to complete a physical education credit before graduation. Their next unit was going to be archery, and Matt had asked Mr. Manning if he was able to bring in his own bow—after all, he'd told him, he made it himself. Mr. M didn't see anything wrong with that, so long as he left it in his office and didn't bring any arrows to go with it, which would be grounds for suspension. Matt assured him he wouldn't, and when they finally started the unit, he proudly displayed the bow for all who cared to see.

Which was nobody. Because the two dozen sweat-smelling teenagers were too easily amused with the county's equipment, the bows in the old bucket nothing more than dry-rotted pieces of shit, to pay any kind of attention to the craftsmanship of Matt's handmade beauty.

Matt appraised the piece of old wood. It had seemed so much more impressive when he'd made it years ago, but he supposed that the joy of creating it all on his own had made him blind to its flaws.

He watched as Mr. M instructed each of the boys to shoot at the straw-backed target. "One at a time," he emphasized. "We don't need anyone going to the emergency room."

But Matt didn't need a lesson, and he watched with amusement as his classmates clumsily plucked their bowstrings, slipped with the arrows, and shot them into the ground. If he'd been capable of laughter, he would have done so.

Clowns, he thought. *All of you.*

He watched as this procession of stupidity continued until it was his turn. And as Mr. M stood beside him and placed a reassuring hand on his shoulder, Matt didn't bother pretending that he didn't know how to shoot. He just took an arrow and raised the bow, eyeing up his target.

"All right," Mr. M said, "we've got Billy out there adjusting the target, so wait until he clears out of the way."

But Matt didn't hear a single word his teacher said, his mind consumed instead by what the arrow was telling him. *Shoot me*, it said. *Shoot me. Relieve the itch. Soothe the fire.*

"Another few seconds and you'll be good to go. Just make sure that Billy—"

Matt released his grasp on the bowstring and let the arrow fly.

His mind was calm in the silent seconds that always followed a shot, but it wasn't long before his attention was broken by the class's chorus of horrified screams.

Maybe they were cheering for him, Matt thought. Maybe they were shocked at his precision and accuracy and how drastically they'd underestimated him. How they'd always underestimated him.

Matt looked out into the field. The straw-backed target was devoid of arrows. He'd missed the target, yes, but his arrow had still penetrated something solid. Namely, the stomach of Billy Hughes.

Billy moaned and writhed on the ground as the boys descended upon him like boardwalk seagulls to dropped French fries, gawking dumbly at the arrow protruding from his bloodied torso. As Mr. M realized what had happened and squawked for help on his walkie-talkie, Matt stood silent and alone, removed from the bodies and screams that sounded farther down the field.

Later, after the ambulance had taken Billy away to the hospital, Matt heard the same comments he'd come to expect:

"Fucking freak."

" . . . tried to kill him!"

" . . . some kind of psycho or something?"

"It was an accident," Matt said plainly, without the slightest touch of sorrow or pity in his voice. And while Mr. M and the police officers on the scene eventually left with the same conclusion, Matt could see it in their eyes when they questioned him that they weren't totally convinced.

And, to be honest, neither was Matt.

He'd aimed for the target, sure. But what, he pondered, had his brain perceived as a target? Was it the straw-backed circle with the tri-colored rings, or was it the pot-bellied seventeen-year-old boy standing next to it? Just how much did that itch inside his brain demand to be scratched? And to what degree did he have control?

What he did know, however, was that Billy Hughes survived the incident with thirteen stitches and a cool story about almost dying at school. Frankly, Matt thought, he should be thanking him. It would probably be the highlight of his dumb, boring life, something he could tell his children one day, should he ever manage to land someone to have them with.

The story coming from Matt's end, however, would be considerably less cool. Because although he was off the hook for what he'd done, he realized just how close he'd come to being found out—especially if the police attempted to talk to his father or found the slew of red-tipped feathers sticking from the piles of dead things in the backyard. Or saw his browser history with dozens of searches of crime scenes and autopsy photos.

He could not allow that to happen.

He knew he was different from everyone else. *Fucking weird*, as his classmates said. That what he did, eliminating the burning itch deep inside him, wasn't exactly the kind of after-school activity that kids his age signed up for. Because while his classmates remained shaken up days after the incident, Matt was cool as a mid-October breeze. He did not cry. He did not sulk. And even though it was ruled an accident, he showed no remorse. The only thing he'd felt was the fluttering of elation in his stomach as the arrow had landed, the release of that pressure valve inside his brain that came with the realization that, had Billy died, there'd be one less asshole in the world. Justice would have been served.

Registering the probing looks of his peers, his teachers, policemen, and the counselor who had been assigned to talk to him after the incident, Matt had the most important realization of his life:

From then on, he would have to be careful.

Because although he did not know what normal felt like, he knew enough to know that what he did, how he acted and felt, was not normal. And if people caught onto that, if he wanted a chance at life outside a prison or psychiatric facility, he needed to learn how to fit into society. Or, at the very least, how to fake it.

He would need to study—when to laugh or look sad, how to smile and make friends. Maybe even join a club or sport. At least until he was out of high school. Then the real game would begin, and Matt would no longer be protected by the excuse of being an angsty teenager, or a forgiving juvenile justice system.

But how long could he keep up the act, all the things that were so foreign to him?

If he didn't want to die, if he wanted to keep relieving that burning nagging deep inside his brain and feel the ecstasy that came with it, he knew he'd better be able to keep it up for a very long time.

36

THEY DINED ON overpriced burgers and fries in the hotel's restaurant before Matt said that he had some things to do. "Preparations," he said when Charity pressed him for details.

He paid the bill and walked across the marble floor to the front door with a flimsy black bag slung over his shoulder. Charity's mouth dripped burger juice and confusion as she watched him leave the hotel and make a left on the city sidewalk.

Preparations?

Why hadn't he told her before? And why wasn't he including her?

A wave of anxiety swept through her, and she yearned for the calming melodies of The Crystals and The Chiffons on her iPod instead of the restaurant's awful smooth jazz. Instead, she rose from her chair and started for the restaurant doors, nearly colliding with a black-vested waiter carrying a tray of sweat-beaded glasses of ice water.

Out on the heat-baked sidewalk, the towering buildings surrounding her seemed to close in on her like a trap. Though she was familiar with city life in Baltimore, the area of Manhattan in which she now found herself—towering hotels and skyscrapers, the incessant and obnoxious blurting of taxi horns—was a culture shock. She'd always thought of New York as a magical place, and she supposed it was, once she knew where to look for it. But as she walked down the graffiti- and gum-covered sidewalk, all she felt was tension and anxiety. She couldn't imagine living here.

She looked to her left and spotted Matt among the flow of businessmen and bag ladies approaching a crosswalk. Charity stood on her tiptoes to keep him in sight in the converging masses.

Where is he going? she thought again. *And why didn't he tell me?*

Charity shuddered as she followed Matt down a pair of side streets, each narrower and emptier and darker than the last. Matt had been to the city many times, which automatically put him at an advantage. But Charity hadn't. What if she got lost?

Or jumped?

Or raped?

She'd heard that those things could happen to unsuspecting tourists, and then she'd be screwed. But the alley where Matt had stopped did not seem extraordinarily dangerous or unsafe. It looked like a junkyard, filled with the garbage city-dwellers were too lazy to dispose of properly, like rusted bicycles, broken furniture, and discarded sculptures and pieces of art. In that way, at least, New York wasn't so different from Baltimore.

She peeked around the corner, placed a hand on the bricks, and watched with bated breath as Matt scanned the area to make sure no one was around. Seemingly satisfied, he reached into the flimsy black bag he'd brought with him, unzipped the side, and withdrew the object he had shown Charity that afternoon. Shadows from the surrounding buildings cast it a darker hue, the smoothness of the wood and pointed tips making the bow look like a weapon from another time and place.

Charity pressed her face to the building's cool concrete, one nail-bitten hand clutching a corner stone. Anxious confusion settled upon her as Matt raised an arrow from the bag and brought it against the bow.

What's he aiming at? There's nothing there.

Out of the corner of her eye, she saw the quick blur of movement behind a trio of trash cans as Matt raised the bow and lined up his shot. And as the scurrying creature cautiously poked its head from the tall, weedy grass, he let the arrow fly. The propulsion forced it from its hiding place, and Charity saw that it was a rat. With its squirmy tail and meaty brown body, it was perhaps the biggest she had ever seen.

But why had he shot it?

Her quiet pondering was broken by a swift *woosh, woosh* as Matt fired two more red-feathered arrows into two additional Garfield-sized rats.

Charity jumped, careful to keep a hand to her mouth to stifle her surprise.

Matt swiped the sweat from his forehead and reached down to grab another arrow, but Charity wasn't sure what he was planning to shoot. There were no more rats that she could see, no living things of any kind.

As if on cue, a scruffy golden retriever turned the corner of the sidewalk and entered the alley. With its red collar and dangling gold tag, it obviously belonged to someone. But wherever it belonged, this alley was not it. The animal had strayed far from home.

It sniffed the ground, padding happily along as it weaved through the alley's many piles of trash and rejected treasures. Matt was so still that she wondered if the dog even saw him as it walked right into Matt's line of fire. He held a fresh arrow against the bow, his stance of someone who meant to shoot.

Charity's heart sank but was quickly buoyed. *No. He wouldn't do that. Not to a dog. Not—*

Her thought was severed by Matt's arrow.

"No!" she screeched.

Matt whipped around, startled, as if he'd been caught doing something he shouldn't have, scrambling to stuff the bow and arrows back into the bag. But when he turned and saw Charity, he dropped his head in relief and set the bag back on the ground. There was no anger or surprise in his voice as he said matter-of-factly, "What are you doing here, Cherry?"

She didn't know what to say at first. She couldn't tear her eyes or thoughts away from the dog that lay dead or dying atop a heap of empty beer cans. "You didn't tell me," she said, finally, her breathing ragged as she struggled to inhale.

"I needed to be alone for a little bit."

"Why didn't you tell me?" she wheezed. Her voice trembled as she pointed a shaking finger at the dead golden retriever behind him. "Why didn't you tell me about that?"

"Sorry," he said, though there wasn't a trace of sorrow or remorse in his voice. "I'm just used to being alone. Not having to answer to anybody. I hope this doesn't change things."

Charity was shaking, her eyes glazed with moisture. This was not part of his proposal, killing innocent animals in back alleys. These were not the grand plans she'd had in mind when Matt had enticed her with the idea of getting back at those who had wronged her.

"Why are you doing this?" she asked, her voice choking as tears snaked their way down her cheeks. She gestured again at the rats and the dog crumpled on the gravel with arrows protruding from their bodies. "*They* didn't do anything to us."

Although Matt looked directly into her eyes, she felt a tremble of fear at the idea that he wasn't really seeing her. As if he were a robot or sleepwalking. Where was the engaged, smiling, and charming man who had offered her a hand and words of encouragement back in Baltimore?

"This is my preparation. For tomorrow." Then, as if he'd been contemplating saying something he knew he shouldn't, he muttered, "It scratches the itch."

Charity didn't know what to think. What was he talking about?

Scratches the itch.

"Wait," she cried in the moment after she put it together and understood what he was saying. "You've done this before? What, for fun?"

"Shhh," he soothed. "Everything is going to be all right."

She took an involuntary step backward. Just as when she'd been on stage in front of all those people laughing at her, Charity knew that going with Matt had been a mistake. If she had never talked to him, or auditioned for that stupid show to begin with, none of this would have happened. She'd be back in Baltimore, back to her life. And as small and inconsequential as it was, returning to it would be better than someone tricking her into thinking that it could get better.

"You're sick," she said, still moving away from him. "You need help."

"Cherry," Matt said, holding out a calming hand. "Don't think about it. It just is."

As he crept closer, Charity turned and started to run. Her feet kicked up gravel as she reached the corner of the alley, but she was no match for Matt. It took him only a few strides before he closed the gap between them and swallowed her in his arms. She shook and wriggled as he turned her to face him.

"Get off me!" she yelled, pounding his chest. "Get off!"

Matt held tight, absorbing her blows as she thrusted her fists against him. "It's okay," he calmed. "Get it out. Yell. Get mad."

"Shut up! Let me go!"

Why is he still talking? Doesn't he get it?

"Go on, Cherry. Use that power. You don't have to push it down anymore. Shout. Scream."

His binding arms enraged her, but she was also furious at herself for how else they made her feel—safe and secure, as his restraint turned to an embrace. The loud, guttural cry that came from her throat startled even her. "Damn you," she shouted. "Damn you!"

"That's it," Matt said as if he were talking to a vomiting child. "Get it out. Embrace your anger. Let it fuel you."

Charity writhed in his arms, but it was a losing battle. "Screw you!" she yelled.

She was both horrified and exhilarated to realize it was the most severe curse she'd ever said aloud. Her pounding fists slowed to half-hearted slaps before her will to fight weakened and left her completely. But, she realized, as angry as she'd felt, she couldn't deny that it had energized her—made her feel *alive.*

"Relax," Matt said as Charity's muscles untensed. "You can do this."

"I can't," she sobbed. "I can't. I thought I could, but seeing it . . . " She shook her head, trying to purge her mind of the dead dog. "It's different. And if I can't even watch . . . " She grew limp in his arms as if ashamed by her weakness.

"Cherry," Matt said, placing a delicate finger under her chin, unknowing that it was a gesture her father had done when she was little to soothe the traumas of childhood—losing her pet goldfish or falling off the monkey bars. It calmed something inside her. "Look at me," he said.

She did.

"You *can* do this. You're stronger than you think. Just by the simple fact of being here today. By surviving. But if you don't want to, if you don't want to watch what we do, you don't have to."

She looked up at him, a child asking a parent to confirm a promise. "I don't?"

"I mean, it changes things a little, but it's nothing we can't work through. There are other ways you can contribute." Then, smiling, he added, "This plan doesn't succeed without you."

She continued to shake her head in self-doubt, loose strands of hair sticking to her freckle-dusted cheeks in the tracks of her tears.

"I don't know if I'm built for this."

"You are," he soothed. "Trust me. Remember those people who laughed at you?"

How could she forget?

"Don't they deserve to feel the way you felt? The way they made you feel—worthless and humiliated. Helpless and alone?"

She looked into his eyes, his words once again sparking that deep connection she'd felt when he'd first knelt beside her.

"Promise me something," she said.

"Anything."

"When you're down there, when it's time, promise me that you'll take care of *them* first."

He didn't need to ask for clarification to know that she meant the three people seated at the judges' table. The three people who had laughed at her and snatched her dream away.

"Whatever else happens, I want them to go first. Especially *her*. Take away their chance right off the bat. The order is up to you."

Matt didn't even blink.

"Consider it done."

Just like that.

She gave him a shy, admiring smile, and when she laid her hand atop his, he allowed it to stay.

"We'll show them what it means to feel pain and embarrassment," he said. "To be kicked when you're down. To be broken. And when we're through, when everyone has seen what we are capable of, when they realize that they brought this upon themselves, they will kneel before you and beg for your forgiveness."

37

MATT LOOKED AT his face in the mirror and automatically knew it wasn't right. Though he'd gotten a new haircut as he'd intended (asking the stylist for something shorter, something popular among guys his age—*something normal*, he'd thought but did not say), his expression was wrong. His cheekbones were too high and his smile too wide, his lips upturned in an exaggerated grin that showed too many teeth. The stack of magazines on the sink with their glossy covers of movie stars beaming artificially whitened smiles seemed to mock him. *You'll never be like us,* they said. *You can practice all you want, but you'll never get it right.*

He'd known he'd needed to start mirroring others, but he didn't think it would be as hard as it was proving to be. Mimicry shouldn't have been difficult. Animals did it all the time in the wild, so why was he having such a hard time? His exaggerated expressions of joy, sadness, and surprise were more caricature than anything else, never seeming to match the given situation as he'd intended.

What was wrong?

It was the same question that the school guidance counselor had asked him after the Billy Hughes incident. She'd known Matt from middle school and, by chance, had transferred to his high school when he was a freshman. Ms. Katie, it seemed, with her watered-down blue eyes, chronically sympathetic gaze, and relentless desire to *help* and *understand*, could not be outrun.

Matt knew that she'd suspected there was something off about him from her observations of him as a child. He'd refused to play or interact with his peers, wrecked others' art projects without remorse, and was prone to staring off into space, as if his thoughts were infinitely more interesting than anything in the real world—because they were. He knew he was quiet and solitary, but it was of his own choosing rather than an inability to communicate. And if he never raised his hand in class, he knew it wasn't because he lacked intelligence. He was smarter than nearly all the college-bound mouth breathers in his classes, just bored. Besides, why should he waste his time responding to questions he already knew the answer to?

Sure, he didn't have any use for friends or building relationships with his peers, but he'd never been angry or violent. He'd never gotten into a fight with another student or told a teacher to fuck off. So why did Ms. Katie always look at him from the corner of her eye as if convinced that he was some kind of psycho or deviant? He'd read up on mental illnesses for his abnormal psychology class and knew that they were the kinds of things that had to be formally tested for. You couldn't just observe that someone was socially uninterested and slap a diagnosis on him. He did not remember anyone—a doctor, psychologist, or even Ms. Katie herself—ever testing him for any cognitive or behavioral disorder. Not that his father would have given his permission for such a thing to begin with. He supposed that he'd been too young back when she'd first met him, but now that he was in high school, it made sense that she would be desperate to evaluate him. He knew that if she didn't manage to test him now, in the final months before he turned eighteen, that would be it. There would be nothing she or anyone else could do to uncover whatever it was that she suspected was wrong with him. Which was fine with Matt. His behavior didn't bother him nearly as much as it seemed to bother others. He imagined the mix of sadness and pity on Ms. Katie's face that she would surely display years from now when referring to Matt as one of the hundreds of kids who had been allowed to fall through the cracks each year.

Although Matt's student file had been relatively devoid of concerns (Matt had peeked through the manila folder atop Ms. Katie's desk when she'd excused herself to use the bathroom), Ms. Katie's years of training and observations of his behavior through the years had evidently convinced her that *something* was wrong with him. Apparently Matt's action of shooting another classmate with an arrow was enough to get Ms. Katie's principal to agree with her.

"How do you feel, Matt?" she'd asked him that day.

"Feel?"

"Yes, today must have been very . . . traumatic. How does it make you feel? How are you doing?"

The truth was that he felt fine, but—thinking of his peers and teachers who now looked at him with cautious, side-eyed glances—he realized that would not be the smartest thing to say. "Sad," he said instead, knowing that it was the right answer. "I guess it's . . . unfortunate."

Ms. Katie nodded as if both agreeing with him and relieved that he'd acknowledged this. "Yes, it certainly is. But, Matt," she soothed, "don't worry. We're here to talk about it. This is all about you."

An uncomfortable silence descended upon Ms. Katie's concrete shoebox of an office as she looked into the blank, unblemished face of her young pupil.

"Matt," she said delicately. "Before today, have you ever felt compelled to hurt another student?"

Another student? he thought before repeating it aloud.

"No," he'd said as if the question was absurd. After all, it was true.

But he needed to prove it. To convince her and everyone else that he was normal.

He put his practice to the test the following day, smiling widely as he thanked a barista for his coffee, the words coming in jagged starts and stops with misplaced emphasis that did not match his smile. "Thank you," he'd said. "*So much.*" It wasn't any better when glancing up at the corner television to see a news report for a Florida hurricane. "So terrible," he said, in a low monotone. When the barista met him with a confused, uncertain stare, Matt realized he'd still had his best imitation of a friendly, normal-guy smile plastered on his face, making it seem as if he reveled in the storm's destruction.

Was that where he'd gone wrong? Or was it his word choice? His tone? He had long since deemed emotion useless and unnecessary. Something that he'd never lamented not having. But he'd also underestimated how difficult it would be to feign. The way things were going now, someone would be able to spot his shortcomings from a mile away. And if it happened to be when he was in the act of extinguishing the fire inside his brain . . . well, it wouldn't end well for him.

When he returned home, he screwed up his face in the bedroom mirror, trying his best to imitate the joy he saw on the faces of celebrities gracing the glossy covers of *People* and *Us Weekly*. But his smile was too wide and eyebrows too high. He couldn't mimic their effortless jubilation without looking crazed. His smile could improve, he knew. So could his tone and his empathy. But his eyes . . .

His eyes never seemed to lose their faraway gaze, their soul-lessness. But maybe that was okay since he didn't think he had a soul anyway. As he turned away from the mirror, feeling the closest approximation to hopelessness as his mind allowed, he sat on the edge of the bed and listened to the local NBC affil-iate report that a pair of men had just been apprehended after breaking into the house of their former drug dealer. A pair of mugshots popped onto the screen, both men looking bedrag-gled, all uncombed hair and rough, tattooed skin.

But their smiles.

Their eyes.

There was something in them, as if Matt automatically knew what those men were thinking and what they had tried to do. What, if they were ever released on bail, they would try to do again.

Have you ever felt compelled to hurt another student? Ms. Katie had asked.

The cogs inside his brain turned and spun as he stared at the mugshots, considering the horrors those men had commit-ted and the release they must have felt. The same release that he felt each time he scratched the itch. Something clicked then, as real as the fire deep inside his brain. Because if he was going to feign joy or sadness or anything, he had to observe the people who were most like him, the ones who got pleasure how he got pleasure. People whose joy he could use to simulate his own, to help him fit into society and trick others into thinking he was someone else.

"No, I've never wanted to hurt another student," he'd said to Ms. Katie half-truthfully.

But now that I have, he thought to himself that day in the bathroom, *I know that I want to do it again.*

And by then, he would fit in real good.

He would make sure of it.

38

THOUGH THERE WAS no one scheduled to be inside the theater during the day, Matt said they'd wait until dark to make their move. There were things they needed to do inside the building that night if they were to succeed tomorrow. Everything they needed, Matt said, was already there. So, when darkness settled over the city, streets flooded with the bright lights of taxis and limousines chauffeuring the wealthy wherever they wanted to go, they left the hotel with nothing but a pair of silver keys on a neon green plastic ring.

The theater was not far from their hotel, and they arrived at the Sixth Avenue venue after a brisk ten-minute walk. As they stood across the street and waited to cross, Charity's attention was commanded by the theater's wraparound marquee. Its blocky concrete exterior and marquee of cursive lettering in neon reds and blues combined to create what she considered to be the perfect melding of past and present. To Charity, the old building signified not decrepitude, but sophistication. She'd seen the theater in panning shots of the city when NBC did their tree lighting every year, and she'd thought the only way it could look more magical was if the Christmas tree they set atop the marquee every November had been present, filling the New York City dark with the magic she'd known existed.

The little glowing man told them that it was safe to cross, and when they finally extricated themselves from the waves of crossing pedestrians—*Doesn't anyone say excuse me?* Charity marveled—and stood under the marquee near one of the theater's ticketing windows, Matt said, "Come on," and led her around the building.

He had worked inside the theater many times since joining the *Talent Now!* road crew, so he was already familiar with the venue and its security procedures. "Plus," he said, dangling the set of keys in front of Charity with a smile, "easy access."

"What if we get caught?" she asked, not so much nervous as pragmatic.

"There's no show tonight. We won't. But if we do, I'll just show them my ID badge and say that I wanted to show my girlfriend around the theater."

Charity was flummoxed. *Girlfriend?*

Matt saw her blush and said, "Relax" as he smiled that wide, charming smile. "That's just the story we'll go by."

They turned right and came to a metal door with a set of dual locks and a sign that read, DO NOT ENTER. ONLY STAGE CREW PERMITTED BEYOND THIS POINT.

"I guess you pass," Charity said playfully.

Matt slid the neon green band off his wrist and inserted the first key into the first lock, turned the bolt, and repeated the action with the second. There would be no additional security or alarm to navigate, Matt assured as he held the door for her.

The spacious backstage area in which Charity found herself was not that different from the one in Baltimore. They were surrounded by scores of scattered television production equipment and machinery, as well as a multitude of large black crates marked TALENT NOW!.

Matt closed the door behind them and led Charity by the hand across the floor, as if he knew exactly where he was going.

Her heart fluttered when he grasped her fingers with his, and she couldn't help the butterflies that rose inside her as he navigated through the quiet room. Maybe he was right, after all, she thought. Maybe no one *would* be here.

"Almost there," he said, as Charity saw a sliver of light ahead.

The set of cascading black curtains made her flash back to her horrible audition, and she found it hard to believe that it had only been two days since she'd met Matt. Right away he'd managed to understand her and the indignities she'd been faced with, her insecurities and anxieties.

But the rats, she thought. *The dog.*

It seemed to come so easily to him. *Did he enjoy it?* she wondered. *Had he done it before?* And then, recalling his empty expression after killing the dog, she wondered, *Should I be scared of him?*

He'd been charismatic at first, smiling that charming smile and saying all the right things—that she wasn't useless, that everyone was a bit socially awkward, that she could do great things and be somebody. But that charisma seemed to fade little by little with each hour she spent with him—the smiles a little smaller and the enthusiastic lilts to his voice coming less frequently.

He liked to keep to himself and never seemed to be in the mood for small talk, even on the few occasions when Charity tried to engage him in conversation. After all, wouldn't their plan work better if they acted as a cohesive unit? He talked about himself rarely and about their plan only sporadically, as if he'd worked out the details long ago. Though Charity was satisfied to go along with whatever he suggested or instructed to make the plan work, a small, nagging voice in the back of her head told her she was just fodder for a plan that was Matt's alone. But then the light squeeze of his soft hand made her think that she was crazy for even considering it as she followed him past the black curtains and into a pool of dim lighting.

When she stepped onto the stage, what she felt was not the fear or nervousness or humiliation she'd felt in Baltimore, but all the emotions her audition should have come with: joy and excitement, the sense of a dream coming true. The dark, polished floor sent her footsteps echoing throughout the empty theater as the massive stage swallowed her up, making it feel as though both she and her problems were so small in the grand scheme of things. Ironically, standing here by herself beneath the soft stage lights, she realized, was one of the few times in her short life that she hadn't felt alone.

She barely blinked as she marveled at the floor-to-ceiling LCD screen behind her that, come tomorrow, would bare the *Talent Now!* logo and whatever other glittering graphics the production team deemed necessary. Though unlit, each of the three judges' exclamation marks dangled above the bare stage at a dizzying height, sleeping monsters of metal and Plexiglas. Her eyes followed them to the series of high arches that rose across the stage like a thick metallic rainbow, and Charity knew these would also glow at the show tomorrow, lit with silver sparkles and patriotic patterns that would illuminate those seated in the first dozen rows of the audience. It would be remarkably beautiful, and she lamented that she wouldn't be here to see it. If what she and Matt had agreed upon still held true, she wouldn't be anywhere near the stage.

She heard a whistle and saw Matt beckoning her to join him at the edge of the stage.

"What?" Charity whispered anxiously. "Is someone here?"

"I want you to see something," he said as he pointed above.

"What am I looking at?" She was more worried about losing her balance and falling off the edge of the stage.

"You see those two huge barrels?"

After a moment of searching, she did. They flanked the judges' three giant exclamation points that tomorrow, like the rest of the stage, would come to life with a brilliant glow. "Yeah. What about them?"

"They're already filled. Probably yesterday or the day before."

"Filled? With what?"

"They're confetti cannons. They fill them for every audition in case Larry, Portia, or Hans use their 'judge save' to automatically send a contestant through to the next round."

She looked ahead at the darkened judges' table with disgust. It seemed to mock her. *Hans*, she fumed, hating the rise of heat that colored her cheeks. *Portia*.

"And why do we care about confetti?"

"Because there are four other barrels," Matt said. "Four barrels that haven't been filled or put in place yet."

"Barrels," she repeated, sure there was something more important they could be focusing on.

Matt pointed at the massive metal arch that soared seventy-five feet above the theater's massive orchestra section and the long, transparent Plexiglas of the judges' platform. "One goes there," he said, pointing to the left side of the arch, "another in the center, and two more on the far right."

Charity scrunched up her brow. She'd known the audition tomorrow would involve the bow, but why was he so hung up on confetti cannons? What did she care who got the judge save?

"Okay, so they haven't been put into place yet. So what?" she said. Her tone was dry, a bored child eager to move on to a new activity. "Why does that mean anything to us?"

"Because," Matt said, a sinister grin spreading wide across his face. It was the self-satisfied look of a child who enjoyed killing ants with a magnifying glass. "We're going to fill them."

Charity scoffed. "With more confetti?"

"No." Matt withdrew his iPhone from the pocket of his black jeans and swiped the screen a few times before turning it around for Charity to see. He could've told her the single-word answer to her question but favored the dramatic flair singular to photography. His lips curled as he waited for her awed reaction. "With this."

The picture's background was dim, but it was clear enough for Charity to make out the focus—a cluster of large barrels amid a battlefield of clutter—and the single word printed on each in white block letters:

GASOLINE

39

ON THE AFTERNOON following his high school graduation, Matt packed up his few belongings, told his father goodbye, and finally left the hole in the dirt he had called home for the past eighteen years.

But not before one final task.

He stepped from the sweltering living room and onto the porch, holding two beers with the tabs already popped. He offered his father one of the Buds, beads of water clinging to the can, and took a seat on the adjacent rocking chair next to him. He had not been happy to hear that Matt was leaving, and his mix of anger and intoxication had resulted in the barrage of insults he now directed at his child: that he was a sorry excuse for a son and a lousy farmer; that he was heartless for leaving Fred to fend for himself during the cold winters and harsh summers; that he was just like his mother, abandoning him for greener pastures. This last one was especially rich, considering that his father hadn't even bothered to come to his own son's graduation that morning—not that it mattered to Matt.

Matt listened and waited patiently through his father's homily of disappointment as the intensity of his insults, and the rapidity with which he spoke them, began to slow.

"You're nothing, Matty," he spat. "You . . . you never were and . . . and . . . " His words morphed into bursts of wheezing and coughing as a fine gloss of blood began to paint his bottom lip.

Matt sipped from his own can quietly as he appraised his father. He was amazed at how quickly the rat poison had taken effect. He knew it'd be fast, but he'd hardly finished half of his beer.

His father stared confusedly at his can, then at his son, and in the final moments of Fred Manson's pathetic life, Matt saw the dawning, wide-eyed realization on his face. It was as if he was recalling the image of his young son beside the mounds of dead animals in the yard and finally understood what he was capable of. *You did this to me*, his expression said.

Yes, Matt thought. *I did.* Because to start over, he had to cut ties with the past. With the people who held him down. But he'd known what he was going to do for a while—since the day he'd shot Billy Hughes. Needed to make sure his father was both silent and unavailable if law enforcement or one of Matt's old teachers should ever come poking around and decide to ask Fred Manson if his son had ever exhibited any unusual or cruel tendencies.

His father dropped his can with a trembling hand and slouched forward, tumbling off the rocking chair and onto the dry-rotted porch with a hollow *thump*. The sound nestled comfortably in Matt's brain as he realized that one of the itches that had been bothering him since he was a child had been permanently scratched.

He finished his own beer and set the empty can on the porch beside his rocking chair, then stood, withdrawing the silver lighter from his pocket. He'd soaked the porch in gasoline before leaving for graduation while his father was still sleeping off the previous day's hangover, giving the thirsty wood a good couple of hours to drink it up. Now, he flicked the lighter's wheel and watched as a blue-centered flame sparked to brilliant life. Just this once, he forced himself to look away from it as he spoke to his father for the last time.

"Get out of here, Dad. Leave your son be," Matt said to the crumpled, wheezing lump. "You know how I am about my fireside time." And then he tossed the lighter into his father's piss-stained lap.

Flames instantly blanketed his father's torso, greedily eating through his dirtied clothes and bedraggled graying hair. He did not move. As Matt watched him burn, he once again thought of *Baby on Fire* and was instantly transported back to the day in art class when he'd been struck by the painting's arresting beauty of bright yellows and oranges. He hadn't understood then why it had such an effect on him, but now he knew.

As he watched the fire spread, the one inside his head began to diminish. His muscles slackened as endorphins flooded his brain with dizzying speed. Matt closed his eyes against the euphoric flashes of luminous yellow blooming behind his lids. He basked in the satisfying prickle that ran over his flesh as his mind flashed back to that night in front of his father's fireplace, the one he had been banned from enjoying, and the promise he had made to himself. *Everything comes full circle*, Matt thought, his lips curling into a twisted smile as he watched his father's skin blister and char. He had given nothing to Matt, and his son would leave him with the same.

Matt opened his eyes to the crackling flames as they greedily ate the corpse and dry-rotted wood beneath. The breeze now carried bits of ash and dust, and the remaining cows on the Manson farm mooed in protest. *They'll die out here*, Matt thought matter-of-factly as he grabbed his backpack with the bow sticking out and started down the porch steps. It wasn't long before the entire house was alit with fire. Soon there would be nothing left.

He did not look back. Just kept walking down the dirt road, toward a new place and whatever life came with it. And the next day, when news of the house's smoldering shambles made it into the paper, people in town would read it and think some version of, "Isn't that Fred Manson's place? I wonder what happened there. Didn't he have a son?" But if Matt did his job, if he moved far enough away and did his best to observe and mimic and blend into the society that had both shunned and tried to understand him, they would never find out.

40

CHARITY LOOKED AT Matt with a mix of horror and thrill in her eyes, her brows rising as if to say, *Are you serious?*

He was.

They kept gasoline backstage to power the theater's backup generators in case of power outages. A blackout on national TV—live or taped—would be a regrettable PR disaster.

"And we just fill them up and hope that the stage crew will put them in place?"

"Exactly. I'd supervise it myself but, as you know, I'm putting in my resignation tomorrow. Can't audition if you're affiliated with the show."

"Yeah, I remember."

It might work, but there was still that nagging, worried voice that forced her to consider the minute details of their plan and the many ways it could possibly go wrong.

"How do we know they won't check the barrels beforehand and think that they're surprisingly heavy for holding pieces of ripped-up paper?"

"Because they don't lift them," Matt said, staring at the theater's ceiling as if he could see the starry night sky through the many layers and feet of concrete, wood, and plaster. "They use a crane."

Matt left her for a moment and disappeared around a darkened corner. When he returned minutes later, he was rolling a large metal cylinder like a barrel of whiskey. She could hear the liquid sloshing around inside.

"Where'd that come from?" she said.

"The mechanical room."

"Let me guess," she ventured sarcastically, "you had a key."

"Guilty," he smirked.

Matt rolled it onto a manual platform lift and began pumping the handle to raise the barrel higher than the one that held the confetti. When he finished, he found a rubber syphon in a nearby box and, after using one of the keys on his ring to unlock both barrels' lids, got to work. He stuck one end of the transparent rubber hose into the gasoline barrel and sucked deeply on the other end as the urine-colored fluid snaked through the tube. As it reached the tip, Matt shoved the loose end into the smaller confetti barrel, but not before catching a mouthful of gasoline. He spit it into an empty water bottle, wiping his mouth on his shirt.

"Gross," Charity said. But she couldn't help her curiosity when she asked, "What's it taste like?"

Matt's lips were slick with gasoline. "Hot oil mixed with paint fumes and shit. Care to try?"

She waved away the offer. Her curiosity didn't extend that far.

You came all this way to let him do all the work? said that nagging voice inside her. *When all this is over, don't you want to be able to say you did more than just watch?*

"Wait," she said, stopping Matt with the tube halfway to his mouth. She walked over and held out her hand. "I guess I should try."

Matt gave her a greasy smirk and passed her the tube.

She did as he instructed. It was like sucking on the straw of the world's biggest milkshake. The urine-colored liquid slowly snaked its way up the transparent tube before spilling into her mouth. She looked frantically at Matt and pointed to her chipmunk-full checks as if to say, *What now?*

Matt eyed her slyly. "Spit."

Gasoline sprayed from Charity's mouth as she coughed and gagged. "You didn't tell me it was going to burn!" she said.

Matt crossed his arms loosely over his chest and kept his unblinking eyes fixed on her as if mentally taking notes on her performance, like a father supervising his teenager change a flat tire for the first time.

After she had regained her composure, they took turns syphoning until each of the confetti barrels was full. Their endeavor had barely made a dent in the large containers of gasoline, both of them purposefully tapping an equal amount from each.

When it was done and Matt had relocked the barrels, Charity regarded their work with pride. Matt wiped his hands on the front of his jeans and offered her a Tic Tac. "Now that that's done," he said, "let's go over your part."

They took one of the small flights of stairs down from the stage and walked along the aisle against the soundproofed wall. The incline caught Charity by surprise, but it was far from unmanageable. She marveled at the sheer number of red velvet seats waiting to be filled with the people who had hurt her so deeply. If the website she'd checked on Matt's phone was accurate, there were over two thousand seats on the floor level and three tiers of wall-to-wall balcony seating.

They pushed through one of the six sets of double doors that lined the wall opposite the stage, above a glowing green

EXIT sign. Charity felt her scalp prickle as the door nearly clicked shut behind them, but Matt stuck the lime green ring of keys between it and the jamb.

"Good save," she said.

Matt pointed to the long, curving row of mezzanine-level exit doors where they now stood. "Look. There are six pairs on this level." He gazed down the row of doors that led into the theater. "Whether they try to exit from here or any of the upper tiers, they'll all have to funnel down through here."

"Meaning?"

"Meaning that this row of doors is the only one that matters. That when the people in there"—he pointed inside the theater—"try to run, these are the doors they'll be heading for."

"What about the orchestra level? Won't they be able to get out without us down there to stop them?"

"Unfortunately," Matt said with noticeable lament, "some will get out. We can't be everywhere in a venue as big as this. But with any luck, we'll get them from above. Or at least slow them down a bit."

Charity nodded as if it was understandable that there would be some escapees.

"But what about the doors at the front of the building?" she asked. "And the ticketing entrances in the lobby at ground level? There are too many to keep track of. We won't be able to prevent anyone from coming in to stop us."

"Cherry," he said, smiling the way a parent might smile at a child who had failed to grasp an obvious concept, "they won't be able to exit from the same doors they entered. It's posted all over the theater. All we need is for people to show up," he said. "And when they do, they'll look for the closest, most convenient exit." He gestured to the row of mezzanine exit doors. "And besides, by the time someone manages to call the police or fire department, it'll be too late. They can try to come in all they want. Our work will be done."

"So how does this involve me?" she asked. "What's my part?"

Matt withdrew something from his back pocket and placed it in Charity's hand.

"A bike lock?" she said, clearly unimpressed.

"Just an example," he said. "The actual chains we'll be using are much bigger and don't have child-protective plastic casing around them like this one."

"And you have them? Back at the hotel?"

He nodded.

Charity held the lock uncomfortably. "So, I just hook the chains around the door handles and lock them?"

Matt laughed.

"No, Cherry. Not *just* lock them." He stepped closer and began to slowly, tenderly, wrap the bike lock around her wrist. "You do it slowly, savoring the moment." Then he wound it around the other one, his face only inches from hers.

Charity's mind shouted *danger!* But she could not seem to move.

"You think of the pain they caused you. The embarrassment. The irreparable damage to the dreams they took from you."

He had bound both of her wrists together now, and Charity trembled at the feel of his soft hands slipping across her knuckles. She began to relax, the fear and hesitation slowly abating.

"And when each chain has been placed and each door locked, when you look inside that theater and hear their screams, take a step back and savor the moment of your revenge. Because when you hear their shouted pleas and pitiful apologies, when their lives are in your hands and the power they took from you has been returned, then you'll know"—he paused as the bike lock clicked into place above her wrists—"that you've won."

Charity had never liked to be touched, but as she felt the hot plastic of the bike chain around her wrists, her heart thumped wildly. No one had ever spoken to her that way, in soft seductive whispers. Matt's words seemed to stroke a part of her brain and body that had been asleep. Her skin buzzed with prickles of passion as the moisture dried from her mouth and a lump formed at the back of her throat. Feeling his soft hands atop her own, her body shuddered with a thunderbolt of impatience as she realized that she wanted him more than she'd ever wanted anything in her life.

Just as abruptly as he began, Matt released the lock and began to unbind her. When she was free of the chain and had settled herself, she asked, "Aren't there cameras in here? Won't there be security guards stationed outside the doors?" She already knew the answers to these questions but needed to say something to keep Matt's attention off the rise of color in her cheeks.

"Absolutely," he said. "But not for long. Once they see the first hint of something wrong on stage—if they're smart enough to realize that it isn't part of the act—they'll be called into the theater immediately. And that is when you make your move. You've got to be fast, though."

"So, I won't actually be on stage with you."

"That's what you wanted, right?"

She looked down, slightly embarrassed.

"Hey," Matt said, softly cupping her cheek. "You're still an integral part of the plan. You'll be here the whole time, free to watch them suffer just as they watched you."

"And what about you?" she asked, wringing the bike chain. "What's going to happen to you in there? How are you going to get away?"

Matt's tone was soft and level. "Well, I'll try to make a run for it afterward, when the time is right. But this whole thing was never about escape."

Charity felt an inner tremble, a fear she hadn't known was there. "What *is* it about?"

"The same things we discussed in Baltimore—revenge, retribution, payback against the people who don't understand us. They want to put us in a box, Cherry. Stick a label on us. And we can't be labeled. We're different. Separate from society's labels and rules and expectations. That's why they won't see us coming." He stopped to take a breath. "And once they've seen what we're capable of, when they've seen what they brought upon themselves, that's when we've won."

"The chances of you getting out of there . . . "

"My name will be all over the news." He shrugged. "If I run, they'll follow. Somehow, no matter how good I am at hiding or blending in, they'll find me."

It was a melancholy thought but a result she had to be prepared for.

"I'll try to get back to you, but if I don't, run. You've got a better shot at it than I do."

Charity's eyes shimmered with the realization that had just dawned on her. "Tonight might be the last time we're together."

"Shh," he said, pressing a gentle finger to her lips. "Let's not think about that. We knew going into this that nothing was guaranteed."

But his words could not erase the defeat she felt weighing on her mind and shoulders.

"Just think how lucky we are," he continued. "We understand each other, Cherry. That's more than most people get in a lifetime. It's nice to be loved, but it's profound to be understood."

Charity nodded her silent agreement. As exhaustion began to creep its way into her body and mind, she knew it was the best they could hope for. They'd done what they'd come here to do, and the rest would play out on the stage tomorrow.

They turned and walked back down the theater's main aisleway until they reached the stage and the back door they'd entered through. As Matt stuck the silver keys into the twin locks, he and Charity slipped out of the cool theater and into the muggy New York City night, the wild honking of taxis and sulfurous odor of sewer grate smoke filling their ears and noses once more. Matt locked the door behind them, and they left the theater without seeing a soul.

41

THOUGH IT WAS well past ten when they arrived back at the hotel, throngs of people and taxis clogged the streets as the flashing signs and marquees in nearby Times Square charged the city with life. It seemed as if it was time for a mid-afternoon stroll rather than sleep. The air was buzzing with electricity as couples headed to bars or late dinners, the sounds of karaoke and jovial laughter leaking onto the litter-filled streets. Clusters of backpack-wearing college kids chatted and fished crumpled dollars from grubby pockets as they stood in line at the pretzel and hotdog carts occupying nearly every corner.

But Matt and Charity were not among the crowds. It was the night before their big day, and they agreed that a final rundown of their plan was necessary to avoid any missteps. They would not, they knew, be getting a second chance. Matt recapped his role, detailing what and where he'd be shooting from, and he reminded Charity to wait for his signal before locking the doors with the chains he'd told her about.

"And here they are," he said, unzipping the black backpack filled with industrial-sized chains and padlocks.

Charity looked inside, eyes widening with apprehension. "There's a lot in there." She lifted the bag with one hand. "Stainless steel?"

"My, my," Matt said, impressed. "My Cherry knows her metals."

"And heavy, too."

"If they weren't heavy, they wouldn't work."

"Yeah, but I doubt I'm going to get inside with them. Aren't they gonna check my bag at security or something?"

"Cherry," he said, narrowing his eyes, "did they check your bag when you auditioned in Baltimore?"

She had to think about it for a second. "No. They didn't."

"There you go. And as far as anyone knows, they're part of my act."

"And they'll just believe you?"

"Sure. Who ever heard of someone being threatened with a chain?"

"No one, I guess." She shrugged. "I get the chains, but why not guns instead of the bow? We *could* just shoot up the place, you know."

Matt laughed, real as she'd ever heard from him. "Now, where's the fun in that?" he said. "Besides, guns are lazy. Artless. Anybody can buy a gun. Anybody can point and shoot. But what we're using . . . what I made . . . " His eyes fluttered closed as he pictured his bow's sanded wood and the slick Minwax finishing stain. "When I use it, it's not just a piece of wood and string. It becomes part of me in a way that a gun would not."

The corners of Charity's mouth wrinkled with uncertainty as she tried to understand where he was coming from. Guns still seemed better.

"This is a talent competition . . . a reality show. Think of the kinds of people that watch this shit. Do you really believe they're going to think anyone would try something at a talent show?"

"Probably not," she said, wondering how it was possible that no one had tried anything before.

"And that," Matt said, holding a finger in the air as if his point had been made, "is part of the reason they deserve what's coming to them. Because after all this is done and news makes its way to the papers and TV and the Internet, the only thing everyone's going to wonder is how come something like this didn't happen sooner."

As they readied for bed, Charity asked, "You don't think the plan is too simple? Shouldn't there be, I don't know . . . more parts?"

Matt gave her the expression she'd come to both love and fear, a smile that stretched his lips farther back than they should've gone. There was a glint of amusement in his eye that made her wonder if he was considering something darker than what he let on. "Cherry," he said, his too-wide smirk revealing the tips of pointed canines, "all the best plans are simple. It's simplicity that's our secret weapon."

She supposed there was some truth in that. Besides, elaborate plots had more opportunities for mistakes and things to go wrong. Matt, it seemed, had thought of everything. As she listened to him speak, she once again felt the familiar fluttering inside her stomach. She touched his bow with a smooth palm and felt the same arousal as when he'd wrapped the bike chain around her wrists. Charity closed her eyes and leaned towards him, her lips inching closer to his.

"Cherry, what are you doing?"

Her eyes snapped open. "I-I just . . . I'm sorry." Her cheeks turned bright pink as she turned away from him and faced the window.

"Hey, I almost forgot," Matt said, either not understanding or ignoring what she'd tried to do. "I got something for you."

A present? Whatever it was, she hoped it would be something to erase her memory of the last ten seconds.

Matt reached into one of his black canvas bags and pulled out a similarly colored square with curved corners and placed it in her palm.

"Open it."

Charity felt the pliable nylon of the CD case in her hands as she unzipped its sides. She lifted the front flap and felt her heart flutter when she saw the title of the first and only disc staring back at her. The Mamas & the Papas, the yellow disc said. *Greatest Hits.*

"Matt," she said, swelling with surprise and gratitude. "I-I don't know what to say."

"You don't have to say anything," he said. "I know you had an iPod, but the music sounds better this way." He pointed at the CD case. "Keep going."

Charity flipped through the remainder of empty slots. "There's nothing else in here," she said. But then her finger grazed on a fat brown leather case at the very back. She looked at Matt with a mix of confusion and anticipation as she unbuttoned the top and slowly extricated the object inside.

"In case anyone tries to stop you tomorrow," Matt said, but Charity didn't need further explanation.

She eyed the black-handled blade in the moonlight seeping through the window. The mere action of holding it made her feel powerful, wielding something that could so easily take a life in the swift and careless way that so many things had been taken from her. As she gripped the hilt, she thought she was finally understanding what Matt had said about his bow becoming part of him, an extension of his body.

"And if you ever feel like you can't go through with it, remember why we're doing this in the first place. Think of all the people who laughed at you. Remember that when you slice them open."

She couldn't help it when she rose from the edge of the bed and kissed Matt on the cheek. This time, she did not blush.

"It's perfect," she said.

42

MATT RELUCTANTLY LET her kiss him. It was fine. It meant his gift had worked. That she hadn't spotted the truth behind its offering—or its source.

He did not tell her that he had stolen both the CD and the knife. Or that the weapon, with its sharp blade and scuffed brown leather case, had been taken from the homeless man he had killed in the alley before Charity had found him.

She didn't need to know.

In fact, his entire plan hinged on her not knowing.

Not knowing a thing.

43

CHARITY SLIPPED BENEATH the covers and stared out at the glimmering lights of the New York City skyline. From this height, the chaos and traffic below were invisible, leaving only the distant illuminated buildings and blinking towers. *It's so beautiful*, she thought. And, quite possibly, it would be the last time she would ever see it.

She'd only been here for a couple days, but she wasn't the same person she was when she left Baltimore—the timid girl who hid behind her iPod at family gatherings or searched for the calming presence of her mother every time she had a panic attack. In fact, she had barely thought of her mother since she'd snuck out her bedroom window on audition day. What had her mother thought when she'd come home from work and hadn't seen Charity in her bedroom, or in the living room watching *Ellen*? That she was in some kind of trouble? That she'd been kidnapped and left to die in one of those ditches mothers were always talking about? Did she wait all night for her daughter to come home, or had she called the police right away?

Had she cried?

Despite her mother's hovering, Charity loved her and always would. But as deep as her love swelled, she now understood that her mother was part of what was holding her back. After all, Charity had done things over the past two days that she never would have dreamed of. She wasn't perfect, and she still had a long way to go before she could feel completely comfortable shaking hands and making eye contact with strangers, but she was beginning to worry less and carry herself more confidently, qualities she could've mastered a long time ago if her mother had bothered to nurture the potential Matt had seen in her. Because if she was going to get what she wanted out of life, it was these qualities, she knew, that would help her get it.

With these thoughts fresh in her mind, Charity slid under the cool, expensive sheets and closed her eyes. If she could just hold on to them until tomorrow, everything would be okay. She was fine, she was safe, and she would wake up in the morning to begin the life of whoever she was going to become.

44

THEY LEFT THE hotel in the morning with whatever they'd come with. For Charity, it was only the small purse she'd bought to go with her audition outfit. If she'd left anything behind that could be linked back to her, she didn't care. Caring less was another thing she was learning to do.

They walked the same familiar blocks of midtown Manhattan, once again standing across from the Sixth Avenue theater they'd visited the night before. This time, it would not be empty. The line of potential contestants wrapped around the block just as it had in Baltimore, scores of people sequestered between steel barriers like cows to a slaughterhouse.

After a couple hours in line, it was their turn at the sign-in table where Matt completed the necessary paperwork that asked for information like his name, birthday, address, and occupation. At the bottom it said: *Please list the names of all performers in your act and their roles.* Matt scribbled, "MATTHEW MANSON—ARCHERY". As such, it was a no-brainer to check the box entitled DANGER under the act category headline. Then, before signing his name, the final box asked: *Are you affiliated in any way with the production of* Talent Now!*, its creators, producers, judges, or anyone involved with the making or*

broadcast of the show? Matt checked the box next to the word
NO. As of this morning, he was unemployed. He'd spoken to
his boss before they'd left the hotel and informed him that he
was quitting in order to audition for the show.

He handed his paperwork to the young woman at the
check-in desk and received his Contestant ID sticker in return.
As he stuck it on his shirt, the woman pointed between him
and Charity and asked, "Are you two together?"

"Yes," Matt said, "but she's just here for support. She's not
auditioning."

"Aww," the woman said, addressing Charity as the corners
of her mouth rose to show that she was visibly touched, "that's
so sweet of you. You know, the world needs more people like
you two, rooting each other on."

"Yes," Matt agreed, smiling his best practiced smile,
"they do."

The short-haired woman handed Charity a sticker that
read, "Contestant Guest" before saying, "And what's in your
backpacks?"

A hot, nervous tremor shot through Charity. She'd anticipated this moment. Thankfully, Matt had it all figured out.

"A bow, arrows, and some chains," he said, gesturing coolly
to their open packs. "I wrote it all on the form, so the crew
knows I don't need any additional materials for my audition."

"Well," the check-in lady said, impressed, "aren't you thorough?" Then she leaned over the desk conspiratorially. "I do
have a question for you, though, if you'll indulge me."

"Sure," Matt said.

"I get the bow and arrows, but what are the chains for?"

"Oh," Matt said with practiced cheer, "if I told you that,
then it wouldn't be a surprise." He turned to Charity. "Would
it, Cherry?"

She nodded her silent agreement.

The woman shot them a playful smile. "Well, then, I guess I'll just have to wait."

They walked away and had nearly reached the theater doors when she shouted after them.

"Hey!" she said. "Maybe if you're good enough, you'll make it on TV."

Matt smirked. "Yes," he said. "Maybe we will."

They funneled into one of the theater's many waiting areas. Space was limited, so instead of allowing all contestants to congregate in one large room as Charity had done at the Baltimore Convention Center, they let seventy-five people into each of the theater's three rehearsal rooms. It was there, behind a door marked REHEARSAL ROOM #2, that Charity and Matt waited silently for the moment Matt's number would be called and their work would begin.

Though auditions had not yet begun, black-shirted and headset-wearing production assistants fanned throughout the theater as they funneled audience members inside. They would fill the orchestra section first, followed by the three sections of wall-to-wall balcony seating. Because *Talent Now!* often panned the crowd for shots of the enthusiastic audience, the producers wanted every seat filled (as did Charity and Matt). After all, they wanted to make it look like the show was a hot event, something that everybody was clamoring to get tickets to even though they were free.

While Matt strummed his bow string to make sure it was taut, Charity emptied the trash from her small purse until the only items remaining were her wallet, ID, and the leftover pack of peanut butter crackers she had brought in line to her audition. With this task completed, she took stock of how differently this room felt from the one in Baltimore. Where the air had once been full of excitement for the chance of acceptance and inclusion that had lay before her, it was now replaced by a calm reverence and mental steadiness in preparation for what came next. She'd made her peace with what they were about to do. Matt had helped her realize that they could not pick and choose who would live and who would die. That innocent people would be caught in their crosshairs was inevitable.

Looking around at elderly ballroom dancers, little girls in tutus, and large choirs and dance troupes practicing excitedly, Charity shook her head.

"What's wrong?" Matt said.

"It's nothing." Her tone was one of resigned disappointment. "It's just that my mother wouldn't believe I'm here." She looked into his eyes with a sense of calm that was new to her. "You know she didn't even want me to audition?" she said. "Didn't even think I could."

"And?"

"And what?"

"And look where you are now. I'd say you've proved her wrong, wouldn't you?"

"Yeah," she said with a small smile. Freed from the weight of her mother's thumb and hundreds of miles from her watchful eyes, Charity found that she was capable of more than she'd imagined. She had talked to strangers and asserted herself and even walked around a new city by herself. Her hands had still been clammy and her heart had still thumped with anxiety, but she'd done it. And all the while, she had not relied on the comforting presence of her iPod to drown out the sensory overload that once would have sent her into a corner with her eyes closed and hands pressed tightly against her ears. "I think I would."

Silence descended over them once again as Matt stared blankly at the hordes of contestants scattered around the room. "Cherry," he said after a moment. "Have you ever seen a fire?"

"Of course," she said, caught off guard by the question. "Who hasn't? My uncle took me camping once and we made a campfire. Plus, there's always a story about burning buildings on the six o'clock news."

"No," he said, the corners of his mouth drawing up in a dimpled smile. "A *real* fire. Close enough where you can see the changing colors of the flames and feel your skin turn slick from the smoke and heat. That kind of fire."

"No," Charity said, her brows knitted in confusion as she twisted the hem of her shirt. She was about to ask him if he had ever seen that kind of fire, but the longing way that he looked off into the distance with his glazed and unblinking eyes told her that he had.

"Then, Cherry," he said. "You're in for a real treat."

45

"MATT?" CHARITY SAID, forcing him out of his reverie. "Thanks for believing in me."

"You got it, Cherry. You're worth believing in."

Her heart swelled as they were enveloped by the room's mix of instruments being tuned and the zippy pop music that was pumped in from hidden speakers. Shortly after, a skinny guy with a young face and shaggy brown hair appeared before them.

"Hey, buddy!" he said to Matt, startling Charity as she looked up to see the word CREW printed in white on his black T-shirt. "Heard you quit to audition for the show."

"You know it," Matt said, smiling and shaking the man's palm with one hand and slapping his back with the other.

"You know him?" Charity asked suspiciously, concerned that his sudden appearance would put a wrench in their plans.

"Sorry," he said. "I'm Carter. Me and Matt work—well, *worked*, I guess I should say—on the show's crew together."

Charity nodded, her anxiety abating.

"Well, hey," Carter said, turning back to Matt and clapping his hand on his shoulder. "Living the dream, huh? Right on."

Okay, Charity thought, *I may have overreacted.*

"Anyway, if you want to come with me, I can get you through a little faster," he said with a wink. "Figured you might want to bypass all the waiting."

"Hell yeah," Matt said. "That'd be great. Thanks, man."

Carter offered Charity the opportunity to wait backstage as well, but she told him that she had somewhere else she needed to be—which was true. But she knew that her "Contestant Guest" sticker would be helpful if she ended up needing to come up with a plausible excuse as to why she was loitering outside the theater's mezzanine doors with a suspicious-looking backpack.

Matt collected his own pack off the chair beside him and rose to follow his former coworker, even though he already knew where to go.

"Break a leg," Charity said, eager to say something, anything, in case it was the last time they would speak.

Matt, it appeared, was considerably less affected by this possibility. He stepped back beside her and bent close to her ear. "Stay sharp, Cherry. Wait for my signal. You know what to do."

"I will," she whispered. "And Matt?"

"What?"

"Don't miss."

His eyes were a blank slate of brown steel as he turned from her and was whisked away from the elegantly carpeted room. She imagined him walking through a maze of hallways that presumably led to the backstage area, where he would wait for his turn on stage.

With Matt gone, the pressure of her role now weighed heavily upon her. Her breaths became shallow and rapid, her palms swampy with sweat as a fresh wave of anxiety bloomed.

What if he misses? What if I don't get to the doors in time? What if someone stops us?

But there was no time for second-guesses. This was it. They each had their part to play, each dependent on the other. In another hour or so, Matt would text her using the burner phones they'd bought at 7-Eleven the day before. That would be her cue to go to her spot. His next signal, the one meant for her to make her move, would not come by text. She would be able to see it through any one of the doors that ran the curved length of the theater's mezzanine level, each made of the same bulletproof acrylic used in banks across the country. *No one gets in, no one gets out*, she mused. They would surely be discovered if they attempted the same stunt at the heavily secured orchestra level but in the middle, Matt had assured her, there would be fewer security staff milling about.

She knew that there were people there who did not deserve what was about to happen to them, but there was no way to pick and choose who would be caught in the crossfire. It wasn't fair, but their deaths would be the sacrifices their plans demanded. And the more victims they racked up, the higher chance that their deeds would make their way into the papers and news broadcasts—not just in New York but across the country. Then everybody would realize the real-life cost of their ignorance and hatred. That you couldn't hurt someone and walk away unscathed. Because although karma was a bitch, she was a *slow* bitch. She and Matt would be there to pick up the slack.

Because I'm somebody, she thought. *I matter.*

I have feelings, too.

She looked around the room at the costumed acrobats and jugglers, guitar-playing country girls, and scores of other talented performers with the dream she'd once had. Though she had a new purpose, the desire was the same: to be confident, to be herself, to be *seen*. After all, she had begun to realize that others' acceptance was overrated. And if no one was willing to accept her for who she was, maybe they deserved to burn.

Maybe they all did. Because bystanders to injustice were no better than the perpetrators.

Soon, she thought, many of the people in this room would cease to exist. It reminded her just how quickly life goes by, which led to the sobering realization of how much of her own life she had wasted by allowing herself to be sheltered and self-conscious and tormented. As if it were normal, her cross to bear.

If only things had been different, she thought.

But this was the way things were now, the way they had to be.

The time had come.

She would be seen.

And though she wouldn't be on stage, it would be the performance of a lifetime.

PART III

SHOWTIME, 2013

As the weak masses fall and the smoke rushes higher,
legends aren't born—they're made in the fire.

—*Black Wolves, runners-up of* Talent Now! *Season 3*

All the world's a stage.

—*William Shakespeare*

46

THE DARKNESS WAS the same as it had been each time before: deep and all-consuming. Jordan again felt the disorienting sense of being pulled backward on a high-speed roller coaster. When the accompanying nausea had settled, he slowly began to open his eyes like a child peeking through closed fingers to see if the scary thing under the bed had disappeared. Everything was too bright, and he could only focus on the harsh pounding in his head. It felt like someone was cutting into his brain with a sharp, hot knife. He pressed his hands to his temples and gritted his teeth against the building pressure. He wanted to scream but knew that if he brought attention to himself, there was no knowing what repercussions there would be. Instead, he knelt on the floor and puked on the carpet.

As the pain in his head began to abate, he wiped a thick line of spittle from the corner of his mouth. Peeking out from the familiar, red-curtained alcove, he allowed himself the briefest of relieved sighs.

It had worked.

He was back.

Which was good. Because if the increasing pain and headaches were any indication, this was his last chance before his body or mind couldn't handle it. Either the past didn't want him here, or he was right: there *was* some kind of radiation or strange energy involved. Even though the decrepit VHS tape and selling of Pop's house had already made the decision for him, Jordan knew that this was the last time. The deep throbbing in his head was like nothing he'd ever experienced. If it had been this bad with so few trips, he couldn't fathom what pain further visits would inflict. He recalled the slip of paper with Pop's tally marks, each mark a separate time he had visited the past, and wondered how he had done it. What was his secret? He had been decades older than Jordan and somehow had managed to survive dozens of trips.

Jordan glanced at his watch. He'd already wasted two minutes that he could not afford to lose. Each one was precious, and he was down to fifteen.

He stepped from the alcove and bypassed the row of acrylic exit doors that ran the length of the mezzanine level, instead opting for one that was set into the wall. He still needed to get as close to the stage as possible, and taking a side exit would enable him to bypass the theater's numerous lobbies to get directly to the main floor.

With a quick look back to make sure he was not being watched, Jordan pushed through the door. He breathlessly raced down the flights of carpeted stairs, barely registering signs beside each stairwell door that read, BALCONY TIER 3, BALCONY TIER 2, and BALCONY TIER 1. He kept going until he ran out of stairs and reached the coffee-colored door with the sign that read, ORCHESTRA LOBBY. He reached out, ready to push the exit bar, but then froze as he felt a searing pang of worry roiling in his stomach.

What if this was a fire door and sounded the alarm?

But if that were the case, he knew the alarm would've sounded the second he'd opened the door on his balcony level.

Jordan breathed deeply and reminded himself to be more careful, to think before acting. Because even though time was not a luxury he could afford, neither was carelessness.

He pushed through the door that opened onto a long, deserted lobby. A carpet in shades of deep red and tan extended as far as he could see, below matching walls and large floor-to-ceiling mirrors. Shiny gold touches on the door frames, knobs, and railings accented the large room, which was lined with a multitude of shimmering crystal chandeliers. The neat sophistication of it all made him feel as though he were inside a painting of a French museum rather than the lobby of a Broadway theater.

The show's remaining ticket holders were funneling through the front entrance as ushers guided them to their seats, but aside from these stragglers, the massive lobby was nearly empty. With the show's novelty and popularity in 2013, he assumed everyone lucky enough to score tickets wanted to be in their designated spots on time.

Which included Jordan.

He sped through the lobby, observing the room with furtive glances: the islands of ticketing counters, smiling ushers near the theater doors, and the excited chatter among a trio of middle-aged women wearing homemade T-shirts that read, "I ♥ HANS". He did not, however, see the person standing in front of him. He knocked her down with a force unexpected to both of them and lingered only to say, "Sorry" to the waif-like girl with a black backpack before continuing onward.

He needed to find some way to get backstage. When he and Sam had researched the theater, they'd found nothing that would help with getting there discretely or quickly.

Jordan checked his watch.

The rapidly decreasing numbers on the small digital panel at its center ratcheted up his nerves. Another three minutes had passed, meaning he only had twelve minutes left to do what he had come to do.

He scoured the lobby for something that might resemble what he was looking for before spotting a roped-off door in the corner of the large room with a sign that warned, EMPLOYEES ONLY BEYOND THIS POINT. Ignoring it, he reached behind the red velvet ropes and tugged on the door handle.

It was locked.

Of course it was.

Fuck.

Ushers were in the process of closing the main doors to the theater as the show was about to start. The announcer's deep voice leaked into the lobby. "Now, please welcome your judges!" he boomed, "Larry . . . Portia . . . and Hans!" The volume increased as the crowd chanted the names of their favorites, the roar of sound drawing Jordan's focus so that he nearly missed seeing what was happening behind him. A large man in a black T-shirt with two black satchels slung over his shoulder entered the theater from the street entrance, flashed a laminated card at a woman at a ticketing counter, and bumbled toward Jordan.

Shit, Jordan panicked. *Security.*

The man sweated profusely as he ran toward Jordan with a speed that promised tackling.

"Excuse me, buddy," he said.

Jordan was silent as he threw up his hands in surrender. His heart thumped double-time and exacerbated the queasiness in his stomach that made him think he was about to vomit again.

"Please," Jordan said, his eyes bulging with terror. "I was just—"

The man bypassed Jordan as he unlatched the velvet rope in front of the door and slid his tremendous weight through.

As he did, Jordan noticed the big lettering on the back of his shirt and felt his stomach unclench. *CREW.*

Again, his carelessness had made him blind to something so obvious.

A crew member, he marveled. *A very* late *crew member.*

Before he could appreciate his luck, he stuck his hand between the door and the jamb, catching it before it clicked shut. With a final look back to make sure no one was watching him, he wiped his palms on his jeans and slipped through the gap, failing to notice the small security camera with the blinking red dot planted firmly above the door.

47

WHEN MATT WAS gone, Charity left the rehearsal room and walked into the theater's large lobby. The remaining audience members were funneling in through the theater doors, each entryway filled with a gaggle of excitable Americans clutching crumpled ticket stubs as they searched for their assigned seats. *Idiots*, she thought, bypassing the crowd as she headed around the corner to the place Matt had shown her the night before.

She had worried that the area with the curving rows of glass exit doors would be brimming with people. But as she looked around the long, carpeted space with sporadically placed abstract sculptures, she was relieved to find it empty. Aside from her shallow exhalations, the only sounds came from the subtle whirring in the air conditioning vents above. For now, at least, she was alone.

She walked assuredly to one of the doors and cupped her hands to the glass to see the dim silhouettes of the thousands seated inside the theater and the *Talent Now!* logo on the bright LED screen behind the stage. The house lights were still up, but when everyone had taken their seats and the doors to the theater had closed for the taping, they would dim as the show's announcer declared in his booming voice, "This is . . . *Talent Now!*"

Idiots, she thought again.

In another few minutes, the show would be underway. All she had to do was wait for Matt's signal. Then she would get to work. She wondered why there was such a lack of security, like Matt had predicted, but supposed that it wouldn't make sense to expend the resources for an area where there was nothing going on.

Charity sat on the floor and sighed with relief as she dropped the chain-filled backpack from her shoulders. She stretched, straightened her white top (the same one she'd bought and worn especially for her own audition), and waited patiently for her moment to shine.

The time came quicker than she thought it would.

She was sitting on the floor and watching the acts on the stage below when she felt her phone vibrate against her thigh. She fished it from her pocket, flipped it open, and looked at the yellow envelope that appeared on the screen.

The message was short and sweet but said everything she needed to know:

NEXT IN LINE. BE READY.

Her heart beat faster as she read the words, but it wasn't from nerves or fear. No, she was not afraid. She was excited.

Her fingers fluttered above the phone's buttons as she tried to decide how to respond. Finally, after deleting two drafts, she settled on:

I'M HERE. DON'T MISS.

She thought that was good. Like Matt's message to her, it was short but direct.

She returned the phone to her pocket, unzipped the black backpack, and sorted through the tangle of heavy chains. She figured she had another few minutes, but it didn't hurt to be prepared. She worked quietly as she listened to the audience booing the most recent act. It sounded like a singer, and she felt a pang of empathy.

Charity had always prided herself on being observant and mindful of her surroundings, especially in unfamiliar places. But she had either become too comfortable or too preoccupied with thoughts of the task ahead because she barely registered the sound of footsteps behind her.

48

MATT WAS AWARE of the chorus of sound that filled the cavernous space around him, but the world inside his head was mercifully silent. He waited backstage, tuning out the audience's cheering, the crackling of crew members' headsets, and the horde of other miscellaneous sounds of a well-oiled television production. His exhalations were normal, heartbeat relaxed. Though emotion was lost on him, he felt a tingling mixture of exhilaration and wonder that his plan was now in effect after so many years in the making.

He'd always known that his life was building up to something big, some grand conclusion. Because that's what this was, wasn't it? The ending of one life and the beginning of another. And he didn't mean Heaven, though he didn't condemn others for subscribing to such a concept. For him there would be only darkness, the sweet nothingness he'd experienced all his life that teachers and counselors seemed to think was such a torturous burden. But his concern was not with where he would end up after all this, neither physically nor spiritually. Because if he succeeded and everything went according to plan, he would transcend death to a state of being desired by many and attained by few:

Immortality.

His name would be remembered for years and decades to come. Even if he got out of this alive, putting himself and his actions on display in front of thousands of people would ensure that his years of anonymity, of hiding who he really was, would draw to a close. They would hunt him. Play and replay his name on TV and in newspapers and on amateur crime sleuthing websites. The kind of John Walsh shit that got people like him arrested or institutionalized. He wasn't stupid. His face would be everywhere, and everyone would be looking for the man wanted for one of the deadliest home-grown terrorist attacks on American soil. After all, the only goal of a terrorist was to cause terror.

And he planned to do just that.

Escape or any kind of life after this was not a guarantee, but it was a risk he was willing to take. To feel the rush of blood pulsing through him as he stepped onto the stage and experienced the sights and sounds that would envelope him in their embrace—the acrid perfume of gasoline and smoke, the burning of fabric and metal and flesh. A large risk for a large reward.

Backstage, half inside a beam of light, he caressed his bow as the fiery itch inside him was momentarily replaced by the feeling of a pressure relieved, as if someone had turned off an invisible steam valve. He felt the warm tingle running under his skin and down his spine, his eyes closed in ecstasy. Maybe his mind was trying to tell him something. *This is what you're supposed to do. This is the next logical progression, the next step in your evolution.* Because it wasn't the slingshot or the bow that had ceased to scratch his never-ending itch, he knew. Because when his arrow had struck Billy Hughes and he heard him call out in surprised terror and pain, Matt realized it was not the tool but the target.

And that's when he started thinking it: How would it feel if he did it again?

And again?

He'd always been smart and careful, but there was always that monotonous, nagging voice that had said, *What if you forget something? What if you miss something?* It was a voice he couldn't ignore. The satisfaction would be great, but it would hardly be worth the consequences. The only way it would be worth it was if it was a lot of people. He'd thought that if he could somehow manage to get away with striking a flock of birds with a single stone, he'd be satisfied. But he never thought he could pull it off.

It wasn't until years later when he responded to the online job posting for *Talent Now!* that everything clicked into place. When he realized that what he'd long considered impossible was, in fact, possible. And not only that, but it would be easier than he'd thought.

He didn't watch TV, but he'd heard of the show. Everyone had. It was one of the water cooler topics he'd used to practice talking up his coworkers at his many temp placements, studying their facial expressions and social cues. Normal people talked about current TV shows, after all. But if he was going to do what he was beginning to contemplate, it would require extensive consideration, the careful weighing of pros and cons. He needed time. And a plan.

As he traveled across the country, he was surprised to find that each audition city seemed to be more packed with contestants than the last. It was like they were addicted to it, the thrill of being seen by so many people and getting the attention they craved. But the judges' and audience's reactions were not limited to talent. It was all about the contestants' appearance, clothes, and the hardships they overcame to endear them to the television-watching American public. Their *story*. He'd been to enough auditions to know audiences responded to appearances first and sob stories second. Actual talent, it seemed, was a close third.

It was a joke. All of it. Because he saw what the home audience didn't see: the crying participants, snarky judges' off-camera comments, production assistants priming contestants backstage for answers to questions like "What was the most upsetting moment in your life?" or "What insecurities do you have that your talent has helped you overcome?" All so they could have something inspiring or tear-jerking to put in the opening package before their audition was televised.

And people ate it up.

As he bore witness to costumed contestants clamoring for their moment in the spotlight and scores of audiences cheering and shouting and booing, once again he wondered why it was okay for them to bring out their inner animals when it was socially unacceptable to bring out his. Why did *his* lion have to be caged?

Is this what the world has become? Is this really what it's like?

If so, he supposed they should thank him for what he was planning. He'd had years' worth of mimicry and blending in, but he knew with a deep certainty that this was as good as he would ever get. It was now or never. His whole life, he now realized, had been leading to this moment. The plan was simple, but they would never see it coming.

But he'd known he couldn't do it alone. He'd known he would need help. But who could he have gotten to help him voluntarily, who wouldn't report him or sabotage his plans? He'd needed someone easily manipulated. Someone eager and angry and malleable enough to bend to his will.

There were times in life when things just fell into place. He couldn't predict them. They just happened. And for Matt, an afternoon in June 2013 was one of those days. He'd been backstage listening to the contestants performing (most were shit but there were some that were actually pretty good) and thinking of his plan. So when he turned and saw the pale, blonde-haired girl sobbing among a tangle of black curtains, it was as if she had fallen right out of his mind and into his lap. Then he knew that all those years of practicing in front of the bathroom mirror were about to pay off. After all, he'd become a good faker. And she was just the kind of person he was looking for.

49

JORDAN FORCED HIMSELF to wait a moment before he followed. He didn't want to waste more time, but he wanted to put some distance between himself and the crew member in case he turned around and saw that he was being tailed. When he rounded a corner and was out of sight, Jordan followed him down a carpeted hallway dotted with framed posters of old films and Broadway shows. He'd once read an author claim that books were a uniquely portable magic and, though he could not remember who had said it, he thought it must also be true of film and theater. The joy, the magic, he supposed, was why Granny had come to *Talent Now!* in the first place—the sense of awe contained not in the pages of a book or glass of a screen, but all around her. And somewhere, Jordan thought, picturing the audience beyond this windowless corridor, she was out there.

He knew he was getting close to the stage when he heard the roar of the audience and the harsh *bzzz* that meant one of the judges had slapped their buzzer in dislike of whoever was performing. The sounds overpowered those of his heavy breathing as he reached the end of the long, zigzagging hallway just in time to see the crew member bumbling through the exit door. Careful not to draw attention, Jordan waited ten seconds before he rushed to the door and pushed it open.

Immediately, he was drowned in the sights and sounds of a television production in full swing: the crackle of crew members speaking into headsets or moving camera equipment, squeaky wheels on old floors, the metallic clanging of lights and feet on the catwalks above. There was something happening, to see or hear, everywhere he looked. And beyond the dark walls and black curtains of the backstage area, he was able to catch a glimpse of the vivid LED screen that loomed over the stage bearing the *Talent Now!* logo in red, white, and blue. Along with the swirling strobe lights, the audience's thunderous sounds of clapping and shouting swept over the theater as if it were hosting an AC/DC concert instead of a televised talent show.

He checked his watch again.

Nine minutes left.

The current contestant wrapped up her song and exited the stage as another act—one that Jordan knew quite well from Pop's tape and the viral fame it would acquire in the weeks following the episode—galloped onto the stage and into the spotlight.

Cowgirl Judy greeted the audience with a high-pitched "Howdy!" and a shudder went through Jordan with the knowledge that she was the last act before Matt would stride onto the stage. His mouth ran dry, and his arms trembled at realizing that, although these events had happened over seven years ago, they were now his reality. Whatever happened to him here would be real. But even if he survived, if he wasn't discovered or hauled away in handcuffs, he knew that he only had one chance to do what he'd come to do. There would be no do-overs.

He squeezed his eyes shut, banishing the thought. It was not something he would allow himself to consider. Instead, he quickly scurried to a series of sturdy black boxes with silver locks and trim that gave him a decent vantage point from which to watch the performance, away from the curtains and loitering employees.

Cowgirl Judy galloped around the stage in her red shirt and brown hat as Jordan had known she would, tossing her rope around the necks of wooden horses. Jordan was amazed how good she was, but the judges disagreed. Hans hit his buzzer right away, lighting up his corresponding exclamation point above the stage in bright red. Larry hit his next, followed by Portia, as the audience yelled and booed and crossed their arms in Xs in a visual display of their dislike.

Monsters, Jordan thought. It was as if being in a crowd made people lose the very things that made them human, and his heart ached as Judy stood proudly against the audience's heckling and attempts at humiliation. As much as he wanted to reach out to embrace her or say something reassuring, he fought the urge to interfere. This wasn't what he was here for.

He stayed huddled and hidden behind his crates, watching her walk down the hallway and out of his life forever. The only way to bring justice to her—and to the dozens of innocent lives that would soon be lost—was to stop this fucker from doing what he was planning. What he would do.

As a few black-shirted crew members prepared the stage for Matt's act, Jordan carefully withdrew Sam's gun from his pocket. He quickly filled all six chambers with bullets and closed it. He'd never fired a gun before. What if he missed? What if he shot himself, or someone else? As the roar of the crowd filled his ears and beams of light cast by the stage's strobes found their way backstage, Jordan wondered if he could really kill another human being.

He thought of the countless afternoons he'd spent walking alone in the woods to smash and break and scream, thinking, *If there was a way . . .* And now that he actually had the opportunity to set things right and make whole the parts of him that had been broken, his answer did not waver. In all the years since Granny had died, it had remained the same. *Yes*, he reasoned. To undo the deaths of the dozens who had died, he would kill one.

The revolver was cold as Jordan took a deep, shuddery breath and tried to steady his trembling hands. He mentally recited the instructions Sam had given him ("Safety off. Use both hands. Arms up, aim, fire. And most importantly, don't get yourself killed.") and decided he wouldn't wait until Matt stepped onto the stage. Once he was in the spotlight, there were too many variables: the audience's reactions, observations from the stage crew and security officers, and dozens of others he was sure he'd forgotten. And besides, who was to say the audience's shock of Jordan killing him on stage wouldn't then cause the deaths of many, anyway, thousands of people trampling each other in their panic? Who knew how his merely being here would change things?

No, the stakes were too high. He would take him out before he stepped into the spotlight.

Jordan steeled himself, eyes searching backstage for the face he knew so well. There were many, but not the one he was looking for. He glanced again at the rapidly decreasing numbers on his watch with his heart throbbing.

Where is he? He should be here by now.

Jordan was startled from his thoughts as the audience's enthusiastic applause changed into the thunderous roar of thousands of men, women, and children excited by the promise of something dangerous and exciting. He looked frantically around him as he searched for the reason for their change in behavior, understanding only when he turned away from his makeshift nest of black crates and saw the lone figure standing in the stage's spotlight.

50

THE CLINKING OF the chains mixed with the cushioned carpet masked the muffled steps behind her. But the air felt different, thicker, as if a heavy shadow had fallen over her. It was the same feeling she would get when her mother would hover over her bed at night, checking to make sure she was still breathing. Chains still in hand, Charity slowly turned and peered through a gap in the curtain of her stringy hair to see the figure in the black uniform standing behind her.

He towered over her diminutive size and lanky frame, all six feet of him managing to look threatening despite his broad shoulders and the gut hanging over the top of his belt. There was a silver badge pinned to his chest, but Charity didn't need to look at it or the word "SECURITY" printed in white on his baseball cap to know who he was or what he was doing here. He looked down at her hunched over the black backpack and slowly walked toward her, the fatty folds of skin on his forehead shifting as his tiny green eyes narrowed with uncertainty, not quite sure what to make of her.

"What are you doing here, little girl?" he said. His voice had the deep huskiness of a cowboy. "You lost?"

Charity couldn't tell whether he was being considerate or mocking, his darkly tanned face showing kind but cautious eyes above a thin layer of black facial hair.

"What you got in that bag there? Hmm?"

He crept closer and Charity didn't know what to do. She was frozen, like some small woodland creature trapped in the beam of approaching headlights. *What to do? What to do?* Her temples throbbed deeply, her fear and indecision making it feel as though her head was in a vice, the pressure building and building until she couldn't think.

She couldn't run. That would only cause more trouble, and she'd no doubt lose any chance of seeing their plan through. But she couldn't *not* show him the contents of the bag. That would only make him more suspicious. She saw no possible way out of this, and she mentally berated herself for screwing up and letting Matt down. She squeezed her eyes shut as if that might make the man vanish, like he was an imaginary monster under the bed that she could just wish away. But when she opened them, he was still there. And he was looking inside the bag.

He raised a tangle of chains, his eyes and tone changing from mere caution to grave suspicion as he looked from the backpack to Charity. "What do you plan on doing with these, young lady?"

Charity sat motionless on the floor as the man grabbed his walkie-talkie off his massive belt and clicked the button that would allow him to speak into it.

"Walker here," he said, taking his eyes off Charity for only a second. "I'm in the exit lobby on the mezzanine level. I'm going to need some—"

She didn't know what she was going to do before she did it.

She looked up from the bag and sprang into action with the spry motion of a cheetah pouncing on an unsuspecting zebra. She knocked the walkie out of his hands and leapt onto his back, taking advantage of his massive size. She was careful not to scream, though the rage and fear and adrenaline boiled inside her, yearning to be expressed in sound.

The security guard grumbled, marveling at how quickly the small girl had laced her hands around his throat. "Please," he tried, his words coming in short bursts of ragged breath, "let . . . me . . . go . . . " He tried to pound his hands behind him to release Charity's own from his throat, but his arms were too large, Charity too small and agile. His neck sweated profusely, and Charity's grip—once strong and solid—slid over his skin. She lost it for a second and the guard used it to his advantage, spinning around until one of her arms lost its grip around his shoulders. She hadn't been expecting it, so when he drew back both arms and elbowed her in the stomach, the force was so great that she flew from him with ease and landed on her back, the breath knocked out of her.

The guard took a moment to massage his throat before running toward her with a pair of handcuffs. But as Charity rose to face him, the force propelling him toward her was too great to stop once he saw what was in her hand. The blade of the knife slid noiselessly between his ribcage, Charity's hand gripping the hilt, fully conscious of the weapon's power, *her* power, to take life away.

Her shock at what she'd done quickly faded as the man slid to the ground and slowly collapsed at her feet. He didn't beg for her forgiveness like Matt had promised, and she didn't make him. But in the moments before his stupefied gaze glazed over, Charity bent down so her lips nearly touched his ear. "I'm not a little girl," she whispered spitefully as she twisted the knife, hearing the wet crunch of bone fragmenting among muscle and organ.

The satisfaction, the freedom, the empowerment she felt, however, did not last long. She felt a nervous trill as she thought she heard more people approaching, but it abated once she realized that it was coming from inside the theater. She listened to the chorus of expectant cheers and peered through the glass at the stage far below. Matt stood in the center. From his placement at the microphone, she supposed he had just walked out. The time was almost here.

But first she had a body to hide.

51

FOR A MOMENT, Jordan couldn't breathe or move as he stared in disbelief at the man on the stage. How had it happened? How had he missed him?

Fuck, Jordan thought, mentally reviewing the last sixty seconds. It must have been when he was examining the gun. He balled his fists tight until his nails cut deep crescent moons into the center of his palms. *Fuck, fuck, fuck!*

He'd missed his first shot. Now everyone would watch as Jordan gunned him down, causing who knew what kind of panic. After that, there would be no time to run, and it would be only a matter of time before he was arrested. And unless his shot hit its intended target, it would all be for nothing. But then again, he remembered with a burst of optimism, the tape would be ending soon, and he'd be safely returned to 2020. So let them arrest him. As long as they didn't stop him from doing what he came to do, he'd go along with their security procedures until the countdown on his watch reached zero.

He glanced back down at his battered Timex to see that he only had five minutes left. It was now or never. Jordan propped himself against the crates and eyed up his shot.

He focused on Sam's words: "Close range," she had said. "Head or heart. Anything less than a kill shot is a chance you don't want to take."

Jordan agreed.

As the judges primed Matt for a sound-bite-worthy response, Jordan extended his arms and gripped the gun with both hands, his elbows locked against its certain recoil. He kept it steady, inching his body to the left and solidifying his kneeling stance just as his arm struck something solid. He tore his gaze away from Matt in time to see the large black box to his right toppling from its tower of crates as various pieces of heavy equipment spilled onto the hard, polished floor in a symphony of crashes and clangs.

Jordan slowly turned, trepidation as much a physical part of him as his arms and legs. But despite the commotion both backstage and in the theater, the incident was not lost on the many employees who had whipped their heads around at the sound of the clatter.

Especially the technician looking right at him.

The bald, dark-skinned man stood frozen, eyes protruding from his face as if he couldn't believe what he was seeing. "Hey!" he shouted, pointing at Jordan with a stubby finger. "He's got a gun! He's got a gun!"

Some crew members scrambled frantically away while others stood immobile. No one, Jordan was astonished to discover, had done anything to separate him from the gun.

He had to act now.

He leveled the gun in the window made between the gaps of stacked crates. Matt was in his sights, still answering the judges' unimportant questions. Sweat beaded Jordan's forehead and dripped into his eye, momentarily blurring his vision as his trigger finger—

"Drop it!" someone shouted. "Drop the weapon!"

Jordan was so focused that it took him a moment to realize that the harsh command was addressed at him. He glanced over his shoulder at the pair of black-shirted security officers aiming their guns at him.

Whatever you do, do not give up the gun. One shot. You have one shot.

He looked from the guards, to Matt, and back again.

"Son, I'm going to ask you once more to drop the weapon."

Jordan was still, afraid that even his slightest movement would cause an instinctual reaction from one of the guards' trigger fingers.

Fuck.

He'd blown it. Again. He couldn't save Granny. He couldn't save those people out there who were oblivious to what would happen in the next few minutes. The best he could do now was try to get out alive.

"Okay," Jordan said calmly with his hands up. "Okay. I'm putting it down."

"On the ground," one of the guards said, motioning to the floor with his own pointed weapon.

Jordan placed it at his feet.

"Kick it over."

No sooner had he done so than he was seized by the two security officers, Sam's gun whisked away behind one of their backs. They grabbed him by the arms and forced him to his feet. He felt cold metal around his wrists and heard the metallic *click* of handcuffs snapping into place.

"Wait!" Jordan shouted, startled by their sudden movements and hands on him. "You don't understand! That man is dangerous! He's going to kill those people out there!" He looked back at the stage, which was drawing farther and farther away as the security guards dragged him backward by his arms.

Jordan saw Matt momentarily halt his act as he turned back toward him and the commotion he was making.

Jordan tried to emphasize the obvious danger here, but it was no use. *What the hell was wrong with these people?* He knew he sounded crazy, just like he and Sam had feared he would, but his inability to do anything to stop the massacre from happening made him explode with frenzied adrenaline. "Are you people fucking stupid?" he yelled. "He has a bow and a table full of arrows!"

"Would you be quiet?" one of the guards spat. "It's part of his act."

"It's not!" he pleaded. "Just go and see! As a precaution!"

One of the guards gave a chuckle that revealed he'd dealt with his fair share of lunatics before.

Why aren't they taking this seriously? Jordan panicked. And then, grimly, he realized that this was always how it happened, tragedy after tragedy and school shooting after school shooting, when well-intentioned concerns were brushed off as trivial or unwarranted. Good people tried to help, their warnings went unheeded, and then more good people died.

Maybe Matt knew it would be like this. Maybe he was banking on it.

"We saw you on the security cameras," the thin, muscled one said.

Cameras? What cameras?

He'd assumed there were tons of them in this place—the theater, lobby, hell, probably the bathrooms—but where had he been that had raised suspicion? No doubt he'd been seen in the lobby, at least, but what had he done? What door had he—

Then it hit him.

The lobby door with the velvet ropes and the sign that read, EMPLOYEES ONLY BEYOND THIS POINT. He hadn't seen a camera anywhere, but they were so small and discreet now that it could've been right above the door and he wouldn't have noticed.

"We were watching you but didn't think you'd try to do something this stupid."

"Yeah, hope you had a good time exploring," the large one said with a smarmy smile plastered on his face.

Jordan could take their torment, the injustice of this moment, but what angered him most was that people were going to die if they didn't let him go. "Please," he begged as they dragged him farther away from the stage. He kicked and pulled and fought, a writhing creature tangling his clothes and limbs against the guards who barely budged. "You have to stop the show!"

But neither of them offered anything in the way of sympathy.

"Sorry, buddy," the muscled guard said with not an ounce of sorrow in his voice. "You're going to have to come with us."

52

THE NEON LIGHTS and uproarious audience applause ebbed as the distance increased between Jordan and the man he had come to kill. And as the stage lights dimmed to dramatic music, Jordan knew his act was beginning.

He hadn't been able to change anything. But if he could just survive this encounter, he'd be back in Pop's living room when his watch reached zero. He glanced at the seconds racing by; his time here was quickly coming to an end.

"Let me go!" he yelled with an animalistic rage.

He had less than a minute left.

Jordan closed his eyes, waiting for the moment when he would be free of these people and place and time. For years he'd yearned to be here, in this theater, in this moment. But now, after all he had seen and done and heard, all he wanted was to go home.

He felt the pressure of a hand on his wrist.

"What's this?" the larger of the guards asked. "You counting down to something?"

"None of your fucking business," he spat.

"Yeah?" the guard said amusedly. "Well, whatever it is, it looks like you're out of time."

The digital readout on Jordan's watch displayed two sets of flashing zeroes separated by a colon.

No. It wasn't possible.

He was out of time, so why wasn't he back? He should've been back by now. It should've worked.

Something had gone wrong. Had something happened to the tape? Had he miscalculated a step or inadvertently changed the outcome of things? The questions swirled through his mind as he realized he could be trapped here, seven years in the past, in a theater that would soon be a smoldering ruin.

"I shouldn't be here!" he screeched, voice growing raw. "I'm not supposed to be here!"

"You're damn right," said the muscled guard.

Jordan wriggled his arms against the guards' grip, shifting his torso from left to right, but it was no use. Their arms remained coiled around his own as Jordan's heart hammered with the mix of fear and adrenaline coursing through his body like a deadly dose of caffeine. It struck him then that the commotion of his detainment had caused a hiccup in their timing, Matt's extended pause causing Jordan's countdown to go off before Matt shot the barrels. It hadn't happened yet, but it would. Soon. And whatever happened afterward would be new to him. Anxiety filled him as he imagined the coming horror.

"I'll take it from here," a new voice said, accompanied by the jangling of keys on a ring.

Jordan couldn't see the figure from his backward position, but he could tell from the voice's light cadence that it belonged to a woman. He was sure he didn't know her, but there was something familiar about her voice and her assured way of speaking that he couldn't quite put his finger on.

"You sure?" one of them asked. "He's a squirmer."

"I think I can handle it," the woman said, her hint of sarcasm making Jordan think she ranked higher than the men restraining him.

The two guards exchanged uncertain glances and shrugged, seemingly happy to be relieved of this duty. "Have at it, then. We'll be around if you need us." They dropped Jordan to the ground and walked away, leaving him and the woman in a backstage hallway devoid of people and commotion. If he wanted to, he could run. But something told him that would be a very dumb and dangerous idea.

When he looked up from his cuffed wrists to the woman above him, he almost didn't recognize her. Her normal waves of brown-blonde hair were pulled back into a bun below her black SECURITY baseball cap, and her black tactical uniform pinned with a silver badge were not the clothes she'd been wearing the last time he saw her. As she stepped closer into the light of one of the bare hanging bulbs, the implausibility of the situation rendered him confused and speechless. All he could think was *how?*

"I'd love to catch you up," Sam said, "but we need to go. If we're going to do this, we need to be quick."

53

SHE HELPED HIM off the ground and hurried him back through the maze of backstage hallways with a firm grip on his arm to maintain the appearance that she was delivering him to the police, who were no doubt waiting outside the building.

"Where are we going?" Jordan asked, his words coming in jagged bursts as he attempted to keep up with his cousin's pace. "What are you doing here? Why are you wearing different clothes than when I saw you seventeen minutes ago?"

"Keep your voice down," Sam said with a pointed look. But as they advanced down the hallway, her severe expression seemed to slowly fade away as if she was now contemplating a collection of memories and experiences of which her cousin could not know. "Jordan," she said. It's been seventeen minutes for *you*."

"What are you talking about? You came here after I did. It's been the same time for both of us."

Sam shook her head.

No, that solemn look said. *You don't understand.*

"Jordan," she said, her pained expression etched deeply on her face, "I've been here for eleven months."

Jordan stared uncomprehendingly before shaking his head again, as if trying to grasp the absurdity of her statement. He looked from his cousin to the view ahead, then back again. She had led them in a loop, and they were once again approaching a curve that led into the last hallway before the backstage area from which Jordan had been dragged. The muffled sound of the show—the shouts and chants of the audience, obnoxious sound effects, and snippets of zippy pop songs—grew louder with each step they took.

"Sam . . . "

"We don't have much time," she said. "I'll tell you what I have time to tell you. The rest will have to wait."

54

SAM WAS SPELLBOUND, her vision blurring in her trance-like state, when she first watched Jordan pulse and fade before disappearing from their grandparents' living room in a flash of light and static. After watching all seventeen minutes of the *Talent Now!* tape and the beginnings of the carnage that had unfolded on that day in 2013, tendrils of guilt had probed and weaved their way through her as she waited for Jordan to return. She hugged her knees, a gesture she hadn't done since she was little, and bit the inside of her cheek to keep the tears at bay. *What is wrong with me?* she thought. They'd had a way to change things and she'd backed out. Why?

But she already knew the answer.

Sitting there on the floor of her grandparents' near-empty living room, she wasn't sure there was a more selfish emotion than fear—of the unknown, of what might happen to her, of the possible repercussions of what they were trying to do. It all involved her. She'd given no thought to the fear of the innocents who had died from smoke inhalation or falling debris, or the fear of the first responders who'd spent their time during and after that day helping to save and repair and console. She did not think of the horrors small children had witnessed, their parents dead or dying at their feet, and the years of therapy they'd need to sort through their complicated feelings. She hadn't thought of anyone's fear but her own.

Or of the woman they were trying to save.

Stupid girl, Sam thought now, reprimanding her younger self, the selfish punk in the halter top and distressed jeans. She'd spent so much time believing that her grandparents would always be there, but she'd quickly realized just how wrong she'd been. And though it had changed her—the way she thought, the time she spent with family, the realization that every second mattered because tomorrow was never guaranteed—it was not a concept she would fully understand until she was older, when she had no grandparents left to appreciate.

From the time she'd gotten that phone call in the mall, she'd often catch herself thinking, *If there was a way to save her, I would do anything to change it.* Not knowing that her cousin had been contemplating the very same thing. Because if there was, maybe she wouldn't feel so guilty or hate herself so much.

Maybe Jordan was right in saying that she ran away when things got hard or scary, like she had at Granny's funeral. Or not applying for that job with the *Sun.* Maybe that's why the accusation had made her so upset. Not because it was cruel, but because it was true. She, it seemed, was the only one who hadn't seen what a coward she really was. So much had already been taken from her, and she was scared to find that there might still be more that she could lose, and none of it up to her. Giving up control had never come easy, and the thought of going back to 2013 with Jordan had made her anxiety spike with an almost physical pain.

As she raised her trembling hands to wipe away her tears, she caught a glimpse of the TV screen. The sight of it made it feel like something heavy and hard had dropped into her stomach.

"No."

She stared at it uncomprehendingly, her wide eyes reflecting the light held by the glass. The once clapping and moving figures in the audience were stilled, the sounds of shouting and theatrical audio effects were muted, and the previously crisscrossing strobe lights of red, white, and blue were locked in place. Everything was.

"No," she said numbly as she registered the one thing she had feared. "No, no, no, no."

This wasn't happening. This couldn't be happening.

She pounded her fists against the glass screen, pleading with it to unfreeze. But it did not, and her heart began to race even faster when she saw the wisp of white smoke seeping through the tape slot of the VCR.

"Oh God," she wailed, her hands trembling in front of her. "Damnit!"

She quickly scanned the VCR and found the square marked EJECT, punching it rapidly with the tip of a finger like it was a call button for a lazy elevator.

"Come on," she begged. "Come on!"

At last, her request was met with the burping and whizzing of machinery trying to whirr itself to life.

She tapped her fingers on top of the VCR as its protector flap finally lifted and spit out the tape. She tentatively reached forward before touching it, as if it might bite her, her horror only growing as she gently pulled it out. It looked as if it had been mauled by a pit bull. Long strips of film stretched between the VCR and the tape like sinister party streamers. She didn't have to see much to know it was toast. The film was tangled in itself, torn in some places and worn in others. It had been in poor shape when they'd found it, and it looked even worse now. It crinkled as she handled it, her nail snagging on the film strip and tearing it in half. The terrible sound of it—a flaky crinkle not unlike cheap aluminum foil—was stuck inside her head, replaying over and over.

Jordan.

He was in there, stuck somewhere in 2013. What had happened to him? Was he dead? Had he ceased to exist at all? But no, she didn't think that was the case. If it was, she wouldn't remember him. Right?

She hunched over the disheveled tape with its filmy, eviscerated guts. They had known there was a chance of this happening but had done it anyway.

No, she corrected. *Jordan* had done it.

"You're just the same selfish, self-absorbed bitch I remember," he'd said.

She needed to do something. But what? Who did you call to troubleshoot matters of time travel via television?

She paced on the carpet before sitting in front of the TV and examining the VCR with its array of obsolete buttons and switches. Now, looking at the chunky black rectangle, she praised her grandparents' frugality as she got an idea. The player itself was fine, it seemed. It was just the tape that was fried. She confirmed the button she'd located on the VCR was in working order, quickly rifled through Granny's black box of tapes, and laid them all out on the blue carpet in an order that only she understood. When it was done, she inspected them again before depositing them back into the box until only one remained. She looked at the label on the remaining tape and frowned. It was the closest one. But there wasn't time to think it through. She breathed deeply, knowing very well that this may be her last moment in this house, in her own time, but she didn't let the sorrow linger. She would make things right. She would not run away when things got too hard. Fear would not control her anymore.

Sam knelt before the VCR and pushed the tape in the slot.

Since Granny had died, she'd thought, *If there was a way to save her, I would do anything to change it.* But it was never something she'd seriously considered because the possibility hadn't existed.

But now it did. The chance to change everything was in their grasp.

She pushed the right button on the VCR, unsure if it would work but knowing that she owed it to both Jordan and Granny to try.

Over the past seven years, she'd never seriously considered what the *anything* part of her silent prayer would be. But now, as she watched the beginning seconds of the tape she'd inserted into the VCR and placed her hands at the corners of the television the way Jordan had showed her, Sam thought she was about to find out.

As she shared these things with Jordan, she did not tell him of the fear she'd felt in that moment or the many others in the days, weeks, and months afterward; she did not tell him of the loneliness and isolation of living in a time and place that was not her own; she did not tell him of the people she'd met, the things she'd done, or the precautions she'd taken not to screw up the seventeen minutes they had come here, to 2013, to change. She did not tell him any of these things or the many details that had comprised her life in New York City for the past year. In the grand scheme of things, it was unimportant. And as she had told him, it would have to wait.

55

JORDAN DIDN'T KNOW what to say or think. Between the tape breaking and Sam saying that she'd been here for eleven months, it was all too much.

"So," he managed, "the tape is . . . "

"Fried."

"How did you know it would work?"

"I didn't. I thought if I used another tape that was close to this day in 2013, I could just live through it until this moment and meet you here, provided you lived that long. "But I also knew that it wasn't feasible because—"

"It would only keep you there for the duration of the tape."

Sam nodded.

"But then I saw the button on the VCR. SLO-MO PLYBCK."

The wheels in Jordan's mind began to turn, his eyes gleaming above a sly smile as he understood how what she had done was possible. Time had slowed for her, and she'd faced none of the limits that Jordan had. With her clever use of the slow-motion button, eleven months for her here in 2013 translated to mere minutes in the present. No one in 2020 would even think she was gone.

"I hoped if I slowed down the tape—even if I had to try it a few times with different speeds—it might somehow last long enough to get me here."

"How did you know that it even would?"

She shook her head, sharing his disbelief. "I honestly didn't think it would. And when it did, I kind of just figured that I was stuck here. Like I'm sure you did when the tape died."

"And you've been here, in New York, all this time?"

Sam nodded.

He couldn't comprehend what she had been through and what she had sacrificed to be here with him, in this moment. "I'm sorry I called you a coward," he said.

She waved it away. "It's okay. None of that matters anymore."

But Jordan had so many more questions. Where had she lived? How had she stayed camouflaged? What had she learned? Did she have headaches?

"I tried so hard for so long, Jordan. I thought I'd have enough time. I got this job thinking I could stop things from the inside, figure out some way to change things before the show, before any of this even happened. But nothing worked."

"What do you mean? What did you do?"

"Everything I could think of," she said. "Months ago, I dumped water on the electrical equipment backstage hoping the technical malfunctions would get the *Talent Now!* producers to agree that the theater wasn't a safe venue for the show. All that resulted in was changing the tape date from May to June and the repair—and *strengthening*—of the theater's electrical grid." Sam scowled, a bitter edge to her words. "So, I started getting desperate. I set off the fire alarm a couple times, including once yesterday, thinking that they'd cancel the show for a full theater inspection, but all they did was turn off the alarms while they put in a report for a fucking repair order. So now we know that if anyone pulled the fire alarms on show night, they weren't even working. And you have me to thank for that."

Sam shook her head, eyes wide and frazzled.

"I also sabotaged the security cameras so the theater would buy new, better ones, but they didn't. And a week ago, I told one of the production guys that the confetti barrels looked loose, thinking we could at least stop *that* from happening. I was going to dump out the gasoline when he brought the barrels down, but he only went up in his little cherry picker and tightened them in place. And today I even went outside and started turning people away, saying that the show was canceled due to technical difficulties. People did leave, but the producers went outside and managed to get seat-fillers from off the street."

Sam clenched her fists, frustration and sadness etched in her tired eyes. "I tried, Jordan. I tried so hard but every single thing that I've done has led to the creation of the exact circumstances we've been trying to avoid. It's like the past doesn't want to be changed. Like it knows we're trying to meddle. I thought there might be another way, but you were right. The only way to stop this whole thing is to kill Manson."

Jordan stared at Sam, his eyes shimmering with awe for everything she'd managed to accomplish. Shame radiated from his rosy cheeks as he considered the awful things he'd said to her and how selfish he'd been, so focused on money and school and moving away. Suddenly all of it seemed so small.

"Sam, I tried. I don't know how it's even possible without—"

"Jordan," she interrupted. "If we spend our time chatting, all of this will have been for nothing. We're only here until the tape ends," she said. "Which is why we need to hurry."

56

THE ROAR OF the audience's expectant cheering filled Matt's ears like a symphony. *If they knew what was coming, they wouldn't be clapping*, he thought. Nevertheless, as he felt the intoxicating energy in the room, he understood how some could fall under its spell.

After years of yearning to do something big, to relieve the mounting pressure and the itch inside his brain that had been there as long as he could remember, the moment had finally arrived. He closed his eyes and pictured the people who would soon be stampeding with panic, terror fixed on their faces as the theater erupted in brilliant bursts of fire. And during this cacophony of screams and explosions, this feast of sight and sound and smell, Matt would know it was he who had caused it. *Now I am become Death, the destroyer of worlds.*

All he had to worry about was the girl. But she was so broken, so desperate to be seen and understood, that he was sure she'd follow through with what they had discussed. No, the girl would do as she was told, and everything would end with a bang.

Matt's serenity was quickly interrupted by the same crew member who'd escorted him backstage. He opened his eyes to see Carter's overexcited grin as he informed him that it was his turn. He gave him a good-luck backslap before leaving, and Matt relished the fact that this would be the last time the skinny shit would ever touch him.

The stage's white strobes washed over his skin, beckoning him forward. He supposed this was what death would be like. Only instead of all-encompassing white, it would be black.

He welcomed it.

Matt took a deep breath to steady himself and, with the power of a vindictive god coursing through him, walked out onto the stage to claim his place in the spotlight and begin the performance of a lifetime.

57

JORDAN DIDN'T SEE how it was possible. "No," he said. "I blew it. If those guards hadn't seen me, we might've had a chance."

Sam shook her head, a smile on her face. "We still have time," she said. "Do you think they caught you by accident?"

Jordan didn't follow.

"I was watching for you, waiting to see where you'd come from. Why do you think I'm dressed like this?" Sam gestured at her black uniform and silver badge. "It was my plan to step in once I saw you detained on camera."

"You sent them?" Jordan exclaimed.

"I needed to stop you from doing it before I could get to you!" she whisper-hissed. "Especially since the broken tape gave you more time. And keep your voice down. Besides," she said, leading them around the last corner, "we haven't seen the end of this thing yet. Pop's tape only showed a fragment of what happened here. By my guess, we have another ninety seconds before he starts shooting."

Jordan's jaw was slack with disbelief as Sam propelled him through the hallway. A mix of relief and adrenaline pumped through him as he realized he hadn't blown it after all. They still had a chance.

"Turn around," Sam said, and Jordan obliged as she took a small silver key from her belt and removed his handcuffs.

Jordan rubbed his freed wrists gratefully. "Thanks."

"Don't thank me yet. Here," she said, and stuck her black SECURITY baseball cap on his head. "It's a shitty disguise but it's better than nothing. At least it will make you subtly different to the people who just watched you whip out a gun."

They slowed as the rush of audience applause and near-blinding strobe lights ushered them to the backstage area where Jordan had knelt only minutes ago. They approached the folds of black curtains with equal measures of stealth and caution, squeezing their bodies in the gaps between towers of large crates to conceal themselves.

On stage, Matt had apparently finished the judges' interview because the stage lights were dimmed as dramatic music—*thump, thump, buuuuuuuzz . . . thump, thump, buuuuuuuzz*—played in the background, the kind of soundtrack that televised talent shows used to tell viewers that something dangerous and exciting was about to happen.

If only they knew how right they were, Jordan thought.

Circular targets were set at various intervals around the stage, as they had known they would be. Arrows stuck out from the center of each, proving what a good marksman Matt was. Jordan couldn't remember how many more would be shot in his ruse, only that once Matt turned his bow away from the stage and toward the audience, it was all over.

Another target, smaller than the others, was descending from the ceiling on the opposite end of the stage. As it did, Matt took one of the arrows off the table before him and dipped the tip into a bowl of fire. It caught, flames licking the point, which was met with a chorus of *oooh*s and *aaah*s. The music swelled as the target continued to drop, the wire on which it was attached invisible in the darkness.

"Jordan," Sam said, casting furtive glances around them, "get ready."

Jordan nodded.

The time had come.

He raised the gun with trembling hands and pointed it at the man on the stage. He'd had no problem readying to pull the trigger a few minutes ago, so why did he find it so difficult now? Now that he knew it really *was* his last chance to set things right, the pressure mounted until it was almost a tangible thing swelling inside him. All he heard was the *woosh, woosh, woosh* of blood rushing in his ears as all other sounds were muffled. He was aware of Sam whispering beside him, but her voice came to him as if he were either faraway or deep underwater, her words stretching like putty. "Eaaassssy," she said. "Aaaaaaimm. Taaaaaake yourrrr tiiiimeee."

Jordan focused on his breathing and his aim as he prayed to a god he wasn't sure he believed in to please, please give him the strength and concentration to make the shot, to make things better. For everyone.

Matt was still as he aimed at the target hanging from the ceiling. Jordan tracked him with the gun and closed one eye, the tip of his tongue sticking from his mouth in deep concentration. His aim was perfect.

Nothing would mess it up.

Nothing would stop him.

His finger was on the trigger, ready to pull, but his gaze was broken by one of the few white strobe lights that remained for Matt's act. It swept in his eyes each time he aimed, clouding his vision with a series of diamond-bright pinpricks. Each time, he had to wait until his vision returned to normal before readying to shoot once again. He remembered what Sam had said about the past not wanting to be changed, and thought that maybe she was right.

Jordan readjusted his sweaty grip but was once again distracted by another sweep of bright light. His eyes followed it as it danced off the stage, swept across the judges' desk, and out into the audience, where it grazed the tops of their heads in quick halos of white. Jordan looked at the row where the beam had settled and after a brief moment of letting his eyes catch up to his brain, he felt his wobbling legs threaten to give way, his muscles losing their tension under the weight of his body. His lips parted in disbelief as his attention completely severed from the weapon in his hands. Because although what he had come here to focus on was of the utmost importance, he had not been here, in the past, long enough to be immune to surprises. And this one, equally joyous and heart-wrenching, was the greatest of all. Because a dozen rows back from the judges' long, transparent table, he saw the unmistakable face of his grandmother.

58

CHARITY SLIPPED ON a pair of tight black gloves and dragged the heavy security guard behind the white marble base of a large sculpture on the opposite side of the room. A kneeling gold-plated Atlas supported a sphere of intertwined rings upon his shoulders. Though its ten feet towered over her, the replica was much smaller than the forty-five-foot bronze original she'd seen across the street at Rockefeller Plaza. She was sure there were cameras planted somewhere up here and that someone would eventually find him (and the small spatter of his blood that had stained the goldenrod carpet below), but it didn't matter. All she was worried about was getting the job done as quickly as possible. After that, it wouldn't matter if she was seen on camera. She and Matt would be long gone. There were numerous ways this could go wrong—her surprise visitor had proved that—but she would not allow herself to think, even for a moment, that failure was a possibility. Besides, if what she'd been taught in her social skills classes was true, positive thoughts built positive realities.

She felt no remorse for what she had done. She supposed the man had been just doing his job, but his job was a threat to her, so she had acted accordingly. It was merely a matter of self-preservation. After all, if she couldn't do that—take *one* life—then what came next would be infinitely harder.

She looked through one of the six sets of glass double doors along the curved, carpeted hallway to see that Matt's act was underway. From her spot far above, he was just a faceless figure on the stage. She could not make out his expression and only heard occasional fragments of his responses to the judges' questions through the theater's speakers: that his name was Matt Manson, that he was unemployed (which earned a few sympathetic *awws* from the audience), and that his reason for auditioning was to show America what he was capable of.

Isn't that the truth.

Larry, Portia, and Hans gestured for him to begin his act, the audience falling silent in expectation as the stage lights dimmed and the dramatic background music pulsed. Matt walked to a small nearby table illuminated by the beam of a spotlight. Without an ounce of flair, he tore the thin blue cloth away to reveal his bow. He did the same to another table to reveal a set of red-tailed arrows lined up like soldiers.

Even though Charity knew what he was going to do, she couldn't help feeling that the act's excitement was contagious. She had to remind herself that that's exactly what it was: an act. There was nothing real about his audition. It was a show, a façade, and she would watch only until he gave her the signal. If he was accurate, it would be easy to see from up here.

His showmanship was not grand, and he moved robotically as if his movements were rehearsed rather than organic. But still, there was something about him—a stoic presence, a rugged masculinity, a sense of mystery—that attracted her to him, that made his face and name (the sound of it, even, pleasant and alliterative) inextricable from her mind as her freckled cheeks flushed with embarrassment and desire. If these were the qualities that appealed to who she was now, someone vindictive and vengeful—*a murderer*—then so be it. Maybe it had been building in her all along, just waiting for the right time and conditions to emerge. Like a butterfly from its cocoon. Maybe Matt had only been the catalyst.

A fire burned inside her while Matt raised the bow to the target across the stage. A dramatic horn- and drum-filled soundtrack swelled behind him as he fired, and Charity watched the arrow strike the target with the wondrous intensity of a dream realized.

There it was. There was her signal.

59

THEY ALWAYS WATCHED the show together, counting down the days until their weekly Thursday night spent glued to the television. They'd seen similar variety shows but none captivated them or had the scale or scope of Talent Now!. *Between the assortment of acts and the show's high production value, it all felt magical in the cozy ambiance of the living room's dim lighting as Granny sat on the couch beside him.*

"What the hell?" she'd shouted at the TV when a pitchy country singer advanced to the next round, while a pair of kid salsa dancers did not. "Are they blind?*"*

She voted for her favorites each week, and at the end of the second season, her persistence paid off when her pick—the hip young magician—took home the million-dollar prize. After the thrill of playing a part in choosing the winner, she knew that she had to see the show in person. After all, she'd long-promised Jordan that she'd give in to his pleading and take him one day. Maybe this would be the perfect time. Summer in New York City with her favorite grandson? It didn't get much better than that. Tickets might be hard to come by for a show with top-notch ratings like Talent Now! *but she would do her best to make it happen.*

"*You think you can get 'em, Granny?*" *Jordan had asked hopefully, his eager eyes looking up at her with nothing short of reverence.*

"*You betcha,*" *she'd said.* "*Good things happen to good people all the time. Why not us?*"

And while good things did happen, it would be seasons later before she got the tickets. "*Look at this!*" *she'd exclaimed one afternoon when Jordan had walked into the living room to see her clutching a torn envelope in her hand.* "*I finally got 'em!*" *She beamed her bright smile as she waved a pair of paper tickets in front of him.* "*What do you say? Do you feel like an adventure?*"

Jordan had known his answer immediately but was silent as he pretended to think it over. He didn't want to let her down, especially because he knew how many years she'd been trying to get tickets. "*Hmm . . .*" *he said, making a show of his consideration.* "*Actually, I don't think I really want to go anymore.*" *He looked away as he said it, not wanting to know if her excited smile had faded at his answer.*

"*Oh,*" *she'd said, her softened tone betraying her surprise.* "*Are you sure?*"

"*Yeah,*" *he said, scratching his arm nervously. There was a time when he would've wanted nothing more than to go, when he would've said yes to anything she had proposed. She had a way of making even the most mundane tasks into adventures—mailing bills by challenging him to a race to the mailbox or buying groceries by seeing which of them could collect their items the fastest. But Jordan wasn't six or eight or ten anymore, and though he still enjoyed doing things with her, a hot summer bus ride to New York City did not appeal to him any more than spending another day listening to his parents' incessant arguing.* "*I mean, the show sounds cool, and being there would be fun,*" *he lied,* "*but it sounds like a lot of standing and waiting around and stuff. And besides,*" he said, risking deepening his guilt by glancing up at her, "couldn't we just watch it on TV?"

"It would be an adventure," she said, as if trying to convince him. "Like when we used to watch the show together. Like old times." She seemed to force a smile. "Besides, what could be better than a trip with your ol' Gran, huh?"

"Hey," he said in the cheery tone he used when trying to make up for something he'd done wrong or a disappointment he'd caused, "why don't we do something when you come back? It's a daytrip, right?"

Granny nodded. "Only a day."

"Let's play Scrabble or pick a movie or something."

Her smile downturned almost imperceptibly, but Jordan saw it. Her disappointment and hurt—and perhaps even her fear that her only grandson was outgrowing her—was poorly concealed.

"Are you sure you don't want to go?"

"Yeah. I think so. Is that okay?" he said, knowing that he had to ask unless he wanted to feel guilty until she came back. "I mean, will you be all right?"

She corrected her subtle frown into a smile, her coffee-stained dentures beaming. "Of course it's fine," she said, waving the suggestion away with her free hand. "I'm sure you've got other things you want to do. Besides, you're twelve years old. I doubt you want to be spending time with your old Granny."

"That's not true," Jordan said. He knew that she was joking, though he was unable to push away the idea that she was right. He'd spent years doing things with her—years of adventures and saying yes—so why did he feel so guilty for saying no this one time?

"Come 'ere," she said, wrapping her arms around Jordan and squeezing him tight in a hug that only increased his shame. "No matter how old you get, you'll always be my pal."

The phrase hadn't struck a chord with him then. His grandmother was only expressing her love for him. After all, she said it all *the time. But if he had known that it would be the last thing she'd ever say to him, he would've made sure to soak up her words and her soothing tone and the feel of her arms squeezed around his chest a little more, a little longer. Because as he left his grandparents' house that afternoon with Granny waving goodbye on the front porch, there was no way he could have known the guilt that would soon plague him, or that her goodbye, usually a goodbye until next time, would be a goodbye forever.*

60

SAM WAS YELLING at him, though her words barely registered.

"Jordan! Now! It has to be now!"

His gaze was fixed on his grandmother in the red velvet seat not far behind the judges' table. He yearned to run to her and tell her to leave the theater, that he was sorry he hadn't come with her, that he loved her. But he could not make his lips or feet move.

"What are you waiting for? Shoot!"

Despite the horrors about to take place, Jordan knew that, in this moment, his grandmother was filled with contented joy at finally attending the show she loved so much. "The magic," she'd always said, her eyes lighting up as she pointed at the TV as if it were a portal to another place and time, "is *there*."

"Damn it!"

He barely felt it when Sam tore the revolver from his hand, aimed it at Matt, and fired.

But it was too late.

Matt fired his flaming arrow above the audience in a brilliant arc of orange-red. Its track through the dark theater stole Jordan's attention from his grandmother as he watched the arrow land in one of the theater's balconies. *It's over*, he knew then. *It's all over.* Because this was the way it had happened. The way that, despite Sam's best efforts to change things, it was always supposed to happen.

Jordan had long thought that the seven years of guilt from not having gone with Granny to the show was the worst pain imaginable, but he hadn't realized until now that the ultimate punishment would be to watch her die all over again, knowing that he was the one who'd sent her to her death.

61

JORDAN HAD SPENT so many years telling himself that Granny's death was Matt's fault that he began to believe his own lie. But Matt Manson was no more to blame than Jordan. It had just been easier to dump it on someone else. Because dealing with the hate and disgust and selfishness churning within him was too painful. He'd long wondered why it seemed that it was easier for everyone else in his family to move on, but it had taken him until this moment to realize that coming here, to the past, couldn't erase his feelings or stop the progression of time any more than saving Granny could.

Over the years, he'd never known how badly he needed someone to listen. But the person who'd showed up was not at all who he had expected. He'd always had his criticisms of Sam, but now he knew that he'd been wrong about her, his disgust for her yet another product of his own hatred and jealousy and guilt. After all, Sam had waited for him here for nearly a year, not knowing if she herself would be safe. She'd tried things and had been braver than he ever could have been. But none of that seemed to matter now.

He registered Sam firing two more shots—*three left*, he thought absently—but they both missed their intended target, the dual *pop*s lost amid the blaring background music. But as the screams that began to rise from the arrow-stricken balcony above were quickly muffled by the swelling of Matt's deep, orchestral soundtrack and the applause and excited cheering of oblivious spectators far below, Jordan stared disbelieving as the audience still seemed to believe that it was part of the act.

62

SAM ATTEMPTED TO shake Jordan out of his motionless daze, her pulse quickening with the realization that their window of opportunity was closing. "What are you waiting for?" she shouted over the sweeping orchestral track. "Shoot!"

Soon the chances they'd taken and the lives they'd risked would be for nothing. They would just be another two people trapped in the soon-to-be inferno. And if they died here . . .

A cold shudder snaked down her spine.

She could not let that happen. After living in this city for the past year, everything she'd done and sacrificed to get to this moment, she would not let it be for nothing. She tore the revolver from her cousin's hand and fired twice. But when Matt remained on the stage, unscathed, she couldn't decide which of the two realizations was more horrifying: that the shots had missed, or that there were only three bullets left. Her heart galloped in her chest as she tried to figure out how they were going to get out alive. Because it was all over now. It was no longer a mission of prevention. Their only goal now was survival.

"She's there," Jordan mumbled with a glazed expression.

Sam had no idea what he was talking about. If he had checked out, too shocked or scared to do what needed to be done, how the hell were they going to get out of here? Her head felt like it was in a vice, the pressure building and building, as she considered the frightening possibility that she might be on her own.

"She was right there the whole time. It was a mistake. Stopping this was too much. Too much. Too—"

A sharp *crack* sounded between them, the red mark of Sam's hand slowly appearing on Jordan's cheek. "Jordan, snap the fuck out of it."

Sam had been looking for excitement in her life, but this was not what she had anticipated. She had wanted to feel alive again. She did not want to die. And it occurred to her then, with a sharp stab of clarity, that if she hadn't been laid off, she never would've gone to Pop's in the first place. Never would have seen Jordan. Never would have continued down the path that had led her here.

"It's too late," Sam said. "We messed up." Her eyes darted madly around the theater. "We need to find a way to get out of here. We need—"

Her speech was broken by the sound of panicked screams rising like a wave across the seemingly endless rows of seats, migrating from section to section like a virus. She turned to the audience to find its source and pressed her trembling hand to her mouth as she realized that it was coming from everywhere. People struggled to rise from the upper balcony where the arrow had landed, trampling others in their panic, while the flames around them grew higher and higher. It was worse than the image on the grainy VHS tape, worse than she'd imagined it had been or ever could be. She wanted to turn away from the horror she was witnessing but found her gaze bound to the tableaux before her as if it demanded to sear itself into her memory. *Look at this*, it seemed to taunt. *Look at what you could not stop.*

Sam felt a flutter of optimism as two burly, black-uniformed security guards sprinted up the stage steps with their Tasers pointed at Matt, but it quickly dissolved as he spun on his heels and fired an arrow into each of their chests. She watched as momentary confusion bloomed on their faces as they staggered backward and collapsed to the floor.

"Oh my God," she whispered. She hadn't noticed that she had spoken the words out loud, but she knew that if God existed as she thought He did, He was nowhere to be found.

63

CHARITY WATCHED AS the arrow struck the suspended target. It was all she needed to know that the moment had come. With nimble hands, she extricated one of the chains from her black Jansport and slipped it though the gold-plated door handles of the first door—*clink, clink, clink*—until both sides hung limply. She wrapped the excess chain around and around before finally securing one of the padlocks around two massive links and snapping it shut. She took only a moment to examine her work, blowing the sweat-dampened hair from her eyes as she pulled on the handles to test the strength of the thick chain. The lack of slack assured her that when the time came, no one would be able to slip through. She stole a glance at the theater beyond to see that everyone's gaze was locked on the stage below. Charity half-expected to see lines of drool falling from their faces as they stared at the black-booted contestant with the bow and arrows.

Idiots, she thought. *All idiots.*

She speedily unraveled another chain from the tangle, cursing only twice when it would not cooperate, before finally wrapping it around the handles of the next door. She moved quickly and steadily, willing her subtly shaking hands to cease their tremble. Because if she didn't do this right, if she couldn't get all six sets of double doors locked in time, all of their preparations wouldn't matter. Sure, the wreckage inside the theater would claim its share of lives—and it wasn't necessary that the doors be locked for that—but the whole point was to take away their one chance, just as they had taken Charity's away from her.

One day I'll fit in, she'd thought on many sleepless nights. *One day, I might even have a friend.*

But then her mother's caustic voice would chime inside her head with faux consideration for her daughter's wellbeing. "You don't need friends," she'd say, the same response she'd offer each time they had this same conversation. "Other people don't understand you like I do, honey. They're not nice to people like you. People with your . . . quirks."

Now, as much as Charity hated to admit it, her mother had been right. She could almost hear her say *I told you so* in her high-pitched tone of self-congratulation.

"And now none of it even matters," Charity said aloud, a layer of bitterness coating her words.

But there would be no sadness today. She would remember the cruelty of her tormentors, but the awful memory of all they had done, all the pain they'd caused her, would fuel her fire. She willed away the tears and withdrew another chain from the backpack, winding it through the handles of the next door with one hand and swiping at her eyes with the other. With two down, the third was easier, Charity imagining that she was wrapping the cool stainless-steel links around the necks of Hans and Larry and Portia. She looked over her shoulder as she worked to make sure that no one had snuck up behind her. That there wasn't a battalion of police officers or security guards with their guns raised and a swarm of thin lasers aimed at her chest.

There weren't.

She cautiously craned her neck to the gold-plated statue in the corner as if to make sure that the body of the security guard she'd dragged behind it hadn't come back to life. She'd only stabbed him in the chest, after all. If this was a horror movie, he'd come back just in time for Charity to realize her mistake of not having gone for his neck when she'd had the chance. But this wasn't a movie, and the guard was just where she'd left him, still and silent and invisible behind the sculpture of Atlas. She had nothing to worry about—for now, at least.

She snuck a peek into the theater as she worked, her mental clock ticking as Matt began stringing his last arrow. Before long, the audience's applause and excitable cheers, sounds of joy and safety, would turn to panicked shouts of terror and confusion. A pleasurable tingle worked its way down her back as she imagined it—the screaming and explosions and fire. It would be chaos. A symphony of chaos.

Charity worked faster, feeding the chains through the door handles like a kid feeding a ribbon of tickets into an arcade counting machine. As she moved to the last door and fumbled with the remaining padlock, she reveled in a small jolt of adrenaline, her arms jittering from the thrill of nearly completing her task. With the backpack empty (though for some reason it still had some heft to it), she looked back with a satisfied smile at the curved row of doors. Her body was slick with sweat, but she'd managed to finish.

She considered leaving now, but she had come too far not to witness the result of their efforts. She'd run away after the embarrassment of her own audition, but now that she was the one who held the power, she would stay and watch what she'd done. And this time, she would be the one laughing.

A grim smile broke across her face as she knelt at the last set of doors at the end of the hallway, peering through the glass at the speck on the stage below. As Matt demonstrated his prowess with the bow, hitting every target, she felt a deep swell of pride and longing. He'd rejected her previous attempt to kiss him, pushing her away with an emotionless, "What are you doing?" but maybe he'd just been caught off guard. She could understand that. But she'd also spent her life waiting on the sidelines, and she was done waiting. The next time she saw him, she would put it all out there. It was time she started getting what she wanted.

Her heart leapt as Matt began shooting the real targets. Metal struck metal as the barrels exploded one by one, Charity blinking each time they morphed into an airborne fireball, the theater erupting into chaos she couldn't have imagined had she not witnessed it herself. The panicked cries and sounds of fearful scrambling rose and leaked through the glass double doors, satisfying her primal need for retribution against those who had hurt her.

I did this, she thought.

Those seated in the orchestra section began to rise as the gleaming judges' table caught her eye. The three people once seated there now stood frozen. *This isn't part of the act*, she knew they'd be thinking. *Something's wrong.* Charity was rapt as an arrow struck Hans's chest and he fell atop his buzzer. The obnoxious *booomp* sounded throughout the theater, startling Portia, who froze as an arrow struck her in the side of the neck. When she collapsed, Charity's spine tingled with pleasure. Her only regret was not having been close enough to see the shock on their faces as the life drained from their eyes. Larry had managed to escape after jumping off the raised platform and onto the floor below, but that was okay. Matt had gotten the important ones. And two out of three wasn't bad.

Sections of the audience rose in waves as tiny figures crowded the aisles in search of escape. *Good luck*, Charity thought. *You won't find it.* The rapid-fire pounding of fists on glass turned her attention to the set of double doors farthest away, the ones she'd started with, near the sculpture of Atlas. She saw the floods of people swarming to the exit doors, banging and pounding like zombies hungry for human flesh. It only grew louder and more panicked as they began to realize that they were trapped.

But something was different inside the theater. Something had changed. It took her a few moments to recognize that it wasn't something that had been added but subtracted. Matt's background music was gone. It must have cut off, or the audio equipment had been damaged from the roiling smoke inside the theater. Both were viable conclusions, and she would have believed either of them if a new sound hadn't replaced the old. It started low and slow, the smooth and calming opening notes to a song she knew all too well. A song that had once given her hope and optimism in the face of adversity but now only reminded her of the great shame she'd been forced to endure. Before she could question its sudden appearance, the smooth, lush voice of Mama Cass was easing its way through the theater's speakers, her voice growing louder as she reached the chorus of the sunshine pop hit, "It's Getting Better."

The song's cheerful lyrics and upbeat melody perfectly contrasted with the chaos and hellish terror of flames spreading through the stampeding thousands below. Why had Matt's music abruptly switched to this? It could've been an accident, a mistake made in the sound booth during the ensuing pandemonium. But of all the songs . . .

Matt was still on stage, seeming to soak up the chaos. Although he was down below, countless rows and balconies away, she was able to see his face on the two large LED screens that hung from either side of the stage. Charity watched one of the screens as Matt looked directly into the camera and winked. She knew that it was meant for her. He was the only one who'd known what that song meant to her both before and during her audition. Her stomach dropped, heavy inside her. Was it some kind of sick joke, one that only he found funny? Or were there more sinister implications? Now, seeing him smirk as she listened to that song for the first time since they'd met, Charity wondered if she'd been wrong about him. If she'd underestimated what he was capable of.

The song's chorus continued blaring over the screams and stampeding spectators. She pressed her hands to her ears against the song's intrusion, the growing sensory overload, her eyes clasped shut against the barrage of thoughts flashing in her mind like quickly snapped Polaroids: the convincing look of sweet understanding on Matt's face when she'd met him in Baltimore; his faraway gaze as he'd shot the dog in that alley; how he'd seemed to take charge of all aspects of their plan, only revealing details when he'd deemed her ready to know them; his silence everywhere they'd gone, as if he lived inside himself.

Charity shook her head, unable to believe the possibility that she'd been fooled. That all of this—all of *him*—could've been a lie. Why hadn't she seen it before? Was there ever a tender moment he'd shared with her, a shred of vulnerability, an authentic look at his true self? Her stomach quivered as a horrible thought blossomed in her mind: what if he *had* shown her his true self—cold, emotionless, and concerned only for himself? Because if he had, then she'd never mattered to begin with. She was only a pawn.

But what did it mean? Was he mocking her? She turned from the theater doors with tears in her eyes, the mere possibility making her chest ache as if it was about to implode.

All we've done together, she thought. *All we planned.*

She should've seen it coming. Should've known it was too good to be true that someone had accepted and seen her. Her eyes grew red and puffy as she berated herself for falling for such a charade.

I never should've gotten on that bus to begin with. I never should've even looked at him.

Charity fought to suppress her sobs as she gathered her supplies. She no longer cared if she stayed to see the totality of what they'd done. She'd seen and felt enough already. She was ready to go home and forget that any of it had ever happened. But even as the thought arrived, she knew that she would not find happiness there, either. And so, when the tears came, she wept not because of Matt's mockery or her unhappy home life, but because of the sobering realization that there was nowhere she belonged.

She opened her fist to grab the black Jansport when she saw a shrouded red dot blink from somewhere inside. It was so fast that Charity wondered if she'd even seen it at all. But her suspicions were confirmed when it blinked again from the depths of the backpack. She pulled apart both sides of the zippered bag and peered inside. The red dot winked again, and she ran her fingers over the spot where she'd seen it, her eyes narrowing quizzically. "What the heck?" It was coming from inside the lining with no way to get to it—whatever it was—unless she cut it open. It began to blink faster and faster, its accompanying *beep, beep, beep* rising in pitch and speed like a heart monitor on someone about to flatline.

Charity had a bad feeling but wasn't sure why. And as Mama Cass belted out her nearly fifty-year-old lyrics throughout the theater, and Charity ran her pale fingers over the blinking, beeping red dot, she only had time enough to register that Matt was no longer on the stage before the explosion from inside the backpack knocked her backward and her world went white.

64

THE ARROWS SOARED over the audience faster than Sam could count them. Just as she tracked the flaming tip of one as it shot across the darkened theater, Matt had another loaded and ready to go.

It's too late, she thought, the words repeating in her mind. She knew they needed to leave now, but all she could do was watch the chaos unfolding around her. Portions of the lower balconies were now ablaze, flames catching and spreading outward like radial cracks in a bullet hole through a glass window. They licked the audience seats before greedily consuming the old fabric. Even here at stage level, Sam cringed as pained and helpless screams rose, knowing that it wouldn't be long until the crackling fires obscured both the wailing voices and the trapped figures they belonged to. Their shadows elongated and danced on the theater's walls like all the souls of Hell were begging for release.

During all the times that Sam had been to movies or plays or performances with Dave, she couldn't help but wonder what the venue would be like in the event of an emergency when evacuation was necessary. Would theater staff be prepared with clear, concise directions? Would the audience pay attention and act with calm organization? Now, watching in horror at the edge of the backstage area, she had her answer.

Crew members and security guards stormed past her and into the audience, but she wasn't sure what they thought they were going to do. In a place this big and a situation of this magnitude, what *could* they do? Where would they even start? While Sam knew what the outcome would be, the naïve guards had no way of knowing that their efforts would amount to nothing. All they could do was scramble, wait, and watch the world burn.

The background music was still blaring through the theater's speakers, the deep horns and earthy drums swelling over the audience like a tidal wave as smoke danced and swirled dreamily among the flames. It was too much of a sensory overload to comprehend that any of this could be real. But everything around her—from the smell of ashy smoke and burnt fabric to the sounds of frightened families—told her that it was. She watched parents and children stumble as they clumsily funneled to each of the six main exits and began banging on the doors. And when she realized why they weren't making any progress, why the doors weren't opening, she felt a swell of nausea rising.

She'd known this would happen from the beginning and had tried to get the theater to change the doors for this very reason, but all it had resulted in was a replacement set of doors with bulletproof acrylic. If she hadn't said anything, if she hadn't intervened, would these people be free? Would Sam be spared from having to bear witness to the crowd swarming the doors as each darkened, nameless silhouette clawed and clamored for escape?

Her attention may have held forever had it not been torn away by the brilliant rod of orange-red slicing through the air above the orchestra section. The arrow inched higher on its upward trajectory, much higher than the others. Sam's eyes glistened as it struck one of the large barrels like a plane into a skyscraper, both arrow and barrel consumed by an enormous explosion of metal and flame as the fireball mushroomed and charred the ceiling's ornate molding.

"Oh my God," she whispered. It was the only thing she seemed capable of saying.

Bits of metal encased in tendrils of fire shot outward, the blast engulfing those in its vicinity. Panicked screams struggled to rise above the roar of the flames that cackled mockingly. They lit the right side of the theater, while the opposite remained drenched in darkness. Sam wasn't sure whether that was something to be grateful for because wherever she looked, she saw the frantic movements of flailing arms and clumsy feet, and wherever she listened, she heard the sounds of hoarse screaming from raw throats. Through blurred vision, she watched the slow progress of a wheelchair-bound elderly couple as they attempted to push themselves up the aisles. They were quickly enveloped by the mob of surrounding evacuees, each indistinguishable body looking out only for themselves or their loved ones, paying no attention to the slow or the weak or those who fell behind and collapsed to the floor, trampled in the panic of hundreds.

The exploding barrel seemed to be the final trigger that made the audience realize they were in true danger—that this was not an accident nor a drill. Everyone who hadn't already done so began to rise from their seats in a frenzy. Sam watched in horror as many of them wasted precious seconds to grab the material belongings—purses, sweaters, cell phones—that were completely replaceable. Sam looked up at the ceiling and grew lightheaded and queasy as she saw several other barrels suspended along the curved arch above them. The horror she'd just witnessed was far from over, she realized. It was just beginning.

Another arrow flew and exploded a second barrel over the orchestra section in a ball of fire. It charred the ceiling, chunks of plaster and metal falling like rocks. She cringed at the heavy *thunks* as they connected with heads and limbs below and stray spurts of gasoline ate their way through plastic and carpet, clothing and flesh. The long, theater-length arch groaned high above them and began to sag. For a second, Sam thought it would hold.

She should've known better.

It wasn't long before it loosened and dragged itself and the remaining barrels down like a strand of old-fashioned Christmas lights. The groan of hot metal as it crashed joined the sounds of the relentless background track and the pounding of thousands of footsteps. As the remaining barrels exploded on impact, the mixture of heat and trapped air felt suffocating, every labored breath tinged with smoke and gasoline. Tendrils of fire shot across the room, the flames devouring the stage's scalloped curtains as they spread across the plaster ceiling. Water began to fall from the sky, and at first Sam thought it was raining, that somehow one of the explosions had torn a hole in the ceiling to let in a weak summer shower. But when she looked up, the ceiling was still intact. The water was coming from all around the theater as the sprinkler system finally activated, shooting down thin spurts of pressurized water that were no match for the strengthening flames.

Another burst echoed in the theater, like fireworks in a cave, as the first balcony that had caught fire began to bend and sag under its own weight. The top few rows broke apart in a flurry of concrete and plaster before it bowed forward and crumbled in a torrent of seats and exposed support beams. It was only when the charred pieces continued to fall, when Sam saw that they were flopping and flailing and wearing clothes, that she realized they weren't pieces of plaster. They were people.

She turned away from the nightmarish tableaux and the chorus of guttural screams as something inside her broke. She never could have imagined that such a horror was possible, that she could witness something so scary and so wrong. Would things have turned out differently if they'd tried harder to evacuate the theater instead of only worrying about Granny? Would she feel less responsible? Her head swam as she turned to Jordan for the first time since all of this had begun. In his eyes, she saw her own despair and disbelief reflected back at her.

One person did this, she thought. *One person was responsible for all this.*

How was that possible?

What she did know was that they had failed. She'd thought she was doing a good thing by coming here, atoning for her guilt of abandoning Granny and leaving Jordan to do this alone. That it would somehow make her better and stronger, healing her in a way that living in her own time could not. And in a way it had. But she'd had her chance, and now it was time to pay the piper. And so it was there on the edge of a nearly deserted stage in 2013 that Samantha Jones accepted her fate. There was nothing left to do or plan, nothing left to run to or from, and nothing left to control. She would stand here and wait for her world to end.

65

JORDAN SAW SAM'S eyes glaze with resignation as she knelt on the floor as if in prayer or surrender, her posture that of someone who knows they've been beaten. He was sorry for guilting her into coming here and regretted finding that damn box in the first place. He'd had a chance to change things but had blown it by not taking down fucking Manson when he'd had the chance. If he hadn't been so selfish in his quest for revenge, maybe things would have turned out differently. And while this was the reality now, he would not allow it to be for nothing. He couldn't save Granny or anyone else, and he couldn't prevent this day from happening, but he *could* rid the world of the man who'd caused it. He plucked the revolver from Sam's hand and flipped out the cylinder. There were only three shots left, but it was enough. All he needed was one. He'd messed up the first time and would not do so again. He aimed at the man on the stage, holding the gun the way Sam had shown him, cursing Matt's movements and the numerous distractions inside the theater that prevented him from getting a clear shot. He needed to get closer.

But before he could, Matt abruptly turned and darted across the stage. Jordan watched only for a moment before he abandoned reason and instinct took over. He sprung from his spot beside his cousin and bounded toward Matt as he disappeared through the stage's long black curtains.

66

MATT SAVORED THE acrid smoke from burning plaster and fabric like it was a finely crafted perfume. It enveloped him, tickling his nose as it weaved its way up his nostrils and into his brain. He'd thought about this day each night before sleep took him, but now, observing the chaos and flames and panic all around him, it was even better than he'd imagined. The fear inside the room was palpable as if it was a tangible thing, and Matt allowed himself the briefest of moments to close his eyes and bask in the sounds washing over him. Because this was it. This was the moment he'd been waiting for. And if he made it out alive, he knew this would be the memory that would define his life, the one he'd return to when he needed to *feel*. When he needed to feign happiness or joy, he'd conjure the screams; when he needed to simulate sorrow, he'd consider those who had managed to escape. There was not an emotion conceivable to Matt that this moment would not allow him to fake.

During the other times he'd been able to temporarily relieve that fiery tingle deep inside the folds of his brain, it had never gone away completely. The release had only lasted so long. But now, as Matt probed his mind, the itch was nowhere to be found. He knew it would return eventually, but for now, the physical manifestation of his dark desires and impulses was gone. His mind was clear, his thinking fogless, and Matt was able to focus on what was in front of him with his complete attention.

He saw a crying child in a nearby aisle and was transported back to elementary school. He saw himself quietly standing on the fringes of Circle Time, unwilling to contribute to Morning Share. Even then he'd known that he was different than the other kids. Something about him, he knew, was off. And when he saw the other kids' joy at playing with a new toy or gleeful anticipation for the weekend, Matt knew that he was missing out. Though he hadn't felt a desire to belong to a group or to feel what his peers felt, for a brief moment, he *wanted* to want to.

Teachers and school psychologists who'd tried to get him to talk and open up would ask him questions about his father and home life, hinting at the idea that something traumatic might have happened at home, something to cause Matt to have a psychological break. But Matt knew better. Living with his abusive, alcoholic father sure hadn't helped preserve his innocence, but it wasn't the root cause of why he was the way he was. He didn't think it was any one thing. He'd just been born empty. But then he'd think of the times his father had hit him with his beer bottles or shoved him beneath the floorboards, and he'd wonder if that was true.

Now, he looked down into the first row of disheveled seats at a woman lying motionless on the ground. He could not discern the color of her hair since it was on fire, but as the flames encased her body and nipped hungrily at her clothes, he thought of his father on that last day, drunk and collapsed on the porch. He hadn't turned back to watch him burn, but thought that it must've looked something like this woman, the flames eating through the layers of her skin as it blistered and seared and charred. He almost wished he had stuck around those few extra moments to see it.

He had considered the possibility that this would be his final act on Earth. And if it was, he'd be content to die and enter that black, silent nothingness he knew waited for him. But as he stood at the center of so much chaos and felt the seductive power of a god coursing through him, he thought, *Why should I die?* There was more to live for, after all, especially if he could do this again. The feeling was too great to willingly give up. He had been prepared to die today, but that did not mean he wouldn't try to escape.

He was about to run when he heard the blast at the row of exit doors in the back of the theater, which meant all loose ends had been tied up. It was unfortunate, but it had to be done. The girl had completed her task, outliving her usefulness. And on the offhand chance he should be caught, he didn't need her serving as a character witness against him in court. It hadn't taken much to bring her over to his side, and he couldn't have cared less about who had wronged her, but he had shared her belief that these people deserved to die. Their value on talent and fame and ratings, eager to judge and condemn, disgusted him. *So, goodbye to them, and so long, Cherry. There will be countless others just like you.*

Matt dropped his bow and started for the end of the stage, the long flaming curtains swaying gently as he disappeared behind them. He quickly reached the backstage door but found it blocked with a mound of chairs and crates, lights and ladders, haphazardly strewn about during the mayhem. He wasn't sure where the stage crew had run off to, but it most certainly wasn't through this door. Which meant that he wasn't getting through it, either.

Footsteps pattered behind him, and he realized he was being followed. He looked back only long enough to see the blurred forms of two figures running behind him. Who were they? He didn't know and didn't want to waste time finding out. His only goal was getting out of this building. Everything else was inconsequential.

Matt turned away from the door and carved a path through the deserted backstage area, which led him back around to the opposite side of the stage. From here, there was only one way to go. He would jump off the stage and blend into the screaming crowd of thousands to find an alternate way out.

But before he could leap into the crowd below, one of the figures behind him shouted, "Stop!"

Whether it was the hard edge of the shadowed figure's command or Matt's curiosity at who had demanded such a thing from him, he paused and turned. He was not sure what he was expecting, but it was not what he found: a young woman and an even younger man racing toward him. And one of them was pointing a gun at him.

67

JORDAN DIDN'T KNOW what he was going to say before the words came in an exasperated torrent. The built-up hate and disgust for the person in front of him flooded his mind as he tried to comprehend that he was now in the moment he'd wished to be for the past seven years. He planted his feet as he pointed the gun at Matt. The rising flames at the edge of the stage reflected their frozen figures onto the slick onyx-hued stage as if it were a lake of black ice.

"There's nowhere to run!" Jordan shouted, his voice threatening to tremble. Out of the corner of his eye, he saw Sam beside him and felt himself steady.

"Who are you people?" Matt said, shouting to be heard over the chorus of screams and roaring flames. There was no emotion in his voice—no anger or irritation or fear. Soot smeared his forehead and gray smoke roiled around his feet, giving the illusion that he was floating on his own personal cloud, a dark angel coming from below to wreak havoc on Earth. "What do you want?"

What could he still want that hadn't already been taken from him? What he'd long wished for had proved to be impossible, though killing Matt was still within the realm of possibility.

But as he stared at him, only feet away, Jordan realized that there *was* something else he wanted. Something that only the orchestrator of such a horrific crime would be able to answer.

"I want to know why!" Jordan roared.

Matt turned his head, the rest of his body hunched like he was poised to jump off the edge of the stage and start running. "What are you talking about? Why what?"

Jordan fought the urge to pull the trigger right then. Was this some kind of game to him? "Why you did this, you sick bastard." He pointed an unsteady finger out into the audience. "Those people . . . this chaos . . . what was it for? What did you have to gain?"

Matt's lips rose in a grin that didn't reach his eyes.

"You should run along now," he said. "While you still have the chance."

"Answer me!" Jordan shouted, his throat straining.

As Matt's smile grew wider, Jordan wasn't sure what was more infuriating: that dark, misplaced grin, or the fact that the sunshiny lyrics of Mama Cass were playing over the theater's sound system.

"What are you going to do? Shoot me?" His matter-of-fact tone made it seem as if he was genuinely curious. "Don't you know that you shouldn't play with—"

The bullet sounded with a crack, Matt's torso jerking backward as blood began to pulse from the silver dollar-sized hole that appeared in his arm.

"Either him or me," Sam said, the barrel of the revolver still smoking in her hand.

Matt clutched his left arm with his right hand and glanced down at the wound in his blood-slickened bicep, either surprised or pleased that Sam had shot him. There was something off about his face, Jordan realized. Every expression was wrong. Like he'd spent a lifetime emulating emotion rather than genuinely feeling it. His face might as well have been a mask. Because despite his eyebrows raised in surprise and his lips pulled back in amusement, the expressions painted there were just as plastic and fake as something purchased from a costume shop. For the first time, Jordan wondered not *who* Matthew Manson was, but *what*.

"We've come a long way and risked a whole hell of a lot to get here," Sam said, her heat-frizzed hair nearly hiding the left side of her face, "so I sure as hell hope you've got something good to say."

Matt stood stoically, his black jeans and black T-shirt blending into the darkened theater. "It's over," he said. "There's nothing left to be done. We did it," he smirked. "Nothing else matters."

The words Jordan could handle, but that grin . . . that *smirk*.

"You fucking piece of shit," he spat, his fists shaking as he tore the revolver from Sam's clutched, unwilling hand and trained it on Matt. "Do you know what I lost?" he bellowed, rage fueling his words like gasoline. "Do you know what you took from me?" His breath hitched in his chest as he stepped closer and closer to Matt with each word he spoke. "You're the reason for the fucking hole inside of me. *You're* the reason I was empty for over seven years. Seven fucking years when I felt nothing!"

Jordan shook his head, eyes blazing and sweaty hands trembling. "Nothing seemed to matter if it was possible for some stranger to just swoop in and take everything. But after a while, the only thing that started to fill that hole was hate. For *you*. So much of it that there wasn't room for anything else." Jordan's hearing became muffled, his peripheral vision fading as he became singularly focused on the unwavering man he was addressing. "You're the reason for the emptiness inside me," he thundered, bridging the gap between them. "You're the reason I got into so many fights in school! *YOU'RE THE REASON MY LIFE IS SO FUCKED UP!*" Jordan's wide eyes darted with the rapid rise and fall of his chest as he opened his mouth and released a raw, animalistic scream that sounded as if it was tearing his throat apart from the inside.

Although Matt was silent, his nose wrinkled above squinted eyes as if to say, *What the hell is this kid talking about?*

With his eyes once again trained on Matt, Jordan spoke hoarsely: "For so long, I've dreamed what I would do to you. And after all those years of wishing and wondering, now I know." He paused as a wicked smirk rose on his face. "If you're going to Hell," Jordan said, close enough to Matt to smell the smoke on his clothes, "I'll fucking send you there myself."

The moment the words left his lips, Sam felt a weight drop into her stomach. She knew exactly what he was going to do and what his words were building toward. She had always been against the death penalty and retaliation for crimes committed, but now she realized that it was only because she'd lived the bulk of her life without being on the receiving end of such a tragedy. Now, with Granny gone and Sam staring down the person responsible, it terrified her how quickly her stance on the matter changed. So, when she saw Jordan looking to her for confirmation of what he was going to do, instead of telling him to think it through and remind him that he'd have to live with this decision for the rest of his life, she nodded grimly.

Jordan took the final steps toward Matt, who seemed immobilized as if by some invisible force, clutching his ash-dusted arm as a line of blood ran down its length.

Jordan held the gun trained on Matt's head, reminding himself there were only two bullets left. And once this was over, once he'd placed one of them between Matt's eyes, only then would he allow himself a moment to mourn everything he'd taken from him. He would cry for the child who had not known how to grieve, and for the years he'd spent angry and confused and guilty, blaming others for things they had not done. But most of all, he would mourn Granny and the years taken from her, hoping that she forgave him for abandoning her not once, but twice.

Jordan had always thought that he'd hold Matt's gaze as he pulled the trigger, but now he found he could not. Because although he was perfectly willing to do what was necessary to rid society of this monster, he also knew that Matt's soulless eyes would forever taunt him as he waited for sleep. It was not a face or moment he wanted to remember. So, although he kept the gun trained on Matt's head, Jordan looked away as he held his breath and steeled his nerves.

But in the second before he readied to pull the trigger, the ceiling groaned and creaked, and Jordan glanced up to see one of the judges' brightly lit exclamation points cut through the air like a neon white dagger. He jerked in surprise, firing a reflexive shot at the ceiling and stumbling backward just as it crashed to the floor below the stage, breaking free from its plastic façade and throwing splintered, jagged bits of metal and Plexiglas into the air around them. When the giant symbol's exposed wiring touched the gasoline-soaked carpet, a column of flames rose above the stage, joined by tendrils of white smoke that quickly darkened. Jordan peered over the edge of the stage to see the name LARRY below the symbol, its lights now permanently extinguished.

He still had the gun trained on Matt, but it wavered in his grip as another creaky rumbling from the ceiling sent the exclamation point marked PORTIA to the floor with a sonic crack, the deafening sound of twisting steel causing Jordan to fire another reflexive shot. *I'm out,* he thought numbly. *The gun is empty.* He stepped back just as the exclamation point shot more jagged debris across the stage, not noticing the gash on his own arm until the flames reflected off the steady flow of blood. He stared at his wound as if in a dream, distractedly applying pressure as he heard Sam's faraway voice shouting over the clatter. Jordan followed her finger pointed at the metallic framework above. The last exclamation point marked HANS hung precariously from a metal corner, twisting and swaying as it clung desperately to its mounting. It didn't hold long. It crashed to the ground where it joined its two fallen brothers in a splintered, mangled collection of metal and plastic. Each exclamation point sent up an individual inferno, the three columns of flames fusing into a wall of fire that rose above the stage, blocking any view of the struggling people beyond.

"There's no way out," Sam whispered, staring at the wall of fire. Gray ash swirled down from the ceiling like nighttime snow, darkening her sweat-dampened cheeks and lips like some macabre lipstick.

But Jordan couldn't believe that. Because if he did, it would mean that everything they'd done and everything they'd been through had been for nothing. His shoulders shuddered as anger rolled through his body in trembling waves, his fists clenched at the horror and pain triggered by the shadowed man in black at the edge of the stage.

No, Jordan thought. He would not allow Matt to do to anyone else what he had done to him. He rushed forward and kicked Matt in the side of his knee as forcefully as he was able. Matt collapsed to the ground, a giant momentarily toppled. "Open up," Jordan said, as he stuffed the barrel of the empty revolver in Matt's closed mouth. He heard the *clink* of chipped teeth as he forced it in, deeper and deeper, until he heard him gag. "Oh," Jordan said through gritted teeth, smiling grimly at Matt's discomfort and bloodied mouth, "a human reaction after all."

Although the wall of flame prevented him from seeing anything beyond the stage, he could still hear the many screams and cries of pain and panic. They refused to fade. And that, imagining rather than seeing what was happening, was somehow worse. Jordan squinted at Matt through a haze of smoke and was both horrified and disgusted to see that misplaced glee in his eyes. *I won*, his bloodied smirk seemed to say. *I won and there's nothing you can do.*

"Fuck you," Jordan spat, and pulled the trigger—*click, click, click.*

"Jordan, let's go!" Sam shouted, her voice choked with ash and smoke as she bridged the gap between them. "We need to get out of here!"

A piercing scream sliced through the air that made everyone freeze as they scanned the blazing wreckage to see where it had originated.

The young girl stood away from them at the opposite end of the stage, the flames lighting her figure. She slumped to the right as she walked toward them, her arms dangling limply at her sides like a shambling zombie in a Romero film. Both Jordan and Sam stared, horrified.

She looked as if she had crawled her way out of an oven or a POW camp. Her jeans were ragged and charred, her short-sleeved top tattered and stained deep red. The left side of her face was covered in bruises and blood that oozed from crimson craters in her cheeks, chin, and forehead as if she had been struck with dozens of glass shards. Her hair was singed and burnt, and a missing piece of nose and lip made it seem as if she wore a perpetually upturned smirk.

Jordan thought that the expression of someone who had sustained such injuries would have been one of fear or paralyzing shock, but hers was neither. With her steeled posture and bloodshot eyes that exuded a dark confidence, it was immediately clear that she was neither panicked nor afraid. She was obviously hurt in the chaos, but what was she doing here, on this stage?

"Drop it!" the girl shouted, her words surprisingly clear despite her bloodied appearance.

Jordan didn't know who she was referring to. Was she in shock, hallucinating?

"You!" she shouted again, and Jordan felt a jolt of dread as he followed the track of her accusatory finger to where he stood, still holding the revolver. "Yeah, you!" she said. "Drop it!"

Jordan was stunned by the girl's crazed confidence and horrific appearance. He saw the hand hidden behind her back and hastened his obedience. "Okay," he said. "Okay. Just hold on." He began to slowly lower the gun to the ground.

"Hands up!" the girl yelled, voice straining. "I want to see your hands in the air while you do it. And go slow!"

The gun was already empty, useless, but he did as she instructed. She radiated that special brand of self-righteous lunacy that made for unpredictability.

"Good," the bloodied girl said as Jordan placed the gun on the stage. "Now kick it over."

"Jordan, don't!" Sam yelled.

But he did as he was told, watching as the girl grabbed the gun once it had stilled from its spin across the stage. As her body slumped to the side and blood dripped from her torn-away face, Jordan couldn't imagine what she wanted from him. The nightmarish image shimmered in waves of heat as Jordan followed her gaze to the man—the monster—at the edge of the stage. Matt was as close to the edge as he could be without being consumed by the wall of encroaching fire, looking a little too relaxed for the circumstances. The bloodied girl began shambling toward him, the audience's screams serving as the soundtrack to her shuffle through the smoke.

"You," she said when she was closer. "You bastard." She slapped Matt across the face with a bloody hand, grimacing as her remaining eyebrow narrowed in blazing anger. "We were supposed to be in this together. Look at what you did to me! *Look!*"

Matt's stony expression turned to disgusted recognition for the girl staring back at him.

"Cherry?"

"You look surprised. What's the matter? Didn't expect your little backpack not to go the way you planned? What was that, anyway? An insurance policy to make sure I didn't spill the beans on what we planned? Or did you just get tired of your new plaything and decide it was time to throw me in the fucking trash?" Blood dribbled from her mouth, coating her teeth in a slick red veneer, like she had taken a bite out of a still-beating heart before speaking.

Matt was speechless, staring uncomprehendingly at her bloody visage. "How the hell are you alive?" he finally managed, his voice showing less concern for her wellbeing and more puzzlement over how she was still standing.

Charity smiled grimly, leaned her bloody face closer to his, and whispered, "I'm full of surprises."

"But I—"

"Don't speak," she said sharply, raising the gun to his lips as if it were an extension of her pointer finger. "Don't say a goddamn word. I'm not interested in hearing what you have to say. Not anymore." As the gun wavered, so did her voice. "I trusted you," she said, softly now. "So, when did it all start? When did you decide to kill me?"

MATT STARED RAPT as if listening to the voice of someone who had risen from the dead.

"Tell me," Charity said. "Really. I'd like to know. Was it a last-minute decision? What about after I saw you in the alley with your bow? Did you not trust me with your little secret, what you were capable of? Or was it even before that, back in . . . " Her voice caught in her throat. "Back in Baltimore?"

The notion that he may have planned her murder from the moment they met sent a cold shiver down her spine despite the roaring inferno inside the theater. She felt like she was shrinking into herself, becoming smaller and smaller. Matt hadn't spoken or moved since she'd silenced him, but now, instead of his refusal to answer her question, his silence signaled something far more sinister: affirmation. He'd planned this all along. And with that realization came the awful confirmation of the cold and calculating monster he really was.

Charity felt like she had on the occasions she'd been hit with the dodgeball in her middle school gym classes. The breath was knocked out of her and replaced with sadness and shame and hate—for his seduction and lies, her gullibility and trust. She felt dirty. *Defiled.*

"All this time," she marveled. "You had this planned from the moment I met you backstage. Why did you even bother talking to me?"

Matt shrugged, his first real response. "I needed you," he said matter-of-factly, the surrounding smoke making his voice hoarse.

"No," Charity smiled, showing her bloodied teeth once more as she wagged the gun back and forth. "No, that's where you're wrong. You didn't need me. It could've been anyone else in the world, and it wouldn't have made a damn difference. What you needed was a victim." She was crying now, the full realization of his betrayal crashing down on her like a concrete wall. "So, what was it about me, then? Why me over the dozens of other girls in the audition room? Because I was young? Because you thought I would be an easy mark? That you would just come over, tell me what you thought I wanted to hear, and that would be it?" Her volume rose and she pointed at her chest. "Like I mattered?

"Well," she continued, "I guess the joke was on me then. Because . . . " She trailed off, her face loosening in a faraway expression of recollection. She lifted her chin, bloodshot eyes peeking from behind the thin, matted curtain of her hair. "Because I believed it," she said finally, exhaling deeply as if speaking the words had taken a great physical toll. "I believed all of it. I never meant anything to you. I never mattered."

Matt's eyes reflected the wall of fire, the floating flecks of ash, and the empty gun pointed at his head. "Cherry," he said, "you do. You do matter. You matter to me." He held up his hands as he said it, lightly pleading.

"Lies," she muttered, looking down and away.

"I couldn't have done this without you. Look around. We did this together."

She looked at the still-falling debris and fire that continued to inch steadily closer.

"Think about it," he said. "We are—we always were—in this together."

He hadn't apologized for his deceptions, but maybe this was his way, the only way he knew how. Maybe, she thought hopefully, he was sorry.

"What do you say?" Matt said, looking up as steel groaned somewhere high above them. "Let's get out of here together. Let's leave this place and let these people get exactly what they deserve. Let them burn as we turn our backs." His mouth moved but his eyes lacked expression, as if they had been covered with a fine layer of wax, a depiction of a face that was hard to distinguish between human or sculpture.

He extended his hand again and Charity's thoughts swam in her aching head. Her conflicting feelings ricocheted inside her so that it felt as if it was being torn in two. She clasped her hands to her ears, the side of the gun cold against her temple.

"Cherry," Matt pleaded, as if he had suddenly begun to realize that his control over the situation was slowly slipping away, "let's get out of here. Let's go home."

"I don't have a home!" she snapped.

"Then let's make one." His eyes glistened, his cadence low and calm and seductive. It was a glimpse of the person she knew was still inside him somewhere. At least, she wanted to believe it was.

Matt's gaze bore into Charity's as if he were trying to telepathically influence her to lower the gun. After a moment of trembling hands and quivering lips, she did. Looking at the weapon she held, she turned away and threw it into the wall of fire. A burst of sparks appeared where the cold metal touched the flame before eating it up greedily, hungry for more.

Tears shone in her eyes as Matt gestured with his hands, asking for permission to stand.

Charity nodded.

When he got to his black-booted feet and worked out the kink in his leg, he held his arms opened wide. "Come here, Cherry," he said. "Come to me."

So kind. So sweet. So welcoming.

Her legs trembled before she did as she was told and entered into his embrace, her bruised and bloodied arms locking around his torso. "Oh, Matt," she said.

Matt responded to Charity's relieved exhalations with a smile, and though Charity had already known what she was going to do since she'd woken on the floor outside the row of EXIT doors with her ears ringing and wondering why she couldn't feel her face, that mocking, sinister smile made it easier. Slyly, she withdrew the object she'd been concealing at the small of her back, in the waistband of her blood-stained jeans. By the time Matt saw it, his eyebrows furrowing curiously, it was too late. The hunting knife flashed in her hand like a spark as she thrust it into his stomach. The blade slid into his flesh like a key into a well-oiled lock, quickly and soundlessly.

Matt staggered backward, his eyes locking on her in surprise as she pulled the knife from his stomach and planted it in him again. She could have quit, but it felt too good to stop, savoring the sense of control, of *power*, coursing through her. She plunged the blade in his chest, his side, again and again, until her last attempt caused her shoulder to ache in protest as she let out a pained cry.

Matt stumbled to the floor, and Charity ambled through the red slick of his blood before straddling his torso, sitting above him and his wrong smile. But hers was genuine.

"You messed up," she said, breathing hard from exertion. "You thought you could play me." She held a thumb and pointer finger close together as if squeezing something very small. "I came *this* close to believing you," she said, watching as Matt spasmed and gurgled on his own blood. He could choke on his tongue for all she cared. "But I'm not stupid. I'm not the girl you met in Baltimore, crying in a heap of curtains. That girl is dead. But I suppose I owe you a debt of thanks," she said, "because you want to know the ironic thing? You helped *unlock* her. What I hadn't realized was inside me."

Matt gurgled an unintelligible reply.

"And this?" She held up the bloodied knife, the entire blade slick with red. "A gift. From you."

Blood dribbled faster from his mouth, Matt struggling to raise his arms as if the muscles had atrophied. Charity watched as his face twitched in his attempt to speak. "Push me into the fire, Cherry," he wheezed, his throat thick with blood. "I want to feel it." He mustered some semblance of a smile. Had he found some kind of dark humor in this? Or maybe pride, knowing that his legacy would live on forever. Whatever the reason, it disgusted her. She leaned down to his parted lips until she was able to hear his jagged inhalations and smell the coppery tinge on his breath.

"Sorry, Matt," she said, shaking her head in denial of his request. "I can't do that. But I hope Hell is nice and hot for you." She sighed before looking at him once again, her eyes locked on his. "And one last thing," she said, her voice hardened as she plunged the knife into his heart. "My name's not Cherry."

Blood lined the blade around the wound as she gave it a twist and held it in place, unwilling to believe that he was dead and would not spring back up for one final scare. She gripped the hilt with both hands and tried to hold back the tears as Matt's chest heaved and shuddered like a patient under cardiac arrest. She didn't think it'd be like this—so drawn-out, watching and feeling him struggle and suffer beneath her. She assumed he'd be dead by now.

A halo of smoke swirled around his head. His eyes were dead—they always had been—but his lips still twitched, struggling to part, and Charity almost felt sorry for him. "Cherry," he managed with a gurgling whimper that held surprise and, perhaps, admiration.

His breathing became shallow as his chest hitched a final time and when it did not rise again, Charity knew it was over. She loosened her steel grip on the knife and dropped her hands to her sides, slumping her shoulders in exhaustion as if she could finally rest. Her damp hair hung in loose straggles that framed the intact half of her petite face. Looking at the clean, unmarred side, it wasn't hard to imagine that she might once have been pretty.

Charity looked at Matt for what she knew would be the final time. His misplaced smile was gone, his glazed eyes fixed on something above. His body was still, his mind done its calculations and manipulations. It was perhaps the most human she'd ever seen him. *We are all the same in death*, she mused, unsure where she might have heard it. She heaved the knife from Matt's heart and tossed it into the fire. It crackled as it entered and then it was gone, eaten by the flames as if it had never existed at all. Charity sighed and searched for the tears that she knew were somewhere inside, but the theater was too hot, the air too dry. After everything that had happened and all that had been taken from her, all she wanted to do was cry. And she couldn't even do that.

At the opposite end of the stage, Jordan was still attempting to comprehend everything he had seen and heard. He stood with clenched fists and gritted teeth as he stared at the bloodied girl. If any part of what she'd said was true, she was just as guilty as Matt in planning the awful things that had led to the nightmare they were now living in. But despite the surge of resentment he felt toward Matt, he felt the target of his anger begin to shift as one thought rose above the rest: *he was mine.* He still had so much he wanted to say to the bastard, to make him suffer even a fraction of the pain he'd caused him and the dozens of other families who would soon discover they'd lost someone they loved.

And now *she* had done it.

"You bitch!" Jordan shouted, his temples throbbing. "He was mine! He was mine!"

Charity took a reflexive step backward when she saw him running toward her, but it was too late. Jordan quickly closed the gap between them and entwined his fingers around her narrow throat. His cheeks reddened with exertion and anger as he squeezed. This close to her, he could see every detail of her ruined face. The top layers of her cheeks were shredded and singed. Bits of ash and fabric stuck to the bloodied parts of her forehead where some small pieces of shrapnel still protruded.

"Do you know what you've done?" he yelled, gritting his teeth as spittle frothed between them like a rabid dog. "He . . . was . . . *mine*," Jordan said again, punctuating each word with a deeper grip on her throat.

"No!" Sam shouted, horrified. "Jordan, stop! It's not worth it!"

He barely heard her, though he felt Sam's pawing hands as she tried and failed to pry him off Charity.

"There's no time! We've got to get out of here! This whole place is about to—"

He withdrew a hand from Charity just long enough to shove Sam away with a ferocity that surprised even him.

"You took him from me!" he shouted, his voice ragged and raw. "He was mine and you took him!"

Charity blinked rapidly as she raised her red-slickened hands in feeble attempts to paw him off her. But it was no use. Jordan was stronger.

He looked up from her injuries, away from her gasping mouth and into her eyes. They were big and blue. And scared. *Help me*, they pleaded, and in them Jordan was convinced he saw someone who would give or do anything to get what she wanted—no, what she *needed*. In that respect, at least, wasn't she just like him? Hadn't he been willing to do whatever it took to kill Matt and prevent this day from ever happening? Regardless of what she'd done, as he looked into her wide eyes and squeezed her throat, he realized with sobering clarity that his actions made him no better than the dead man lying at the edge of the stage. He abruptly released his grip and stepped backward in horror, looking at his hands as if they belonged to someone else. Charity coughed and clutched her throat before tripping and falling to the stage, scurrying away from him, as if she believed he meant to do her further harm.

This wasn't how it was supposed to go.

This wasn't what he'd wanted.

I am a monster.

She stopped when she seemed to believe that she had put a safe distance between them, staring at Jordan with cautious eyes as if to assess his next move.

"Go," Jordan whispered hoarsely. Though he wasn't sure where there was *to* go. Flames and piles of debris surrounded them in every direction. "I won't stop you."

Her frozen stare was unbroken as he waved her away.

"Go!" he yelled.

Charity winced as she struggled to her feet, keeping her eyes trained on him as she dragged her bleeding leg behind her toward the center of the stage. Both sets of stairs that led down to orchestra level were encased by the wall of flame, and Jordan wondered where she was planning on going. Maybe she was insane after all.

He watched as her bloodied but nimble fingers swept the ground until she found what looked to be a large metal ring. She slipped the fingers of her good hand into its loop and pulled with a yelp of pained struggle. Jordan watched as a square section of the stage began to rise, two hinges on the bottom holding the trap door in place. With a final fierce heave, it swung back onto the stage, revealing a square of unspoiled darkness below.

She knew it was there. That's how she got up here without us noticing.

She swung her injured leg over the hole, followed by her good one, and let them dangle in the darkness. Smoke swirled around her head in a loose tornado as she looked down, seeming to contemplate what lay below, then back at Jordan. "I'm sorry," she said, straining to be heard over crackling flames and pleading screams that still echoed throughout the theater. "I wanted it to be over."

What? Jordan wanted to ask. *Wanted what to be over?*

Desperation seemed to coat her words, her tone almost pleading for him to understand. But all he understood—all that mattered, at least—was that Charity had been the only one who had gotten the revenge she'd wanted.

As if she'd read his thoughts, she looked to the edge of the stage and the body lying there. It seemed fitting that her last image of this place would be him. Her eyes watered, glassy pupils contracted against the smoke. Jordan watched as she averted her defeated gaze to the dark square below. It was only then, in the fraction of a second before she jumped, that Jordan realized he had questions that only she could answer. "Wait!" he shouted. "Stop!"

But she inched her way off the stage, descending into darkness, and just as quickly and silently as she had arrived, she was gone.

69

HOW DID WE get here? Jordan stared at the empty space the girl had left behind. His chest rose and fell in quick bursts as he tried to comprehend everything that had just happened. The theater continued to burn around them, and panicked, elongated shadows danced up the tall, carpeted walls.

It was all over so fast. There was nothing left to do. They were alone.

They.

He snapped himself out of his daze to see the person he'd momentarily forgotten was there. "Sam!" he shouted. He kneeled to where she lay on her back, collapsed on the stage, firelight reflected around her in its smooth blackness as if she were the object of some Black Mass sacrifice. "Can you hear me?" He bent an ear to her mouth and felt the shallow exhalations of hot air. She was alive, at least. He looked frantically around the stage, paralyzed with indecision about what to do or how to help.

She was breathing, yes, but that seemed to be the only thing that boded well for her. Her hair was straggly and matted as Jordan turned her head to see that it was smeared with blood from the abrasion she'd sustained when she fell. He nearly recoiled as her eyes rolled upward into their sockets.

"No, no, no," he said, panic sliding into his voice. "Sam!" He shook her shoulders, begging her to move as if it was something she could control. "Wake up!"

He lifted her head into his lap as blood gushed from her nostrils in a torrent. It flowed like watery snot, running down her lips and chin before blooming on her shirt in a violent burst of red.

"My head," Sam said, her voice strained. "It hurts so bad."

What's happening to her?

Then he remembered his headaches and lightheadedness, the nosebleeds and vomiting.

But this was her first trip. Why was it affecting her as if it were her fiftieth?

As the answer came, a tremor of fear wormed its way through him. Because what he had been experiencing for a little under an hour, Sam had been experiencing for a year. If Jordan's own side effects after a few short trips were any indication, he could only imagine what kind of reaction it would have on her body.

He adjusted her head in his arms and sat her upright.

"The smoke," she said, weakly waving it away. "Too much."

Jordan grimaced at her deteriorated state. When had she fallen? When he'd pushed her aside? When he'd been strangling that girl? When he'd cursed the injustices that had been done to him, only concerned with himself?

"I'm not dying . . . " Sam wheezed, " . . . like this." She drew in another shallow breath. "Pointless."

"I know. We've got to get out of here."

"There's nowhere left to go."

"There is. Can you walk?"

He helped her to her feet as she careened to the right and vomited. It splashed on the slick stage, droplets spattering the bottoms of their pant legs as they shuffled forward, arms around each other's necks and waists. The trapdoor inched closer, and before long they were standing at the edge. Behind them, the remaining curtains went up in flames as the stage-wide LCD screen exploded in a dazzling burst of glass shards like the shattering of a thousand lightbulbs. A loud groan sounded above them, and both Jordan and Sam looked up in time to see the metal frames of the ceiling's many lighting tracks sag before plunging warped metal spears into the stage and audience seats beyond.

They were momentarily safe from the falling debris as Jordan dropped through the square, then turned back to slide Sam through. When he'd gotten her to the floor, he reached up, enclosed his fingers around the bronze ring, and pulled it backward. He held it open only a foot as he peered out at Matt's lifeless body at the edge of the stage, the flames desperate to reach out and consume it as they had so many others.

Jordan could not see anything through the wall of fire now dangerously close to reaching the ceiling. He imagined the mothers and children and grandparents struggling beyond the flames as they banged on locked doors, desperate for rescue. The chorus of pained screams rose, and Jordan was certain that, unlike the voice of his grandmother, he would remember them for the rest of his life It would be his punishment for interfering, for endangering Sam, for inserting himself in a time and place in which he did not belong. As he stood there in silent waiting, he prayed that he and Sam hadn't made things worse.

He felt a surge of guilt as he peered into the darkened bunker. Just beyond the wall of fire, there were people who needed rescue, people the fire department and various crisis teams would not be able to save. If only he could part the flames and tell them that there was room for them, they would still have a chance. But there was nothing he could do to save them.

Jordan tore his eyes from the horrors beyond and closed the trapdoor against the sweltering heat and screams and falling debris, until all that remained were muffled hints of the chaos and destruction above. And when all he could see was the four thin beams of light leaking through the seams in the door, Jordan climbed down the ladder into the near-darkness and sat beside his cousin.

70

WEAK, SMOKY LIGHT illuminated only a few feet around them, though the many metal support beams told Jordan that the space was much larger than he'd thought, perhaps the size of the stage itself. Charity could be anywhere. But there were other, more pressing matters requiring his attention.

Sam sat on the dusty floor with her back against a wooden girder. The flow of blood from her nose had weakened to a trickle, her chest rising steadily beneath her black security uniform shirt. For the moment, she seemed to be stable, and Jordan ran his hands through his ashy hair as he considered their options.

How did we get here? he thought as he scanned the darkness around them. But despite the many times he'd asked himself, the answer hadn't changed. *Because of me. Because I couldn't leave things alone. Because I had to interfere.*

And now, because of his recklessness and obsession with revenge, they were going to die. It didn't matter that they had found a place to hide; it was only a temporary safety. Death would come to them eventually. Down here, beneath the stage, it would just come slower.

If I could go back . . . he thought, then quickly stopped himself. Because that's what had started all of this in the first place, what had gotten them into the position they were now in. It was all him—*his* wishes, *his* wants, *his* feelings. Never mind what he'd had to do or sacrifice to get it. He looked at the dusty floor with the hot flush of shame on his cheeks.

But it was for Granny! You did this for her!

It was true, but was it the whole truth? Hadn't he done it because he couldn't deal with the grief of losing her? Because he desperately needed to trick himself into the idea that, with her around, adulthood could somehow be postponed? If she knew everything he'd done, he did not think she would be thankful or proud. *No*, Jordan thought. *She would be ashamed.* And it was this thought that weighed on him the heaviest, like a block of ice on his chest.

His legs shook as he slid down the support beam and sat next to Sam, his muscles weak as the adrenaline drained from his body. His cracked lower lip trembled, and he felt like crying. If his eyes weren't so dry and flecked with ash, he might've. He couldn't remember the last time he had done so. Part of him welcomed it—the sense of relief that came with running out of decisions to make, of places to hide, of concerns and risks to consider. But the tears would not come.

Even moments before, he would have cursed Pop or Matt or God himself for his predicament, but there was no one left to blame.

"And now Pop's gone, too," Jordan murmured.

"What?" The word slipped from Sam's nearly closed lips.

"I always thought that he took Granny's death harder than we thought. That he was too proud to ask for help." He rubbed his dry eyes. "He probably was, but now we know the real reason he never left the house in the years after. Why he rarely wanted company and always kept the shades drawn and the

TV on. But . . . it was all for nothing," he wheezed. "I spent so much time wishing I could bring Granny back that I didn't consider that Pop had been feeling the same things. I blamed him for what happened to her, and I never . . . I never said . . . "

Sam placed a limp, bloodied hand atop his. The small gesture was obviously taxing, for she breathed deeply, her chest taking a long time to rise and fall. "Pop would've understood," she said, wheezing with each short sentence. "It's not your fault, Jordan. None of this is. We did our best. We tried."

Granny had said the same thing on those long, sleepless nights. *"None of this is your fault, Jordan,"* she'd soothed. *"You deserve better. You deserve so much better."*

But now, he wasn't so sure he did.

"The way I treated you . . . the things I said . . . "

He saw her pale complexion and dry, cracked lips and struggled not to look away. He'd left her when he'd come here, but he would not leave her now. Not again. Instead, he remained beside her and laid a gentle palm on her thigh. "I'm sorry," he whispered, choking on the words.

Sam's eyes seemed dangerously close to rolling back into their sockets as she merely patted the top of his hand with hers. Anything that needed to be said had been said. All the hate and apologies that had occurred between them no longer seemed to matter.

They sat enveloped in silence as Jordan wondered what Pop would've thought about all of this. There was a reason he'd left the desk to him, after all, and if Pop had viewed him as his last shot to make things right, then Jordan had failed *him,* too. Because he'd managed to do nothing more than hide like a coward from the hellish destruction above. If being alive meant living with the massive burden of all the people he had disappointed, he wasn't so sure that dying would be such a bad thing after all.

"Jordan," Sam said, breaking the quiet and startling him out of his thoughts. "Look."

He thought that this was the end, that Sam was drawing his attention to some blast of roiling smoke or flames, or the sudden appearance of angelic figures only she could see. So, when he turned to face her, he thought his mind was playing tricks on him. But when he blinked and opened his eyes again, he realized that there was nothing wrong with his vision. What he saw was actually happening.

Sam began to shimmer, her body flickering in the darkness like thousands of sparkling pixels. Jordan knew what it meant as soon as he set his eyes upon her. He remembered what she had told him about the tape she'd used to get here and how she'd slowed it down, uncertain when it would expire and catapult her back to their present. It seemed that the time was now. Jordan would be stuck here, but Sam would be safe and go on to live her life. After putting up with his recklessness and giving up a year of her life in a strange place and time, she more than deserved it.

"Looks like your time here is up," Jordan said with a small smile.

She held out her glowing, flickering arms, slowly turning them over as if inspecting a new outbreak of chicken pox. Her body radiated a dull light, millions of bright dots working together to illuminate the darkness around them.

Jordan stared in awe as if witnessing something he'd never seen before. *So, this is what it looks like*, he mused, what Sam had seen when she'd walked into Pop's house to find Jordan on the floor with his hands pressed against the TV. As she'd watched as the impossible happened before her eyes, she had not fainted or ran or denied. She had waited for Jordan to return and explain what she'd seen. And when he did, she listened. Jordan could not say he would have conducted himself the same way if he had been in her shoes.

Sam continued to inspect her flickering form as panic swept over her face like a shadow, her eyes wide and aware as if the full realization of what it meant had hit her for the first time.

"Hold on to me," she said quickly, reaching out to Jordan. Fright lined her words as if she was about to embark on a journey she was afraid to take alone.

Jordan shook his head, knowing what she was thinking. "Sam, you came here using a different tape. Mine is broken. It's your time to go back. To go home."

But her eyes were locked on his, pleading. "Hold on to me," she whispered again. "Please."

"We don't know that it will work."

"We don't know that it *won't*."

He didn't argue. He put his arms around her to humor her, to say goodbye, but they were loose around her chest.

"Tighter," she said.

Jordan obliged.

His vision blurred as he squeezed his cheek against Sam's shoulder, her flickering image shimmering in his eyes like a blank TV station after midnight. If this was it, he was ready. He had made his peace with it—all he had done, and all he had failed to do.

"Jordan," she whispered.

But he didn't hear her.

A dull static rose inside his head like tiny ice picks stabbing his brain. The accompanying ache rose and intensified, and he gritted his teeth against it. He wanted to press his palms into his watering eyes and knead them like dough, but he didn't dare tear his hands away from Sam. He would hold on to her until she faded away and was safe in Pop's living room, leaving him alone to face whatever came next. He held on tightly with his eyes closed against the pain and the horrible things he had seen and done, all the years he'd wasted being angry and resentful.

The time.

It was the one thing he would never get back.

As Jordan sat in silence, considering the things for which he would never be able to forgive himself, he did not notice the warm trickle running from his nostrils as his nose began to bleed.

71

IN THE BEGINNING, there was darkness. There was no time or space as the blackness pulled her deeper and deeper, as if she was falling through a tunnel that had no bottom. Her brain buzzed with the sound of static as she was thrust along the speedy current, the lone survivor of a shipwreck in an unforgiving sea. The pressure inside her head swelled along with her vertigo, and just when she thought that she couldn't take it anymore, a new awareness abruptly replaced that of her freefalling—that she was once again lying on flat, solid ground.

Light began to push away the darkness and a familiar white ceiling came into focus. As it did, Sam realized that she no longer heard screams, or the crackling of flames and crashing plaster. She no longer smelled oily smoke and burnt skin. She looked around the quiet room—at the soft carpet beneath her and the sunken couch against the wall—and knew she was no longer beneath a burning theater stage in New York City. She knew where it *looked* like she was, but was it true? Was it really possible? Or was it just a sick trick of a dying body, projecting one last fantasy before death came to collect her?

The more she regarded the room in which she had spent so many childhood holidays and summers, the more the possibility of fantasy seemed less likely. And whether due to her vertigo or the realization of where she had returned, she could not stop herself as she vomited onto the familiar blue carpet. Her stare lingered on her mess until she heard a cross between a struggling gasp and a wheezing exhale behind her. Sam felt the speed of her already galloping heartbeat surge as she spun around on all fours to see Jordan lying on his side—and breathing.

He was alive. Jesus Christ. They both were.

They were back.

But she did not allow herself to celebrate just yet. *Back* had its own set of questions, and her stomach fluttered with anxiety as she considered them.

She knew where they were. That was the easy part. The question was *when*?

72

THEY SAT ON the couch as they had earlier this afternoon, a time ago that had been much longer for Sam than it had been for Jordan. A quick online search and check of the neighborhood through the windows had assuaged their fears that they had been trapped in a time in which they did not belong. Sam's BMW was still parked on the side of the house beneath the arcing branch of Pop's cherry blossom tree.

Jordan recalled traveling to the *Talent Now!* theater for the second time and returning with a headache and a crumpled Hershey wrapper clutched in his hand. If you could bring things back, it made sense that Sam was able to do the same with a person. A chilly tremor snaked across his neck as he considered what would have happened to him if Sam had not ordered him to hold on to her.

They closed their eyes, relishing the somehow crisp sound of silence permeating the cozy living room that would soon belong to someone else. The only sounds around them came from their own shallow exhalations and the subtle *tick-tick* of Granny's cuckoo clock on the wall. But the stillness between them was broken when Sam turned to Jordan with caution in her eyes. "Should we check?" she asked, nibbling the corner of her bottom lip. "To see if anything changed?"

Jordan tensed as he patted the crumpled news article in his pocket. He scooted onto the cushion next to Sam and watched her wake her iPhone. She opened Google, typed in the title of the article she was looking for, and used her index finger to swipe across the screen. It was one of the first links that popped up and Jordan felt an uncomfortable uncertainty radiate through him as it loaded. If the contents of the article matched the one in his pocket, then they'd know nothing had changed. Or maybe, he thought, his heart beating faster, they had made things worse.

The screen filled with text, the title jumping out at him:

57 DEAD, HUNDREDS INJURED IN TALENT SHOW MASSACRE

He skipped down the columns and read:

> . . . and answers to the questions plaguing the countless victims, injured, and first responders involved in this tragedy are either partial or non-existent. The only thing that seems to be consistent is the lack of certainty about what happened. Various eyewitnesses confirm the act of terrorism was committed by a *Talent Now!* contestant, many claiming that they thought it was part of the show.
>
> The forensics team on site reports multiple traces of gasoline inside the theater. This, paired with eyewitness testimony of barrels falling from the ceiling—barrels that were allegedly to be used for confetti—leads them to believe that this was pre-meditated. "It sickens me," New

York City Police Chief Donald Cartwright said. "We have evidence, we have bodies, but what we don't have is a motive. I like to believe that people are mostly good, but days like this make it hard."

While efforts are still being made to uncover the truth behind this act of terror, another witness who chose to remain anonymous claims there's more to the story. "There was something happening on the stage after the man's act. There were people up there, but I don't know what they were doing. It looked like they were arguing. Maybe they were trapped. The flames got so high I couldn't see."

Regardless, something happened on the stage that led to the perpetrator's body being burned and stabbed at least three times. Which begs the question: who killed Matthew Manson? Was it the same person who killed a security guard outside the mezzanine level? The same person who chained off the exit doors, trapping thousands inside? It's unreasonable to believe that one person perpetrated such a crime. He must have had help. The question is: who was it? And why?

The article continued for another few paragraphs, but Jordan didn't need to read any further. He looked from the phone's screen to the rumpled article he had withdrawn from his pocket, and back again, as if in disbelief of something already proven to be true. From the headline to the number of people dead, from the perpetrator to the same witness testimony, everything was the same. The only difference was that now some of the unanswered questions had answers.

"I don't get it," Jordan said. "We were there. We interfered. Why didn't anything change for better *or* for worse? After all the ways we messed up, something should have."

Sam gazed at the screen, still scrolling with the tip of her index finger.

"Maybe we did it all along," she pondered.

Jordan squinted. "I don't follow."

Sam put her phone down and turned to face him. "No matter what we did, nothing changed. So maybe we *always* went back. That girl *always* killed Matt. You *always* got distracted and missed your shot while he was on stage. Whatever happened, happened. Maybe it was always us and this was just our first time experiencing it."

It was almost too much to comprehend. But then again, if he needed help accepting and believing in the impossible, all he needed to do was consider the past few hours. "How is that possible? That show happened over seven years ago. We were both in different places then, hundreds of miles from that theater."

"Yes," Sam said. "But by going back we became part of it. Like some kind of paradox. A causal loop."

"Causal loop?"

"When something in the future causes something in the past that causes the first event to begin with."

Jordan's face was blank.

Sam sighed, fixing him with a contemplative gaze that made it seem as if she had trouble wrapping her head around it, too.

"Your finding and watching the *Talent Now!* tape and deciding to go back ended up causing the events that happened on the stage—your missing your shot, that girl's interference, maybe even Matt's death—because we were part of them. And the anger your younger self would feel as a result of that, of the massacre, of needing revenge after Granny died, was what led you to Pop's house and watching the tapes to begin with, what made you want to go back to try to change things. Something you did in the future caused the past." She swirled a finger in a circle. "A loop. No matter what we or anyone else tried, it would always end the same."

"But what if we hadn't gone back? If we had chosen not to, what would've happened?"

"We were always going to choose to go, one way or another. Call it fate. Maybe in another universe we might not have, but in this one, you always found those tapes, always got the idea of going back, and always tried to save Granny." She looked down at her lap, as if ashamed. "I always chickened out."

"So what? I probably would've done the same thing if it was me that had walked in on you staring all *Poltergeist* into the TV. Besides, if it weren't for you, I'd be stuck back there. Dead."

"You don't know that."

"There're a lot of things I'm not sure about, Sam, but that's one that I know with absolute certainty."

They allowed the comforting blanket of silence to settle over them once again, knowing that if they let it linger too long, they'd both be asleep in minutes. Though now, fresh off all they'd been through, Jordan found it hard to believe that they would ever sleep again.

Jordan rubbed his temples. "I still can't wrap my brain around this."

"Time travel, Jordan," Sam said with a dimpled smile. "It's not going to make sense."

It was all over, and he wanted nothing more than to sleep. Just a few hours without plans or worries or headaches. But as they laid back on Pop's couch for what would be the last time, his thoughts swam with the realization that although they were back, there were still things to do and decisions to be made. Then again, it was nothing that couldn't wait until morning. And so, despite their halfhearted battle against it, they closed their eyes and let the calming current take them.

Jordan woke, startled to find the opposite end of the couch empty, only a small divot left behind where Sam had been sleeping. The sight of her missing fully jarred him from his sleep. As he sat up, a piece of lined notepaper wafted off his stomach and onto the blue carpet below. He picked it up, squinted, and read the neat cursive printed there.

Couldn't sleep. Call me in the morning. Still some things we need to discuss.

–S

73

JORDAN CALLED SAM once he arrived home in the early, predawn hours of morning, ten minutes after reading her note. He figured he knew what she wanted to discuss but assumed they would have vastly different opinions on the matter.

He was wrong.

"He gave it to you," Jordan said. "Are you sure that's what you want to do?"

He could imagine her nodding over the phone. "After everything we've seen and been through? It's not even a question. It's what needs to be done." She paused. "Why? Do you feel differently?"

"No," Jordan said, allowing himself a brief chuckle, "it's just that I'm used to us not agreeing on things. They're clearing everything out at twelve. Want to meet then?"

"Sounds good. We can use my car. And Jordan?"

A pause hung on the line.

"Don't worry," she said. "We're almost done."

It didn't take long to load the television into Sam's BMW, but that was the easy part. The challenge was getting it down her basement stairs. After they set it on the unfinished room's concrete floor, they huffed with exertion as they stared at the obsolete device that had sat in the corner of Pop's living room for the better part of two decades. The screen was blissfully dark, and Sam and Jordan had vowed it would remain so. "How do we know it's not the electricity?" Sam pondered. "Or something else we could never understand?"

Jordan shrugged. "We don't. But I'm willing to bet that the TV was part of it. A *big* part of it. And if there is electromagnetism, or radiation, or something else under the house, well, we can't fix everything."

"Good. I think I'm done trying to fix things."

"So, we're agreed?" Jordan said, casting a tentative look at the television. "About what to do?"

"You mean bust the shit out of it?" Sam smirked. "Yeah," she said. "I think so."

"When?" Jordan was eager to get it over with, put the whole mess behind them.

"Another day. The important thing is that it's here where we can keep an eye on it."

Another day. It sounded good to him.

They left the TV and walked upstairs into the spartan living room. When they were seated on the lone leather couch, Jordan asked Sam the question he had considered many times over the past twelve hours. "Do you wonder if this was all pointless if nothing changed? I know it's weird to ask but—"

"I think it would be weird if you didn't ask," she said as understanding shone in her bright eyes. "And of course. That's all I've been wondering. And whether or not we're both idiots."

Jordan smiled.

"No," Sam said, "nothing changed. But just because we didn't fix anything doesn't mean we didn't take anything from this whole thing, right?"

As much as he would've liked to take more from this experience than enlightenment, she was right. He knew more about both Sam and himself than he had known going in. And though those realizations did not come without a price, he was glad to have them.

"Besides," Sam said with a cautious smile, "we never would've had this time together."

Jordan shook his head as he looked away from her. "We wasted so much time."

"And we can't change that. We can only move forward."

"But all I put you through—"

Sam held up a hand to silence him. "If this little adventure has done anything, it's wiped the slate clean. Now we can start fresh. And I want to do that, Jordan. I really do." The mix of optimism and relief in her eyes told him that it was true, that they would only remember the damage and wounds they had caused each other to prevent them from happening again.

Sam grabbed her keys off the table. "You ready to head back?"

Shortly after they left, Sam pulled into the alley behind Pop's house. Jordan's beat-up Corolla was still parked on the side street. Sam unlocked the passenger door with a muffled *click* as Jordan thanked her for the ride. He began to walk away before pausing with his hand on the yard's metal gate. He turned around, slid back into the passenger seat of the BMW, and wrapped his arms awkwardly around his cousin. He hadn't known how badly he'd needed some sort of physical contact until Sam echoed his gesture, each consoling the other like children after a shared nightmare that no one else would understand or believe.

When Jordan shut the car door and stepped back to see Sam's face framed in the window, there seemed to be no reason for goodbyes; they would see each other soon enough. After all, they still had some business regarding a television to take care of.

As he watched her drive away, Jordan felt the void inside him begin to fill slightly. He knew that it would get better with time. After all, most things did. He had never believed that before but thought that it wasn't too late to start.

JORDAN STARED AT the faded brick exterior of Pop's house as his Corolla's old motor whirred and sputtered to life.

"After all the time we spent here, it's pretty weird to think we'll never go inside again," Sam had said on the drive over. And while Jordan knew that change could not be stopped, it was no less difficult to accept.

They'd both had good times here—sticky summers with picnics and fireworks, New Year's parties with the entire dining room table filled with food as Granny tried to adorn Pop with a goofy party hat. And the fact that those things had happened, with family and fun and good memories, had to be enough. It was more than some people had or could ever hope for. But just because those times were in the past did not mean they could never exist again. If they chose to, if they put in the effort, there could be new memories, new celebrations and gatherings, new houses filled with laughter.

Nothing stayed the same forever. And for the first time since Granny's death, Jordan was okay with that. He'd been stuck in the past for too long, as if he could somehow burn away the dark shadow that had been cast over his life and hide from the changes and responsibilities that came with age. But all he'd done was stall.

He looked from the patchy garden of tomatoes and strawberries in the yard to the rusted flagpole and overhanging branches of the cherry blossom tree from which both he and Sam had once swung. It was these things he would miss most, the details—the whisper of the wind chimes and the squeaky clothesline swaying in the July breeze. He couldn't choose his memories, the good or the bad, but they were his. The little recollections he had cultivated from his time here that were unique to him alone. He could no more live in the past than he could change it, but that didn't mean he had to forget it, either.

He turned to the black box on the front passenger seat and flipped back the lid to reveal the neatly stacked VHS tapes inside. He'd told Sam he'd get rid of them. That he'd burn them in the fireplace when his mother wasn't home. But now . . .

He wasn't so sure.

They seemed to draw him closer, whisper of the places they led, the people he could see, the things he could experience.

No, he thought. *Never again.*

He would keep the tapes, yes, but only to remind him of his grandmother and all she'd done, someone who had spent her life protecting two others. Maybe he would watch them again one day when he was older or had a family of his own, when his memory became fuzzy and he needed help to remember what she had looked like. But for now, they would remain in the box, and he would try his best to forget they existed. And if he was successful, he might be rewarded some peace.

Jordan glanced at his grandparents' house a final time before pulling away from the curb and driving down the tree-lined street. The pull of the corner rowhome was strong, but he did not look back. Looking back was easy. And so for the first time in a long time, Jordan Jones looked not where he had been and what he had done, but where he was going and what he was going to do.

EPILOGUE

ONE WEEK LATER

JORDAN FOUND WHAT he was looking for in a matter of minutes, but it took him a week before he summoned the courage to act. He knew himself well enough to know that if he didn't do it now, he never would.

He got in his car and plugged the city address he'd gotten from Google into his GPS. He'd anticipated some trouble finding it, but the amount of newspaper articles and public attention had made the resident's anonymity almost impossible. One of the articles mentioned the street she lived on and then he only had to do a quick search to find the house number. After all, there weren't too many people with that name.

He didn't make any wrong turns during his short commute and was surprised to find a parking space on the small side street. He looked up at the slender rowhome with its weathered brick and tin awning and wondered if it was the same one that she'd once shared with her mother when she was young and decided to audition for a talent show.

Though he'd had a week to decide what he was going to say if she came to the door, he was no more certain of his words now than he'd been then. All he'd known was that he needed to see her. There were things about that day only she knew, things only she could tell him. Then again, it had been seven years ago. Would she even remember the details?

Yes, Jordan thought. If someone had survived—had *done*—what she had, it would be more difficult to forget. The question was, would she be willing to tell him? And, if so, would it be the truth? From what he'd read in the papers, she hadn't told the media—or anyone, for all he knew—the truth about her involvement in what had happened that day.

He passed small pots of parsley and rosemary on the brick steps as he stepped onto the porch, minding a small fissure where the grout had begun to crumble. His heart fluttered as he approached the scraggly screen door and the beat-up metal mailbox on the wall that bore her last name. Inches from the door's white frame, he thought of the headlines he'd read over the past week: GIRL SURVIVES NEW YORK CITY TRAGEDY, read one. BALTIMORE WOMAN AMONG TALENT SHOW MASSACRE SURVIVORS, read another. It was hard to believe that she'd always lived just fifteen minutes from his own house.

Police sirens wailed in the distance as he raised his fist to the door but abruptly drew it back. *Stupid*, he berated himself. It wouldn't make sense to chicken out now. But Jordan knew that's exactly what he would do if he hesitated any longer. He raised his fist again and rapped his knuckles against the door's flimsy frame, listening for the sound of footsteps beyond.

Will she even remember me? he mused. Or had her memory of him begun to fade, like his memory of his grandmother?

At last, he heard sounds from beyond the door and froze. He thought it might have been nothing more than a creaky floorboard or the television, but then it was only a matter of seconds before Jordan's ears were met with the sound of nimble fingers unlatching a bolt lock.

The wooden door separated from the frame just enough for the figure beyond to see who stood on her porch but not the other way around. Only her lips and the side of her nose were visible in the gap allowed by the small golden chain. Beyond, the rest was darkness.

"Can I help you?" a woman asked in a small, timid voice.

Jordan thought he would be unable to speak but surprised himself with the speed of his reply.

"I'm looking for Charity Sparks," he said.

"What for?"

"I have some questions I want to ask her."

"I don't want to answer any questions," the voice said.

"Please," he said, "just a few."

The figure's visible eye darted away before returning its gaze to him. "What about? I don't want to buy anything if that's why you're here."

"No," said Jordan. "I want to ask about a specific day."

"What do you mean? What day?"

"June 21, 2013."

She averted her gaze as she spoke, as if she was addressing the floor. "I don't talk about that," she said, her tone nearly a whisper.

"Please," Jordan pleaded, realizing he was slowly losing his chance—for answers, for information, to know why. The door was open only a sliver. All it would take was the wrong word or movement to scare her and seal off his chance for good.

"I don't talk about that anymore," she said again. "Goodbye."

She started to close the door before Jordan shot out a hand and blurted, "I was there!"

She paused.

"Please," he said. "I was there. I just have some questions. I lost my grandmother that day."

Jordan sensed contemplation on the opposite side of the crack.

"Why should I believe you?" she said softly, the suspicion in her voice momentarily receding.

"Because I don't have a reason to lie," he said. "Please. You're my only chance."

The crack in the door held, the girl's single eye blinking against the sun.

"No tricks?" she said.

"No tricks," confirmed Jordan. "Just a few questions."

After a brief hesitation, she unlatched the chain and the crack in the door widened. The darkness lightened, the shadows faded, and before long a face appeared before him.

He hadn't been sure what to expect, but when she turned and pushed her long, brittle, blonde hair behind her ear to reveal the other side of her face, one look confirmed the voice belonged to the person he was looking for.

Her skin was pale on the side of her face that Jordan had initially seen, but the side that had remained hidden by the darkness was a small patchwork quilt in varying shades of beige and tan. The doctors may have tried their best to treat the third-degree burns that had disfigured her face, but the flesh that existed there now was pock-marked and deeply scarred, one of the many physical and emotional reminders of that day made somewhat tolerable by seven years' worth of surgeries, skin grafts, and time. The various colors of flesh that now made up her face made it clear to Jordan that she was wearing a prosthetic nose (or at least part of one), and he tried not to stare. Her eye cast its gaze downward while its twin lolled in its socket, the glass sphere not fitting as well as it should have.

Again, Jordan tried not to stare but was not sure how well he was succeeding. He had just seen her only days ago. And now . . .

And now seven years had gone by. He had to keep reminding himself of that.

How old had the newspapers said she'd been back then—seventeen? Eighteen? But what struck him more than her age progression was the aura of exhaustion surrounding her. Maybe she'd spent the last seven years reflecting and repenting, or maybe she hadn't. But looking at her baggy eyes and hunched posture, Jordan thought better of that. He knew she had to have spent the intervening years perseverating on each detail of that day, wondering how it had gone so wrong and how she had become involved in the first place. Wondering if things would have turned out differently if she'd made different choices or had been dealt different cards. Jordan knew this because they were the same thoughts he had pondered himself on many sleepless, sad, and angry nights.

"Well," Charity said, reaching for something on a nearby shelf masked by the dimness of the living room. "What do you want to ask?"

But as he looked up into the good eye of the woman he'd come to see, the questions he had come to ask—*Why had she done it? How had she hooked up with Matt? How could she live with herself? Why hadn't she gone to the police? Why hadn't she told the truth about what really happened?*—vanished like the last wisps of smoke from a campfire. His attention was drawn to the years of pain and hurt he saw in her eye, as if it had made invisible scars. And as Jordan watched her pull the object off the shelf and onto her head, at least two of the questions he had planned to ask—*Why hadn't she gone to the police? How could she live with herself?*—were answered.

Jordan couldn't tell whether, underneath the blonde wig, she was wearing the shame or the shame was wearing her. She had suffered, he realized. Maybe not enough, but she had suffered. Whatever questions he had planned to ask, whatever information she would be willing to reveal, none of it would bring his grandmother back. And it would make neither of them feel any better.

"Well?" Charity asked again. But instead of expectancy or irritation, her voice was lined with a kind of nervous, childlike anticipation.

It puzzled him at first, but then he understood.

She wanted to talk about it. To share her side of the story—the *whole* story. The one she'd been holding on to for seven years, waiting for someone to listen. Maybe he no longer needed to hear it, but Charity needed to tell it.

She saw him staring at her and held a hand to her face self-consciously, but Jordan couldn't seem to find the words to tell her it wasn't her disfigurement he was focused on. At last, watching her fidget and pick at her cuticles, he said, "Would you like me to come in?"

It was faint, but underneath the hesitation and caution Jordan saw a kind of hopefulness radiating from her tired eyes.

"Or we could just sit out here," he offered. "If that's okay with you, I mean."

That seemed to be better. She opened the door a little wider, and Jordan could see the small, well-kept house beyond. With the right amount of warmth, it even had the potential to be cozy. Charity stepped onto the porch and past the potted rosemary, taking a moment to cast an appraising look at her guest, the first in years. "You look familiar," she said as she passed, not yet making the connection. She adjusted her wig and shut the door behind her before joining Jordan in one of the porch rockers.

Clouds peppered the late summer sky and, if the weather reports were to be believed, it would rain soon, offering a brief reprieve from the humidity. Which was all right with Jordan. It had been too hot for too long, and everything could use some cooling off. He'd always liked the rain—its earthy smell and the calming *ting, ting* sound of drops on glass and metal, the way it made everything clean and new. Besides, as they sat on the small porch, separated by both inches and years, the awning provided plenty of cover. He inhaled deeply, smelling the ozone clinging to the air. Soon the woman rocking slowly beside him would begin her story, and he would listen. For as long as she wanted to talk, he would listen. Jordan was in no hurry. With nowhere else to go, he had all the time in the world. And any day, no matter the weather, was a good day for a story.

ACKNOWLEDGMENTS

A LONG TIME ago, at a university not so far away, when I met with my academic advisor for a career-planning session and shared my aspiration to be a published fiction writer, he told me that I needed to pick *a real career*. I've yet to forget those words—or the shock and horror I felt—almost ten years later. Had I listened to him and given up writing to pursue a *real* career (Goat herding? Avocado farming? Working in a toothpaste factory?) the book you are holding in your hands would not exist.

While writing it was a solitary endeavor (mostly blissful, sometimes maddening), I'm lucky enough to be surrounded by many people who made it a whole hell of a lot easier.

First, thanks to my parents, Rick and Linda Ruszin, for their love, support, and for always asking, "Any news on your book?" A safe and supportive environment isn't necessary for writing fiction, but I'm so lucky and grateful that they willingly and selflessly provided both. Thanks, parents.

Thanks to my sister, Gina Ruszin, for the laughter and inside jokes, always supporting my writing, and bragging about me to her friends long before I had a published product to show for it. (Thanks also for being the one to indoctrinate me into the world of French fries dipped in ranch dressing—which has nothing at all to do with this book, but is a game-changer all the same.)

The love and support of grandparents is the backbone of *Showtime* and I'm lucky to have had four of the best:

To Angela Paetow, for being the perfect model of what a grandmother should be. I'm thankful beyond words for her unwavering support in everything I do, her bottomless well of selflessness, generosity, and positivity, teaching me to appreciate life's small pleasures, and never being afraid to indulge in silliness. Oh, and for keeping me stocked with a steady supply of baked goods.

Santa "Sarah" Cuocci, for her selflessness, emphasizing the importance of family, and loving us with her food. (To my knowledge, she never said a single bad word about anyone, which, in our family, surely qualifies her for sainthood.)

Paul Ruszin, who miraculously had enough love and stamina for ten grandfathers. I'm grateful for our many adventures (it turns out that cemeteries and escalators make for great field trips), his youthful energy, enthusiasm for my writing, and always obliging when eight-year-old me wanted to look at Party City's Halloween masks in the middle of summer.

Clarine "Louise" Ruszin, who inspired *Showtime* and for whom it is dedicated, for her sense of wonder and adventure, her too-good-to-be-true stories of humor and hauntings, and refusing to relinquish her sense of play no matter her age. Without her love (and love of game shows), it is no exaggeration to say that *Showtime* would not have been written.

To the many aunts, uncles, cousins, friends, and co-workers who cheered me on while *Showtime* was being written and beyond, *thank you* doesn't seem big enough to properly convey what your support and enthusiasm means to me. I am spoiled in that there are just too many of you to name.

Special thanks to Amanda Houston, who has kept me sane more times than I can count. Thanks for being there to share in the highest of writing highs, the lowest of lows, and for reading and responding to every rough draft, edit, note, and pestering question in between. Our friendship has kept the writing train moving more than you know, and I'm so grateful for your support and willingness to live in our imaginations. I'd order the skeletons to throw a parade in your honor, but there's no amount of smooth-topped Reese's to repay you.

A giant thanks to my beta readers who enthusiastically agreed to read *Showtime* in its early forms, provided invaluable insight, thoughtful comments, and helpful suggestions: Linda Ruszin, Amanda Houston, Loreta Bradunas, Rusty Ruszin, Deb Laforest, Judi Mercadante, and Matt Cuocci.

In a way, the story of Charity Sparks is one that shows what happens when people allow themselves to be guided by an adult who doesn't have their best interests at heart. Thankfully, I've been lucky enough to have had the positive guidance of more than a few kick-ass English teachers, each of whom has left a profound and unique mark on me:

Loreta Bradunas, for being one of my most thoughtful readers and biggest cheerleaders. Who would've thought that one day I'd be the one giving *her* homework?

Mara Ma, for our post-*Lost* chats and responding to the very first short story I wrote so enthusiastically.

Liberty Grayek may not be an English teacher, but she could've fooled me. I'm thankful for her humor, writing support, and our many discussions about books, movies, and Stephen King.

Michele Summers, for infusing humor and sarcasm into her lessons. If I manage to write sarcastic dialogue well, chances are it's because of her.

Teaching creative writing is no easy feat, but Aaron Chandler does it well. I'm thankful for his passion for craft, his genuine interest in my work, and never trying to steer me away from genre fiction.

Nanette Tamer, for crafting engaging lessons, her infectious sense of curiosity and enthusiasm for language, and talking *with* us instead of down to us.

Kathy Brown, for her genuine kind and gentle soul, love of stories, and for proving that growing older doesn't mean you have to abandon your youthful spirit.

Thanks also to the Inkshares team: Adam Gomolin, for prioritizing character over word count; Sarah Nivala, for her thoughtful suggestions (many of which made it into the novel); Avalon Radys and Pam McElroy, for their incredibly thorough and eagle-eyed copyedits; Kevin G. Summers, for his precise typesetting work; and Tim Barber, for an incredible cover.

The beautiful art that you see throughout the book was created by the amazingly talented Courtney Payne. When I asked her if she'd be willing to collaborate on some interior illustrations, her response was an immediate *yes*. I can't imagine a more perfect collaborator. I'm thankful for her perfectionism, eye for detail, and for going above and beyond to make the book extra special—and for not hating me when I asked, "How would you feel about *one* more illustration?"

Publishing a book is not a quick process, and I'm sorry that there are some family, friends, and readers who were unable to see it come to fruition. Though they are no longer with us, their support was immediate, enthusiastic, and unwavering: Pam Klank, Mary Lou Baier, Cheryl Sparks, and Paul Ruszin.

While *Showtime* would've been written regardless of whether it made it into physical form, your support, reader—yes, *you*—is the singular reason it was able to make the jump from my laptop and into your hands. So, whether you pre-ordered the book three years ago (in which case, your patience is saintly) or recently picked it up at your local library or bookstore: *thank you*. It means the world.

GRAND PATRONS

INKSHARES

INKSHARES is a reader-driven publisher and producer based in Oakland, California. Our books are selected not by a group of editors, but by readers worldwide.

While we've published books by established writers like *Big Fish* author Daniel Wallace and *Star Wars: Rogue One* scribe Gary Whitta, our aim remains surfacing and developing the new-author voices of tomorrow.

Previously unknown Inkshares authors have received starred reviews and been featured in the *New York Times*. Their books are on the front tables of Barnes & Noble and hundreds of independents nationwide, and many have been licensed by publishers in other major markets. They are also being adapted by Oscar-winning screenwriters at the biggest studios and networks.

Interested in making your own story a reality? Visit Inkshares.com to start your own project or find other great books.